BEAS

'WHAT HAPPENED?' ASKED Brustellin. 'For Sigmar's sake, Yefimovich, what happened?'

'It was the Beast,' he replied. 'He struck her down.'

The crowd hissed. 'The Beast, the Beast, the Beast!' Yefimovich could feel the emotions running through the mass of people: grief, horror, anger, hatred.

'Death to the Beast!' someone shouted.

'Yes,' cried Yefimovich, 'death to the Beast!'

He snatched at the bloody green velvet, and held it up.

'I didn't see his face,' he said, 'but he wore this!'

Everyone knew what that meant.

The mob would comb the city for aristocrats, courtiers, palace servants, diplomats. Even anyone who wore green. Then, there would be a glorious bloodbath. A revolution.

More Warhammer from the Black Library

· THE GENEVIEVE NOVELS ·

DRACHENFELS by Jack Yeovil
GENEVIEVE UNDEAD by Jack Yeovil

· GOTREK & FELIX ·

TROLLSLAYER by William King
SKAVENSLAYER by William King
DAEMONSLAYER by William King
DRAGONSLAYER by William King
BEASTSLAYER by William King
VAMPIRESLAYER by William King

· THE KONRAD TRILOGY ·

KONRAD by David Ferring
SHADOWBREED by David Ferring
WARBLADE by David Ferring

· THE TALES OF ORFEO ·

ZARAGOZ by Brian Craig

· WARHAMMER NOVELS ·

ZAVANT by Gordon Rennie
HAMMERS OF ULRIC by Dan Abnett,
Nik Vincent & James Wallis
GILEAD'S BLOOD by Dan Abnett & Nik Vincent
THE WINE OF DREAMS by Brian Craig

· WARHAMMER FANTASY STORIES ·

REALM OF CHAOS
eds. Marc Gascoigne & Andy Jones
LORDS OF VALOUR
eds. Marc Gascoigne & Christian Dunn

A WARHAMMER NOVEL

BEASTS IN VELVET

Kim Newman
writing as Jack Yeovil

*'All men and women are beastly,
and when skinned,
a beast in velvet
is a beast for all to see.'*

– Jacopo Tarradasch,
The Desolate Prisoner
of Karak Kadrin

For Clare, a funny Valentine

A BLACK LIBRARY PUBLICATION
First published in 1993.

This edition published in Great Britain
in 2002 by The Black Library,
an imprint of Games Workshop Ltd.,
Willow Road, Lenton, Nottingham, NG7 2WS, UK

10 9 8 7 6 5 4 3 2 1

Cover illustration by Martin Hanford

A CIP record for this book
is available from the British Library

ISBN 1 84154 235 0

Set in ITC Giovanni

Printed and bound in Great Britain by
Cox & Wyman Ltd, Cardiff Rd, Reading, Berkshire RG1 8EX, UK

See the Black Library on the Internet at
www.blacklibrary.co.uk

Find out more about Games Workshop
and the world of Warhammer at
www.games-workshop.com

PROLOGUE
MARGARETHE

HER LAST PFENNIGS had gone on gin and now all she had to warm her was the sting in her throat. It was late and her legs felt like lead weights threaded through with pain. There were thin, dark clouds overhead, obscuring first one moon, then the other.

The summer was long dead and the autumn month of Brauzeit twenty-six days old. Soon, the winter would set in and there would be lumps of ice in the river. It was cold now, but it would be colder then. The weather scryers were predicting a traditional Altdorf fog.

She trudged down Luitpoldstrasse towards the Street of a Hundred Taverns, noting which hostelries still had 'VACANCY' chalked up on their boards. She could not read, but there were words she could recognize. By the watch station, there was a notice the height of a tall man, covered in scroll-like writing. She could pick out a few words: 'WANTED,' 'MURDERER,' 'FIFTY GOLD CROWNS' and, larger than the rest, 'THE BEAST.' A sergeant stood outside the station, wrapped in a warm wolf's-fur coat, his hand resting on a swordhilt. She kept her head down and walked past.

'Watch out, old woman,' the watchman shouted, 'the Beast is about!'

Not looking up, she swore at him and turned a corner. The officer had called her an old woman. That hurt worse than the cold. She could not stop shivering and wrapped her old shawl tighter about her shoulders. It did little against the fishhook-sharp blast of the wind.

She had no idea where she could sleep. Ten or fifteen years earlier, she could have earned a bed for the night by servicing the night man at one of the waterfront hostelries. Not that she would have bent so low when she was in her prime. She had given herself only for gold crowns. But not now. There were younger girls to collect the crowns. There were always younger girls. She admitted to twenty-eight, but felt twice that and knew that at this hour, by the light of both moons, she must look older still. Next year, she would be forty. Her youth had been used up too quickly. Rikki Fleisch's knife had taken out one of her eyes and left a deep groove in one cheek, a repayment for some imagined wrong, but time had wrought an almost equal damage to the rest of her face.

Her shawl had been good once, embroidered with gold thread. The gift of Friedrich Pabst, a gentleman who had been her admirer, it was now patched and ragged. She was going through her shoes, and they had never been the right size. Her feet hurt more than anything else, ruined by years of tottering on ridiculously high heels through the cobbled streets and across the rickety bridges of Altdorf. The gold crowns were all spent now, mostly by Rikki. He had been sweet to her in the beginning and had bought her clothes and jewels. But the clothes were rotted and the jewels pawned, sold or stolen. They hadn't been worth much anyway. And the few good pieces had had to have the original owners' crests filed off.

Across the rivers, there was music. The Emperor's palace rose above all the other buildings and could be seen from almost everywhere within the city's walls. That was too far away to be the source of the music, but there were other great houses. She had been at balls in her youth, taken along by Rikki as a gift for important men, or even invited on her own by her gentleman – Fritzi, she had called him – during their brief summer together, before his wife had returned from her cousin's place in Talabheim. The ladies had known what she was and shunned her, but their men had come sniffing around her skirts, begging her to dance with them and later soliciting other favours. She remembered their perfumes and their velvets. The music of those days had gone out of fashion, but the gentlemen must still be the same, unchanging, smooth, calculating. Undress them and they were just like Rikki Fleisch.

Once, she had been the prize in a dicing game and was taken upstairs by a courtier. He had been some remote cousin of one of the electors. He was fumbling and clumsy and had popped a dried weirdroot flake into his mouth before joining her in the bed, needing the dreams to inflate his courage. Now, she could not remember his face, just his magnificent suit of clothes. That night, she had woken up to find him twitching beside her in his dream. On an odd whim, she had got out of the bed and pulled his distinctive courtier's green velvet cloak over her naked body, relishing the soft kiss of the fabric on her skin. The courtiers all wore these cloaks when they were in the presence of the Emperor. It was an old tradition. Then, that night, Margi Ruttmann had been fit for an Emperor. She hawked and spat in the gutter, tasting the gin again as spittle filled her mouth.

There was no music on this side of the river. At least, not music like that. She shivered, the memory of velvet on skin like a phantom's embrace. It was a long time since she had lain with a man who used perfume. Or even soap.

On nights like this, the wind blew off the rivers, filling the air with the stink of dead fish and dead men. No wonder this was where the Beast chose to do his bloody business. More people died every year around the wharfs than on all the glorious battlefields of the Empire. Margi had been in the Black Bat earlier, making the few pfennigs she had taken from Gridli Meuser's child last on a tall glass of gin, combing her stringy red hair over the damaged side of her face, pouting at the few sailors and dockhands who came in. They all knew her and no one was interested. Twenty years ago, they would all have been around her, as they were around that pigeon-chested tart Marlene, or the dark girl from the north, Kathe Kortner. But that had been twenty years ago, when she had been ripe. Now, she only got the drunkest of the drunk and then only on nights when it was too dark to see her face. It was a question of on your back under one of the bridges or standing up in an alley and holding your breath so you don't catch the stench of sweat and beer in your throat, hoping it would be over with soon enough to get back before closing time for a glass or a chew. Five children, born in backrooms and sold by Rikki before they could be named, and Ulric knows how many herb-induced miscarriages had ruined her inside anyway. She could never feel anything, which was probably just as well.

Her standards had been slipping recently, she knew that. Where once she would have insisted on the finest wines, now she was guzzling the roughest gin. Anything to dull the pains. She couldn't remember the last time she had made the effort to get any real food. All the coins she could scrape together went on gin. She would take weirdroot when she could afford it and escape into dreams. But these days her dreams were as dull as waking life and she was always pulled back in the end and dumped in her own self, waking up to the pain. It wasn't just in her legs. Her back hurt more and more, and her neck. And the gin was settling into her brain, making her head throb most of the time.

Business was bad all through the docklands, she knew. In the Black Bat, Bauman had been talking about the Beast and how trade had fallen off since the murders started. There were still the waterfront rats and the sailors fresh off the boats, but most of the citizens of Altdorf were staying away from the Street of a Hundred Taverns. If you didn't get cut up and spread around, you were likely to get hauled in by the watch and questioned. Most people said that the Beast was a nobleman from the Imperial court. Or else he was a cultist of the Dark Powers, disgustingly altered by the warpstone, his fingers turned to sharp knives. Kathe said she had seen the Beast once, stalking a child through the Old Docks,

his huge eyes glowing green. She said he had three mouths,
one in the usual place and two high up on his cheeks, that
his teeth had been inches long and that his breath had been
poisoned steam. But Kathe had already discovered the
dream-delights of weirdroot and was out of her skull most
of the time, not caring who took her. She wouldn't last long.
Bauman said he heard that the Beast was a dwarf, killing
because he had vowed to cut the big people down to his size.
The watch didn't know anything. There were posters up in
all the taverns and she had heard drinkers laboriously reading them aloud. The watch were offering good crowns for
any information leading to the capture of the murderer. That
meant they were desperate.

To Margi, it didn't make any difference. All men were
beasts, more or less, with fangs and claws, and women were
fools for thinking anything else of them. Besides, she had a
claw of her own, a nice sharp blade.

She needed a bed now, more than she needed a weirdroot dream. She had spent too many nights curled up
under sacks down by the docks. That was dangerous. Even
if the rats didn't bother you, the company watchmen
always came round and used their sticks on you. She
would always offer herself to them, asking to be left alone
in return. It had been months since one of the brutes – that
hog Ruprecht at the Reik and Talabec Trading Company –
had taken her up on it, and he had been too bloated to do
much. Afterwards, he had kicked her a few times and still
put her out on the streets. She thought Ruprecht had
cracked one of her ribs. With all her other pains, it was
hard to tell. One night, she would go back to the Reik and
Talabec and take out her blade, just to see how many lay-
ers of fat the company man had around his belly. It would
be worth doing soon, before they caught the Beast. He
could take the blame for it.

She leaned against a wall and felt her whole body sag.
Things were bad for Margi Ruttmann.

Whoring wasn't much of a trade at the best of times and
it wore you out in a few short years. She knew that now, but
she had been a stupid girl once, painted and simpering with

the rest of them, dreaming that she would latch on to the younger son of some courtier and become his adored mistress. Marlene and Kathe were like that, but they would learn better soon. She smiled at the thought, imagining the giggling girls gone to rot, shunned by their current crop of admirers. Red-cheeked, plump-titted Marlene would run to fat and drop bastard children yearly in piglet-like litters, and Kathe, who danced like a serpent, would shrivel away to a scarecrow, living more and more in dreams until she walked off a bridge or under a carriage and four. She knew how people aged, had seen it over the years. Margi had just got tough, her soft skin turned leathery, her heart a dead lump like the stone of a peach.

For the hundred millionth time, she cursed Rikki. Without his mark on her face, she would still have been able to get by in her old business. Months after he had carved her, she had slipped into his bed, his own blade in her hand, and cut him a little. She had made holes and let pieces leak out. The memory, too, made her smile. An old woman needed her comforts. The watch had questioned her, but Rikki had too many enemies for them to spend time choosing a likely candidate. That had been during the Waterfront War, when the Hooks and the Fish had been killing each other off up and down the riverbanks. Rikki had been with the Hooks for a while, so he just got listed as another reprisal. The War had not really ended, it just got boring and the gangs lost interest. Earlier, Margi had seen Willy Pick, the current head man of the Hooks, wearing a Citizens' Vigilance armband and walking with an officer of the watch. Until the Beast was caught, there would be some unusual alliances. Most of the Fish were with that agitator Yefimovich, making speeches outside the palace and throwing rocks through shop windows.

Under her shawl, she gripped the handle of Rikki's knife. It was the one he had taken to her eye. It was the only possession she had never pawned. After all, it was her living these days. Her face and body might be ageing like fruit left too long in the bowl, but the blade stayed keen. Tonight, her blade would reap a harvest. Enough for a bed, she hoped, with maybe enough for a few chews of weirdroot to help her sleep, to help her dream.

She tottered down the Street of a Hundred Taverns, looking for a likely prospect. Outside the Sullen Knight, two young, drunken sailors were pummelling each other bloody while a crowd of drinkers looked on and cheered. Kathe was at the centre of the knot of onlookers, her hair loose, her eyes wild and moist, waiting to relieve the winner of his last voyage's wage. Bets were being placed, but neither lad looked to be up to much. That was no good, anyway. Too many people around.

Margi crossed the road rather than walk by the Crescent Moon. She knew what kind of clientele that hostel attracted and she wanted nothing to do with *them*. She didn't mind spending dead men's money, but she was nervous about doing it if the dead man was still walking around.

The Black Bat was closed by now and so was the Beard of Ulric. There was a middle-aged man lying unconscious in the gutter outside the Dancing Dwarf, dressed only in his underwear. He had already been worked over thoroughly: his purse was inside-out and empty beside him, and his knuckles were bloody where the rings had been pulled off.

Two officers of the watch marched past, ignoring the robbed drunk, their clubs out ready to break up the brawl at the Sullen Knight. She stepped into a narrow alley between Bruno's Brewhouse and the Mattheus II, and shrank into the shadows. There was a flickering torch still lit above the door of the Mattheus II and she had to edge close to the wall to avoid its light. There were still a few warrants outstanding on her and the watchmen often pulled her in for questioning. Once, years ago, she had had to service all the men in the Luitpoldstrasse Station just to win Rikki a favour. The watchmen were just like the Hooks or the Fish, with the crest of the House of the Second Wilhelm on their tabards rather than tatty gang emblems. What with the Beast, there were a lot more of them on the streets, hauling in whoever they could find just to prove they were doing something.

She heard the watchmen shouting at the brawlers and the yelps of those who were getting their lumps from the clubs. She hoped they knocked Kathe's silly teeth out for her. Or took her back to the station for a backroom party. That would teach her, the wiry bitch.

Why the watch couldn't catch the Beast and leave the rest of the waterfront alone, Margi didn't know. Perhaps it was because only the drunks and losers who fouled up everywhere else got assigned to the docks. All the shipping lines hired their own men to guard the warehouses and any skipper worth his pay would post his own watches when moored in Altdorf.

It was a long-standing joke in the city that thieves didn't get sent to Mundsen Keep, just assigned to the Dock Watch. The back room at the Luitpoldstrasse Station, where she had conducted her business, was a treasure trove of pilfered goods, stored until the weekly divvy-up. Every once in a while, some officer got too greedy and was hung in chains from the Fork Wharf, but for the most part it was crime as usual. The shipping companies found it cheaper to let their goods be tithed than to make a fuss and suffer from those mysterious fires which often raged around the boats and warehouses of merchants who complained about law and order.

The watchmen passed again, their leather jacks creaking, and she heard the crowd from the Sullen Knight moaning about the spoiled fight. Each of the officers had a chastened sailor on the end of a chain, his thumbs locked together. One of them started singing 'Come Ye Back to Bilbali, Estalian Mariner,' his voice cracked by drink and loose teeth.

'Shut up you,' said one of the officers, administering a thump with his club. The sailor fell down. The officer kicked him. Margi slid down the wall, hugging her bony knees, trying to stay out of sight. A small animal crept by her, brushing her hand with a velvet-furred side. It was gone. Both the officers were kicking the would-be minstrel.

'That's seen for Orfeo here,' said the downed man's keeper, unlocking his thumb-cuffs and wrapping the chain around his hand. 'Let's give his bunkmate some of the same.'

The other officer laughed and also started to free his prisoner. The sailor, a lot less drunk now, protested and demanded to be taken to the station and put in a cell. He was sorry for disturbing the peace.

'Why aren't you out catching the Beast?' said the sailor, his voice wavering, 'instead of–'

The first officer smashed his link-gloved fist into the sailor's stomach, knocking the breath out of him. He took a few more well-aimed shots at the prisoner, then stepped aside to let his friend have a go. The other officer used his chain like a whip and lashed the sailor across the face. The sailor tried to run towards the alley. Margi scuttled back, scraping herself against the wall. The officer flicked the chain out and it wrapped around the sailor's ankles, bringing him down face-first onto the cobbles. His head banged stone and he was probably knocked out. The watchmen kicked him a few times, spat on him and left, laughing. They were typical of the Luitpoldstrasse Station crew.

It was cold in the alley and there was water running somewhere. A chill crept through her. She turned and saw the glitter of water pouring from an aperture in a wall. It didn't smell clean.

There was someone else in the alley. She couldn't make out who or what, but she had the impression of a long cloak. A tall figure, most likely a man. Leaning against the back wall, washing something in the stream. At last, a prospect. She hoped the watchmen were out of earshot.

Margi smiled and pouted. She had practised the expression, to cover up her bad teeth. Under her shawl, she slipped the blade from its sheath.

'Hello, my love,' she said, her voice silly and fluttering like Marlene's, 'lonely this evening, are we?' The figure turned. She could not see a face.

'Come now, come to little Margi, and we'll take care of you…'

She unlaced her blouse and stepped into the light, hoping her skin would look all right. No one would want her if they got close enough to see her. But by then, it would be too late. The prospect would be just where she wanted.

'Come on, my love,' she cooed, her blade behind her. She beckoned with her left hand. 'This'll be a night you'll never forget.'

The figure moved. She heard the rustle of thick material. Fine clothes. She had hooked herself a rich man. Was it her imagination, or did she hear gold crowns rattling in a full purse? This could set her up for a month. She could almost taste the weirdroot in her mouth, feel the dreams blossoming in her skull.

She hung her head to one side and licked her lips. She pulled her blouse away from her shoulder and let her fingers caress her breast, play with her hair. She was like a fisherman, hooking a record-breaking catch.

The figure was close now. She could see a pale face.

She brought out her blade. You could get too old for whoring, but you were never too old to rob a drunk.

She could hear heavy breathing. Obviously, the prospect was interested.

'Come to Margi...'

The shadow-shape was close enough. She imagined a tall man and fit him into the outline she could see, considering where the best spot would be for a first strike. She stabbed out with her blade, aiming for the throat apple.

A hand closed on her wrist, incredibly strong, and she felt her bones grinding, then breaking. Her blade fell and clattered on the cobbles. She opened her throat to scream, sucking in a lungful of cold night air. Another hand, rough-palmed, clamped her mouth, shutting off her cry. She saw bright eyes, aflame, and knew her life was over.

The Beast pulled her into the dark alley and opened her up...

PART ONE
MURDER

I

BARON JOHANN VON Mecklenberg, the Elector of Sudenland, was a good servant to his Emperor, Karl-Franz of the House of the Second Wilhelm. He could not refuse his master a thing, not even an archery lesson for Karl-Franz's son, Luitpold.

'Higher, Luitpold,' Johann told the youth. 'Keep the quarrel and the sight in line.'

The straw targets were set up in the courtyard by the palace stables, and all horses and men had been cleared out of the sometimes erratic path of the future Emperor's bolts. The heir would have preferred to practise in the great ballroom – the only place inside the palace which had the distance to make target practice a real challenge – but an inventory of the priceless paintings, hangings and antiques in the possible line of fire had convinced the Emperor that it would not be a good idea to grant his son that particular wish.

'There,' said Luitpold as he released the crossbow string. There was a satisfying twang. The quarrel brushed the outermost edge of the target and embedded itself with a thud in the wood of a stable door. A horse in the next stall whinnied.

Johann did not laugh, remembering his own shortcomings as a boy. His ineptitude in archery had caused a lot more trouble than merely frightening a horse.

Luitpold shrugged and slipped another bolt into the groove.

'My hands shake, Uncle Johann.'

It was true. It had been true for three years, since the heir had been knocked down by the traitor Oswald von Konigswald during the one and only performance of the original text of Detlef Sierck's *Drachenfels*. No one who had been in that audience came out of the theatre in the Fortress of Drachenfels the person they had been before. Some of them, for instance, had been carried out under a sheet.

Johann was perhaps an exception. For him, life had had its horrors as long as he could remember. Even before Drachenfels, he had become used to struggling with the creatures in the darkness. Most people chose to ignore those things at the edge of their vision. Johann knew that such wilful blindness simply allowed the dark to close in. His years of wandering might be over, but that did not mean the threat was ended. The warpstone was still working its wretched magic on the hearts, minds and bodies of all the races of the world.

Luitpold fired again. He hit the target this time, but his bolt was stuck askew in the outermost ring.

There was applause from above and Johann looked up. On the balcony, Karl-Franz stood, his voluminous sleeves flapping as he clapped for his son. Luitpold reddened and shook his head.

'It was useless, father,' he shouted. 'Useless.'

The Emperor smiled. A thin man with a mass of curly gold-grey hair stood by Karl-Franz, his monk's hood down around his shoulders, his hands in his sleeves. It was Mikael Hasselstein, the Emperor's confessor. A lector of the Cult of Sigmar, Hasselstein was rumoured to be a likely candidate to fill the post of Grand Theogonist once old Yorri finally got through with the business of dying. Johann worshipped at the Cathedral of Sigmar whenever he could, but he could never bring himself to like men like Hasselstein. Clerics

should perhaps not be courtiers. Now, Hasselstein stood by
his Emperor, his face unreadable, waiting to be called upon.
No one could be all the time as cool-headed and even tem-
pered as Mikael Hasselstein seemed to be. No one human.
And Johann was hardly more impressed with his Emperor's
other companion, the pockmarked and olive-skinned
Mornan Tybalt, the Keeper of the Imperial Counting House,
who was intent on replenishing the palace's coffers by levy-
ing an annual tax of two gold crowns on all able-bodied
citizens of the Empire. The agitators were calling Tybalt's
scheme 'the thumb tax,' and gamblers were already wagering
on the percentage of citizens who would rather have their
thumbs clipped than part with the crowns.

'Johann, show me again,' Luitpold asked.

Reluctantly, aware that he was being put on show, Johann
took the crossbow. It was the best design Imperial coin
could buy, inlaid with gold filigree along the stock. The
sights of the weapon were so precise that it would take a
fumblefingers of Luitpold's stature to miss.

Without appearing to look at the sight or the target,
Johann released the quarrel. The target was marked with a
series of concentric red and blue circles. Instead of a bulls-
eye, it had a tiny red heart in its centre. Johann's bolt split
the heart. A tear of red paint dripped from the wound in the
straw.

In his mind, Johann heard the echoing cries of all those
he had had to kill during his ten years of wandering. His
ten years on the trail of Cicatrice the Chaos champion and
his followers, the altered monstrosities that called themselves Chaos Knights and his own brother, Wolf. When he
had set out, with his family retainer Vukotich at his side, he
had been as bad a bowman as Luitpold. But he had
learned. When you shoot at straw targets, it is easy to be
lazy, to settle for less and wait for the next turn. When you
face bestial creatures in battle, you shoot true or you do not
live to draw a bowstring again. Johann would never be as
elegant in battle as a court-educated warrior, but he was
still alive. Too many of the people he had known along his
route were not. Vukotich, for one.

Luitpold whistled. 'Good shot,' he said.

The Emperor said nothing, but nodded at Johann and, with Hasselstein and Tybalt at his side, walked on, vanishing from the balcony into one of the palace's many conference rooms. Karl-Franz had a lot to worry about these days, Johann knew. But then again, everyone had a lot to worry about.

Johann held up the crossbow to his eyeline, checking the sight. He felt the wooden stock against his cheek. Back in the forests of Sudenland, he had learned archery with a longbow. He remembered the tight string against his face, the shaking arrowhead resting on his thumb. When he had fired at a target, they called him Deadeye. But whenever an animal had been in front of him, he had ended up nicking his knuckle and firing wild. Strange to think that, all those years ago, he had had an unjumpable fence in his mind. He had been unable to kill. Now, sometimes, he wished he had never been cured of that particular failing.

One skewed shot and he had lost ten years. At sixteen, he had been too compassionate to kill a deer, and had fired wild, piercing his brother's shoulder. That one mistake had meant Wolf had to be sent home while Johann and Vukotich remained in the forests to finish the hunt, and when Cicatrice and his Chaos Knights rode by intent on ravaging the von Mecklenberg estates, Wolf had been stolen away. Vukotich and Johann had followed Cicatrice across the face of the Known World, learning more and more of the mysteries, the horrors, that were hidden from most. In the frozen wastes of the north, on a battlefield where the monsters of the night fought forever, it had come to an end and Johann had found himself confronting young Wolf, grown into a beastman himself, twisted by a hatred that still writhed in his old wound. Vukotich had sacrificed himself and, by a miracle that Johann still gave daily thanks for, Wolf had been restored to him, a boy again, given another chance. The power of innocent blood had saved his brother and that had been the end of the wandering for Johann.

He gave the crossbow back to Luitpold.

'Again,' he said. 'Try to keep your shoulders loose and your hands still.'

The youth grinned and wrestled another bolt into the groove, cocking the string with a grunt.

'Careful,' Johann said, 'or you'll put a bolt through your foot.'

The heir brought the crossbow up and fired. The shot went wild, the quarrel breaking against the flagstones. Luitpold shrugged. A door behind them opened and Johann turned his head.

'Enough,' Johann said. 'It's nearly time for your fencing lesson.'

Luitpold gently leaned the crossbow against the back of a chair and turned round to greet the newcomer.

'Viscount Leos,' he said, 'welcome.'

Leos von Liebewitz saluted and clicked the heels of his polished boots. Most famous duellists were distinguished by their scars. Johann, with more experience of ungentlemanly scraps than polite contests, was covered with them. But Leos, who had fought countless times, had a face as unlined and soft as a girl's. That, Johann knew, was the mark of a master swordsman. Leos switched his green cloak over one shoulder, disclosing his sheathed sword. The young nobleman had watery blue eyes and cropped gold hair that made all the ladies of the court go weak, but he never seemed to return their interest. Clothilde, grand daughter of the Elector of Averheim, had very ostentatiously made romantic overtures to him very soon after her startling transformation from spotty, spoiled brat to ravishing, spoiled young woman and was now suffering from a severely broken heart. Johann supposed that the young viscount's sister, the notorious beauty Countess Emmanuelle von Liebewitz, had enough devotion to the amorous arts for any one family.

Leos smiled sweetly. 'Highness,' he said, nodding. 'Baron von Mecklenberg. How is our pupil coming along?'

Johann didn't say anything.

'Fearfully bad,' Luitpold admitted. 'I seem to have more thumbs than are strictly required by law. I shall have to pay extra tax.'

'A sharp mind will serve you better than a sharp sword, highness,' said Leos.

'That's easy to say when you're the best swordsman in the Empire,' snapped Luitpold.

Leos frowned. 'My teacher, Valancourt, at the Academy in Nuln, is better. And that fellow they sing songs about, Konrad. And a dozen others. Maybe even the baron here.'

Johann shrugged. He certainly did not intend to get dragged into an exhibition match with deadly Leos.

'I'm rusty, viscount. And old.'

'Nonsense.' Leos drew his sword with one clean, fluid movement. The thin blade danced in the air.

'Would you care to make a few passes?'

The swordpoint darted by Johann's ears, whipping through the air. Luitpold was delighted and clapped encouragement.

'I'm sorry,' Johann said. 'Not today. The future Emperor is impatient to receive the benefit of your learning.'

The viscount's arm moved, too fast for Johann's eye, and his sword was sheathed again.

'A pity.'

An attendant was already clearing away the straw targets and archery impedimenta. A trolley had been wheeled into the courtyard. A fine array of swords lay on the upper tier, while masks and padded jackets were bundled below.

Luitpold was eager to get into his gear. He tried to strap himself into his protective jacket and got the wrong buckles attached. The attendant had to undo the Prince and start all over again. Johann was reminded of Wolf, the old Wolf of their childhood, not the strange young-old boy he had brought back from the Chaos Wastes. His brother was three years younger than him, twenty-nine, and yet he had lost ten years to Cicatrice and seemed no older than his late teens. His body had been restored and his soul purged of all the horrors of his years with the Chaos Knights, but the ghost of the memory was still with him. Johann could still not stop worrying about Wolf.

Luitpold made a mock ferocious face as he pulled his mask down and cut up the air with his foil.

'Take that, hellspawn algebra teacher,' he shouted, thrusting forwards and twisting his blade in the air. 'This, for your calculus and this for your dusty abacus!'

Leos laughed dutifully, fastidiously strapped on his chest-protector and pointedly did not bother with the mask. Luitpold capered, administering a death thrust to his imagined opponent. 'Lie there and bleed!' Johann could not help comparing the lively, unspoiled heir with the withdrawn, brooding Wolf.

He had come to Altdorf not just to do his duty at the court, but to be close to Wolf. His brother was supposed to be studying at the University, catching up on his long-lost lessons. And Johann was worried by the reports he kept receiving from Wolf's tutors. Sometimes, the student would disappear for weeks on end. Frequently, his temper would snap and he would get into some ridiculous fight or other and, holding back at the last moment, would be roundly pummelled by an opponent he should have been able to beat without effort. Whenever Johann saw his brother's face bruised and drained of expression, he could not help but remember that other face he had seen on the battlefield. His brother had been a fang-snouted, red-eyed, luxuriously-maned giant. How deeply had that creature been embedded in Wolf's soul? And how clean had his slate been washed by the power of innocent blood? Which, after all the House of von Mecklenberg had been through, was the real Wolf?

Leos was giving Luitpold a work-out now. Johann saw that the viscount was slowing himself, fencing as if wearing weighted boots and gloves. But he was still an elegant murder machine, prodding the prince's quilted torso with every strike, perfectly parrying the youth's counterthrusts. In a genuine duel, he would have cut the future Emperor into thin slices like a Bretonnian chef preparing a cold meat buffet.

There were a lot of stories about the Countess Emmanuelle's many love affairs and her strange preferences in the boudoir, but they were never told where Viscount Leos might hear them. The exclusive graveyards of the Empire were full of well-born swordslingers who thought they were better with a blade than Leos von Liebewitz. The countess had a lot to answer for.

The viscount was making Luitpold break into a sweat now and the heir wasn't disgracing himself. He was less clumsy with a foil than with a crossbow, and he had the strength. It was the strength of a runner, not a wrestler, but that was what he would need to be a swordsman. Once he learned the moves, Luitpold would be a fine duellist. Not that Karl-Franz would let him get anywhere near a serious fight while still alive and Emperor. Luitpold was enjoying the lesson, even clowning a little for Johann's benefit, but Leos was taking it all seriously. The future Emperor's thick jacket was marked with a hundred tiny tears and the stuffing was leaking.

Watching Leos, Johann wondered about the viscount. During his lost years, Johann had fought many duels to the death, had survived many battles. He had bested men so grievously altered by the warpstone that they resembled daemons. He had killed many. The blood of all the races of the Known World was on his hands. That had not been a courtly game, with seconds and stewards and rules of etiquette.

He was sure that, if it came to it, if it ever got serious, he could take Leos von Liebewitz. But he was not looking forward to it. Not one bit.

Behind the clash of steel on steel, Johann heard something else, a clamour outside the palace walls. Luitpold and the viscount did not notice and continued with their fake combat, Leos ticking off the heir's errors and praising his good moves.

People were shouting. Johann's ears were good. They had had to be, in the forests and the wastes.

Six halberdiers, stumbling as they buckled on their chestplates and helmets, rushed across the courtyard. Luitpold stood aside and Leos, hands on hips, frowned.

'What's going on?' Johann asked.

'The main gate,' huffed a young soldier, 'there's a mob there. Yefimovich is making a speech.'

'Sigmar's Hammer,' spat Leos, 'that damned agitator!'

The halberdiers ran off through the archway, heading for the palace gate. Luitpold turned to follow them.

'Highness,' Johann said, sharply, 'stay here.'

It was Luitpold's turn to frown. Anger sparked in his eyes, but died immediately.

'Uncle Johann,' he complained, 'I–'

'No, Luitpold. Your father would hang me in irons for the crows.'

Leos was pulling off his padded jacket. Johann could see trouble coming to the boil.

'Viscount,' he said, 'if you would remain here to protect the future Emperor. Just in case...'

Leos bridled, but a glance from Johann convinced him. He touched his sword to his nose and bowed his head for an instant. Thankfully, he was not one of those aristocrats – like Luitpold – who had been taught to question every order. The von Liebewitz household must have had a good, strict nanny in charge of the nursery.

Johann followed the halberdiers and found himself in step with a growing number of men as he followed a path through the interlocking courtyards. The noises beyond the gate were getting louder and there were more voices being raised. He heard a rattle and recognized it as the sound of the main portcullis coming down. It was as if the hordes of Chaos were inside the walls of the city, and the Imperial Guard were falling back to the last position of defence. But that could not be the case.

There was such a crowd of soldiers by the gate that Johann could not see through. He judged by the din that there were a lot of people beyond the portcullis gate, and that they weren't happy. It was always something. If it wasn't the incursions of Chaos it was the thumb tax, and if it wasn't some new religious zealotry it was a mob demanding that some unpopular felon be turned over to them for swift justice. The mob of Altdorf was a byword throughout the Empire for unruliness.

He heard one of the halberdiers saying something about the Beast and knew this was worse than any of the other causes. A ball of dried mud and dung sailed through the railings and burst against an arch, showering dirt down on a troop of the Imperial Guard. Halberds were being rattled.

Johann found himself standing next to a tall cleric of the Cult of Sigmar. His hood was up, but he recognized the man as Hasselstein.

'What's happening?'

Hasselstein turned his face and paused a moment – Johann imagined him weighing in his mind whether the Elector of Sudenland was important enough to be told anything – before giving a curt report. 'It's Yevgeny Yefimovich, the rabble-rouser. He's been whipping the mob up into a frenzy about the Beast murders.'

Johann had heard about the Beast murders. The news of each pathetic drab butchered down by the docks had filled him with a secret dread. The slayings were so savage that many could not believe a human being was responsible. The Beast must be a daemon, or a beastman. Or a wolf.

'But Yefimovich is an insurrectionist, isn't he?' Johann protested. 'I understood he was always rabbiting on about the privileges of the aristocracy and the suffering of the peasants. Just a typical fire-breather.'

'That's what's so silly,' Hasselstein said. 'He alleges that the Beast is an aristocrat.'

A phantom blade slipped between Johann's ribs and he felt his heart stop. After a long pause, it beat again, and again. But he would remember that thrust for quite a time.

Very deliberately, he asked, 'What evidence does he have?'

Hasselstein sneered. 'Evidence, baron? Yefimovich is an agitator, not a jurist. He doesn't need evidence.'

'But there must be something.'

Hasselstein looked into Johann's eyes and for the first time the elector noticed how ice-sharp the cleric's gaze was. Something about the man reminded him of Oswald von Konigswald. There was the same ferocious deadness in his eyes, the same compulsion for total control. Johann would not have liked to face Leos von Liebewitz over duelling swords, but he fancied that Mikael Hasselstein would be an even more dangerous enemy.

The cleric reached into his robe and took out the emblem of his cult. It was a heavy-headed hand-hammer. Obviously, it had some religious significance, but it looked as if it would

be mainly useful if the Emperor's confessor ever felt the need
to smash in someone's skull. Johann got the impression that
the calm and suave Hasselstein often felt like smashing in
someone's skull. It was always these icewater-for-blood,
no-emotion-on-the-surface types that ended up in the town
square taking an axe to the market-day shoppers in the name
of some unheard-of lesser godling.

'Let me through,' the cleric said. The halberdiers parted
and a path was cleared to the gate. Another dirt bomb
exploded and Hasselstein shrugged it off. Johann stood
back.

Yefimovich was held at shoulder height by his followers
and was ranting.

'For too long have the titled scum of the noble houses of
the Empire trampled us under their perfumed boots!' he was
shouting. 'For too long has our blood been spilled in the
services of their pointless squabbles. And now one of them
walks the night, dagger in hand, carving up our women...'

Hasselstein looked up calmly at the fire-breather, gently
slapping his hammerhead into his palm.

'If it were duchesses and the like being butchered, you can
be sure that the Beast would be in Mundsen Keep by now,
properly chained and tortured. But no, just because these
women don't have lineages dating back to the time of
Sigmar, the Imperial court doesn't give two pfennigs for
them...'

Hasselstein spoke calmly to a captain of the guard. Johann
couldn't hear their conversation. Yefimovich was shouting
too loud. However, musketeers were joining the halberdiers.
Surely, the cleric wasn't planning to fire on the crowd. The
Emperor would never allow that.

'We know who the beasts are!' Yefimovich shouted, his
hands gripping the bars of the portcullis gate. 'You can see
them in their cage, just like in a zoo...'

He shook the bars, his long hair flying behind him. One of
the musketeers propped his rifle on its stand and took aim at
the agitator, flicking back the flint catch with his thumb.

Johann knew he couldn't stand by and watch Hasselstein
start a riot that would lead to a massacre.

He looked up at Yefimovich. He had heard a lot about the man, had even read some of his pamphlets, but this was the first time he had seen the agitator. He really was a fire-breather. His face seemed to glow as if there were flames under the skin and his red eyes shone like a vampire's. He was from Kislev originally and had got out a few horse-lengths ahead of the Tsar's cossacks. Some said his family had been killed at the whim of a nobleman, others that he was himself of the aristocracy, tainted by the blood of the vampire Tsarina Kattarin, and had turned against his own kind.

'Here I am!' he shouted. 'Are you afraid of me, you lackeys and minions? I drink the blood of princes, break the backs of barons and crush the bones of counts!'

Johann could see why Yefimovich had such a following. He was as magnetic as a great actor. If they ever wrote a play about him, only Detlef Sierck could take the part. Although, considering the fervour with which he advocated bloody revolution, perhaps the late and unmourned Laszlo Lowenstein would have been better casting.

Beside Johann, someone gasped. 'So that's Yefimovich.'

Johann turned. It was Luitpold. Johann felt a knot of anger, but pulled it straight.

'Highness,' he said, 'I thought–'

'It's always "highness" when you're being dutiful, Uncle Johann.'

Leos was with him, his hand on his swordhilt, his face blank. A man like the viscount could be useful just now. Like Johann, he was sworn to protect the House of the Second Wilhelm, and if Luitpold got into trouble, he would need the protection.

Hasselstein had finished talking with the captain, who rushed off to execute some order or other. Calmly, the cleric looked up at Yefimovich. If they had strained, they could have touched one another.

Johann felt as if he were witnessing an invisible battle of wills. It was almost intriguing, the man of fire outside, the man of ice inside. In their hearts, they must have a lot in common.

'Where is he?' Yefimovich was shouting. 'Where is the arch-coward himself? Where is Karl-Franz?'

Luitpold started forward, about to shout back. Johann laid a hand on the heir's shoulder.

'My father is a good man,' Luitpold said, quietly.

Johann nodded.

'Does he care about the murdered women of the dock-land? Does he?'

Yefimovich drew breath, preparing for another speech, but said nothing.

'Citizens,' Hasselstein said in the pause, his voice surprisingly loud and strong, 'you are requested to disperse and return to your homes. Everything possible is being done to catch the Beast. I can assure you of that.'

Nobody made a move. Yefimovich was smiling, the sweat pouring from his burning red face, his hair streaming behind him like flames. He wore many badges on his tunic: the hammer of Sigmar, the sickle of the outlawed Artisans' Guild, the fish of the waterfront gang and the red star of the Kislevite underground. So many symbols, but just one cause.

'The palace, as you may remember, is equipped with many defences,' Hasselstein said. 'During the War of Succession, the troops of the false Emperor Dieter IV besieged this place and Wilhelm II repelled them by disgorging molten lead from the row of exquisitely carved gargoyles you see perched above the main gate. Note the fineness of the detailwork. Dwarfish, of course. The faces are caricatures of the five dae-mon princes the young Wilhelm encountered and overcame during his years in the wilderness.'

The crowd, as a man, started to edge back. Yefimovich was sweating hatred and glaring death. Hasselstein continued with his lecture, as if pointing out features of architectural interest to a visiting dignitary.

'Of course,' the cleric continued, 'those were barbarous times and the current Emperor would never consider using such methods on his loyal subjects.'

Held breaths were released and the crowd pressed for-ward. Yefimovich grabbed the bars again and showed his teeth. He snarled like an animal and seemed fully capable of chewing his way through the portcullis.

'However, it is a simple matter to connect the palace's ingenious sewage and waste disposal system to the old defence pipes...'

He nodded and the gargoyles vomited filth.

A stream of liquid waste hit Yefimovich full in the face and he cried out in rage. His bearers deserted him and he was left hanging from the gatebars. Behind him, the crowd was running from the rain of ordure. People were knocked down and trampled in the panic. The smell wafted through the gates and Johann covered his mouth and nose.

Luitpold laughed out loud, but Johann wasn't sure if it was funny or not.

Yefimovich fell away from the gate. Someone had jabbed him with the blunt end of a halberd. Johann wondered whether it wouldn't have been more sensible to use the business point. The fire-breather slipped on a lump of fecal matter and fell badly. This experience certainly wasn't going to make the agitator change his views and become a lover of the nobility. Children were crying and people, covered in filth, were limping away. The halberdiers were laughing and jeering and making comments.

'You talk it,' one shouted, 'you might as well be covered in it!'

Yefimovich stood up, holding his side, blood leaking from his nose. Bright eyes opened in his brown-coated face. He had a scary kind of dignity, even in his current condition. He spat through the bars of the gate and walked away. The last of the crowd went with him, wiping themselves off.

'There,' said Hasselstein, a thin smile on his face, 'that is that dealt with. The Emperor has authorized me to say that there will be an extra ale ration this evening as a reward for your valorous service in his defence.'

The halberdiers cheered.

'What started this?' Luitpold asked an officer of the guard.

'Some whore down by the docks,' the man replied. 'The Beast got her, ripped her apart.'

Luitpold nodded, thinking.

'The fifth, she was,' the officer continued. 'They say it's a bad business. The Beast just tears them up. It's like he was an animal or something. A wolf.'

A wolf! Johann's heart stopped again as he remembered the face of a boy who was also a beast.

'Uncle Johann,' Luitpold said, 'if the people are unhappy because of this murderer, then it is our duty to catch him and make things right again.'

Knowing better, Johann lied to the boy. 'Yes, highness.'

II

THE BEAST'S FIRST *memories are painful, but exciting.*

'Don't touch yourself there! That's disgusting!'

Then, blows. The Beast tastes blood in its mouth. It sees a face in the mirror, with bruises. A face that could be anything, anyone. It doesn't have to recognize the face as itself. It is lumpy and bleeding, pathetic. It is just the face of the boy-shell. For the first time, the Beast roars. It does not have claws yet, but knows they will grow.

Later: 'Here, kitty-kitty… here, let's play together. There now, there's a nice cat. Whose mama loves you, then? That's right. That's nice. Purr, purr for your mama…'

A sharp claw appears in the Beast's hand. It slides through fur and skin, and punctures muscle.

The cat shrieks like a daemon.

'Here, kitty-kitty… come to mama. Kitty? Kitty!'

Still later, a different voice.

'There now, slip into your trousers. What a fine, hand-some boy you are. You'll make your father proud. What's this in your pocket? Careful, you'll tear the cloth. It's expensive. It's velvet. Like they wear at the Emperor's court in Altdorf. There now, you've torn it. I told you to be careful, boy!'

More blows. By now, the Beast is used to blows. It doesn't feel them, no matter how hurt the boy-shell is. The boy-shell stops crying eventually and with each hurt the boy recedes and the Beast becomes stronger.

When they are ten years old, the Beast kills again, for the first time since the kitten. The Beast is clever. It knows it is not yet as strong as it will become. So it picks Old Nikolas, the family's retired gamekeeper. Old Nikolas had to retire on a pension when gored by a hog during a hunt. His legs are bent and he spends most of the day in his hammock in the old lodge. He is slow and will not be able to escape the Beast. The boy-shell thins and the Beast pokes out its claws, taking down father's two-edged sword from his last campaign. It is heavy in the Beast's hands, but not too heavy. The weight is important. If the Beast can heft the weapon up high enough, the weight will increase the force of the blow, compensate for the weakness of the boy-shell's arms. It has all been thought out perfectly. The sword slices down and parts Old Nikolas's neck as if it were soft cheese, chopping also through the canvas hammock.

The gamekeeper's head rolls free and the Beast kicks it like a ball.

'It's horrible, horrible, horrible. My little boy mustn't see. He mustn't. Don't you understand?'

The Beast waits for a long time, pretending to be the boy-shell. They grow up, are educated in the arts of a gentleman.

On their twelfth birthday, the Beast comes out again and takes an axe to a drunken guest in the garden. It's Uncle Sergius, who had bounced the boy-shell up and down on his knee. He looks strange with the split in his face. The wound reminds the Beast of the forbidden places of the female body. Then the Beast makes its first and only mistake. Kneeling by Uncle Sergius to get a better look at the split, the Beast dips the boy-shell's fingers into the blood, probing the wound.

'Sigmar's hammer!'

It is Natasha, the girl who travels with Uncle Sergius. The boy-shell's father calls her his brother's mistress. The Beast knows what that means. They think that sort of thing is disgusting.

Natasha just stands there, not saying anything, her mouth getting rounder, her arms stuck out like a scarecrow. She looks funny. The boy-shell smiles at her and the Beast takes out the claw from its waistsheath.

'It's all right, 'Tasha. Don't be sad.'

The boy-shell gets up and slips an arm round Natasha's waist. She is shaking, but can't move. The Beast licks her face with a rough tongue. She doesn't flinch.

She enjoys it really, the Beast knows that. Women are disgusting like that. Absolutely disgusting.

The Beast takes its hard, straight claw – eight inches of sharpened steel – and puts it into Natasha's stomach.

She gasps in delight and blood comes out of her mouth.

The Beast takes its claw out of Natasha's stomach and puts it into her chest. Then, it puts the claw somewhere else. And somewhere else.

Split-face Uncle Sergius looks up at the moons. And Natasha doesn't say anything.

This is the best thing the Beast has ever known. From now on, it will hunt only women. It will kill only women. The boy-shell agrees.

Women, it has finally realized, are its natural prey.

Women. Disgusting women.

III

As usual, the tally was coming up three barrels short. Benning, the clerk, was scratching his chin with his quill, squirting a little ink into his beard as he looked in bored bewilderment at the cargo barge moored up by the Reik and Talabec Trading Company Warehouse. Ruprecht, the night man, was yawning enormously, making the point that he wanted to go home and sleep. Judging by his breath, the fat hog could have accounted for all three casks of l'Anguille wine by himself. If the shipyard dog licked Ruprecht's sweaty crotch one more time, it would be as drunk as a priest of Ranald on Trickster's Day.

'Count it again,' snarled Harald Kleindeinst.

Benning, who was sensibly afraid of him, complied, and began checking the cargo against his manifest.

The *River Rat*, pride of the Reik and Talabec line, had the Marienburg to Altdorf run, carrying wines from Bretonnia, cloth from Albion and scrimshaw baubles from Norsca. And, during its twenty-five year life, it had never arrived in Altdorf with exactly the same cargo that had left Marienburg. Rather, while the cargo might have entered

37

Altdorf intact, it always seemed peculiarly diminished by the
time the unloaded goods were inventoried.

Harald was going to do something today that would
change that record.

'I wish you'd hurry up,' said Warble, the supercargo, 'I have
business in the city that won't wait.'

Warble was a halfling, but he wasn't the fey, childlike creature halflings were supposed to be. He was chewing a
cheroot and sitting on a deckstool, calmly waiting for
Harald to let him disembark.

'Take your ease, Warble,' Harald told him. 'Nobody leaves
the wharf until the cargo is accounted for.'

'I'm here on business, thief-taker,' the halfling said.

'So am I.'

Sam Warble shrugged and looked at the pointed toes of
his boots.

The dock crew were also sitting around, impatient. Krimi,
the young foreman, was fraying the end of a rope with a
marlinspike and casting the occasional threatening glance at
Harald when he thought the day watch wasn't looking at
him. Krimi was a Fish, and in addition to the colours sewn
onto his jerkin, had fish tattooed on his cheeks. That
marked him as a war chief and made him think he was a
tough character.

Harald knew better. Harald had met a lot of people who
thought they were tough characters. They usually turned out
to be pussies.

The Fish were losing ground to the Hooks and trying to
get back by throwing in their lot with Yefimovich the fire-
breather. The clerk continued his count, mumbling under
his breath.

It had been a cold night, but it was a warmish day, the last
of the autumn. The heat meant that the docks smelled worse
than usual. The next barge was unloading a cargo of seafish
that might possibly have been caught within the last ten
years, although Harald wouldn't have put a bet on it.
Chunks of ice were fast melting in the sunshine and the
dockers were hurrying the job, trying to get the barge
unloaded before the smell got too bad to bear.

Harald's hand rested on his right hip and happened to brush against the hilt of his throwing-knife.

After all these years, the weapon still hung comfortably in its sheath.

'Come down in the world, haven't you, thief-taker?' said Warble.

Harald raised his upper lip a little.

'The last time I was in Altdorf, you were a captain of the watch. Now, you're just doing sums for merchants.'

Harald looked at Warble, trying to place the face.

'Have I heard of you, halfling?'

Warble shrugged again. 'I doubt it. I keep to myself, mostly. I have a lot of respect for the law.'

'Still three barrels short,' said Benning.

The clerk looked at Krimi before he looked at Harald, which was their second mistake. Deciding to steal from the Reik and Talabec Trading Company, of course, had been their first.

Ruprecht could have stayed out of it, but he was too stupid. He was leaning against a stack of cotton bales on the dock, flapping a meaty hand at a fly that was buzzing around his eyes.

'I told you, Kleindeinst, there's no mystery. The barrels slipped their moorings and rolled overboard. They're with the fish.'

Harald just looked at the night watch. He felt sick to his stomach, as he always did around stupid, contemptible people.

'It's funny how many things just roll overboard on this run, isn't it?'

Ruprecht was sweating more than usual. He must be nursing a hangover from that l'Anguille wine. It had quite a kick and fat people could rarely hold their liquor.

'With the fish, huh? That's a believable story.'

Krimi looked up from his rope and raised an eyebrow. The Fish had originally got their name because they were always the people who seemed to come into possession of goods that 'rolled overboard.'

'Apart from that,' the clerk said, 'the tallies match.'

'Benning,' he said, 'if your tallies match, then you're either a terrible book-keeper or a clever thief. And I don't think you're a terrible book-keeper.'

The clerk jumped, almost falling off the quay. He turned round and his eyes stuck out.

In the quiet, he could hear the creaking of the barge as it drifted into the quay, grinding against the pilings and floated away again. The shipyard dog was panting, waiting for something to happen. Like everyone else.

'Do you have any idea how stupid you've been? These others don't know any better than to steal. But you're an educated man. You should never have doctored the tallies.'

The clerk looked around. Neither Krimi nor Ruprecht met his panicky eyes.

Warble pretended not to be interested and spat the wet end of his cheroot into the water.

'Three barrels, Benning. It's always three barrels. Whenever you count, Mr Fish here unloads and Ruprecht stands around watching, the cargo always comes up three barrels short. You should have varied it. You thought the company wouldn't believe it if there was no pilferage, so you decided on three barrels.'

Ruprecht was shaking, ready to explode. Krimi was gently lashing the dock with his rope. His gang lolled around, half on the barge, half off, leaning on things, waiting.

The halfling exhaled smoke. 'I've been over all the tallies and it comes to a lot more than three barrels a trip. You're a conscientious man, you must know exactly how much you've cheated the company out of.'

Benning was about to crack. Harald could see the water in his eyes.

'I-I-I was… I was fuh-fuh-forced…'

'Shut up, quill-pusher,' shouted Ruprecht, leaning forwards. He slapped his own face, setting his chins wobbling, but still missed the fly.

Harald turned on the night watch and his knife was in his hand, the blade against his palm, hilt pointed at Ruprecht. It was a fine piece of workmanship, with an eighteen-inch blade honed to razor edges. Some men had daggers with designs carved into their hilts and the names of gods etched on the blades. But this was unadorned, a thing of smooth curves and sharp lines. It was not for show.

'It's a tradition of the docks, Kleindeinst... nobody begrudges old Ruprecht his cut...'

Harald didn't say anything. He always felt sick to his stomach when thieves broke down. And thieves always broke down.

Krimi said, 'Yevgeny Yefimovich says that property is theft.'

'Yes, well theft is theft too.'

Harald held up his knife.

'This was made by Magnin the steelsmith,' he said. 'It is the heaviest throwing knife in the known world. To be effective, such a weapon has to be balanced to within a thousandth of an ounce. To be thrown properly, the knife-wielder has to have an accurate sense of time, an unusual strength of wrist and the eye of a hawk.'

Ruprecht backed against the bales. The fly settled on his ear. The night man was blubbering, sweat darkening his shirt.

'You'd better hope, scum, that those five bottles of wine I drank last night have not affected my aim this morning...'

Ruprecht sucked in a breath and closed his eyes, and the knife left Harald's hand, flipping end over end as if travelling through thick liquid...

There was a thud as the knife embedded itself up to the hilt and Ruprecht yelped.

The insect had stopped buzzing.

Ruprecht opened his eyes and found that the knife was stuck into the cotton bale, between his right ear and his skull. He was not even cut.

'Now, do I get a confession, or do things get unpleasant?'

Ruprecht was too busy praying to answer the question, but the Fish weren't impressed. They saw a man without a knife and made the familiar error of thinking he would be easy to take.

Krimi made a move with his eyes and came for Harald. He whipped out with his rope and raised his marlinspike to smash Harald's skull.

It was just like the old watch days. The scum seemed to move slower than a thick syrup, while he darted like a dancer.

Harald caught the rope as it snaked through the air and, with a deft turn, wrapped it around his wrists. He pulled and Krimi was off his feet.

When the Fish was within Harald's reach, he brought his knee up sharply into the other man's groin.

Krimi gasped in agony and his marlinspike fell onto the quay.

Harald let him go and pushed him away.

'Hurts, doesn't it?' he said.

The Fish would be too busy thinking about pain to be any more trouble. Harald picked up the rope and, pulling Krimi's hands away from his bruised balls, tied his wrists.

'Ruprecht,' he said, 'bring me my knife.'

Without thinking, the night man pulled the Magnin out of the bale and handed it to him. Harald sheathed it.

He looked at the remaining dockers. None of them wanted any more trouble.

'What are you waiting for?' he said. 'Get the cargo on the dock and don't forget the secret compartments in the fore hold.'

The Fish snapped to and started moving barrels and boxes like the marionettes of an especially dextrous puppeteer.

Warble stepped off the barge and looked at Krimi, who was still rolling on the dock, his knees locked together.

Harald yanked on the rope, hauling Krimi upright, and slipped an iron collarbrace around the Fish's neck, clicking the catch tight. Spikes dimpled the criminal's throat, drawing a little blood. If he struggled, he would gore himself badly. Harald playfully tugged the collar, drawing a howl from the Fish.

'Tell me,' Warble said, 'is that why they call you "Filthy Harald"?'

IV

'LET ME THROUGH, I'm on the Emperor's business.'

It was not strictly true but, along with his distinctive green courtier's cloak, it impressed enough people to get Johann through the crowd on the Street of a Hundred Taverns. Even discounting the curiosity-seekers and ghoulish layabouts, there were more people in the narrow alley between the Mattheus II and Bruno's Brewhouse than he would have thought possible.

'Captain Dickon,' an officer of the watch was saying to his superior, 'one blanket isn't enough to cover the corpse.'

'Sigmar's hammer,' swore the captain.

More than one person had been sick in the gutter.

'It's incredible,' said a slender elf in minstrel's clothes. 'She's all over the place.'

'Oh, shut up, pointy-ears!'

A scuffle was in the offing. Several, in fact. Johann got the impression that this crowd could be even more dangerous than Yefimovich's mob.

They had already been given their first whiff of blood and now they were thirsty for more.

The officers were standing with two battered sailors, one sergeant asking questions. A watchman produced a pair of handcuffs and rattled them threateningly in a sailor's face.

'It's that sailor boy,' shouted an old man. 'He's the Beast!'

'String him up!' someone shouted.

'It's too good for him,' put in someone else. 'Cut him up like he cut up poor old Margi!'

The crowd was pressing forwards, pushing Johann towards the alley. He felt fingers reaching for his purse and slapped them away. Someone small apologised in a high, shrill voice and scuttled off to rob someone else.

The captain turned, and raised his voice. 'Back, all of you. This man is not a suspect. He found the body.'

There was a palpable air of disappointment. The crowd had wanted to do someone violence. Now, it was cheated. The sailor looked relieved, but his shipmate was too sick to notice his narrow escape.

'Captain,' said Johann. 'I am Baron von Mecklenberg.'

'The Elector of Sudenland?'

'Yes.'

The captain stuck out his hand. 'Dickon of the Dock Watch.'

Johann shook the watchman's hand. Lying, he explained, 'The Emperor has asked me to observe your investigation. He is very concerned with these Beast killings.'

Dickon tried to look as if he was pleased to have an aristocratic overseer. He wore a long coat and a peaked cap with a tiny feather. His nose had been broken and badly set some time in the past. He wasn't in uniform, but he had his watchman's copper badge pinned to his breast.

'Really? Could you do something about my requests to the palace? I've been trying to get the troops down here. The Dock Watch can't cope by itself. We're undermanned.'

Johann wondered if he had got himself in too deep without thinking. 'I'll try my best, captain.'

The crowd were pushing in towards the alley again.

'Look, it's her arm!'

'That's disgusting.'

'I can't see, mama. Hold me up.'

'Ought to be strung up.'

'Where's my purse? I've been robbed!'

'She was a mean old cow, though, that Margi. Vicious.'

'*Disgusting!*'

'Ought to be burned at the stake in the Konigsplatz.'

'Bloody coppers. Never around when someone's ripping your bowels out.'

'They say he eats their hearts.'

'I bet it's a Bretonnian. Filthy people, Bretonnians.'

'Nahhh, it's a dwarf. All the wounds are below the chest. Never touches their faces.'

'It's a curse.'

'We're all doomed. Repent, repent. The wrath of the gods has descended upon the unrighteous.'

'Bloody coppers.'

'Shut up.'

Johann was pushed against Dickon. The crowd was turning in on itself, a few blows had already been exchanged. The dwarf-hater and the woman who had no love for Bretonnians were squaring off against each other. The ragged cleric of no particular god was starting a sermon.

'This is ridiculous,' said the captain. 'You men there, get these people out of here.'

Four officers, one looking distinctly queasy, pulled out their clubs and advanced at the crowd. Luckily, they didn't have to hit anyone. Grumbling, the people dispersed. The taverns were open. Murder was evidently good for business. At least, it was in the daytime when the Beast wasn't about. The cleric loitered a while, telling the officers that the gods were angry. But when a sergeant remarked that the man resembled a pickpocket due to have his fingers trimmed if he were ever caught, the cleric disappeared in the direction of the Black Bat.

'Where's that scryer, Economou?' Dickon asked the sergeant.

'On her way from the temple, sir.'

'I wish she would damned well hurry up.'

Johann and Dickon were near the entrance to the alley now.

'Would you care to take a look, baron?' the watch captain asked, a little insolence oozing into his habitual deference to the green velvet.

'Uh, yes,' Johann said. He realized that the captain thought he was a morbid sensation-seeker, using his position to get an eyeful of the latest atrocity. The watchman evidently had a very low opinion of people. Just now, Johann couldn't bring himself to mind. If Dickon thought he were just another degenerate, then he would never think of checking with the palace to expose his story of being the Emperor's representative. That would make things a lot easier.

Dickon nodded to an officer in the alley and the watch-man bent down to lift the blanket.

In his years of wandering, Johann had come across a great many dead bodies in a great many states of abuse and decay. But this was the worst thing he had ever seen.

'Was it a woman?'

He couldn't relate the remains to anything human, much less distinguish their sex.

'Oh yes,' said Dickon. 'Her name was Margarethe Ruttmann. She was a whore and a thief, and probably killed her pimp a few years back.'

Dickon spat. The officer let the blanket fall. The stains were spreading on the cloth.

'A proper little minx with a blade, too. Let's hope she put up a fight and marked our man.'

An officer who had been on his hands and knees at the rear of the alley, where water was dribbling from a hole in the wall, cried out. Dickon and Johann walked to him, care-fully stepping around Margarethe Ruttmann.

'It's her knife, sir.'

He held up a pathetic little pig-sticker.

'...and here's her other hand.'

'Merciful Shallya!'

The hand lay under the stream, washed white and clean. It looked like a fat, plucked bird.

'Put it with the rest. The scryer will want to see it.'

The copper took out a kerchief and wrapped his fingers, then plucked the hand out of the stream and, holding it with his thumb and fingertips, walked very fast over to the blanket and popped it under the cover. Standing up, he rubbed at his hand with the kerchief. He was shaking.

'Not like thumping drunks and roughing up weirdroot suppliers, is it, Elsaesser?'

The young officer shook his head.

'It's what I have to work with, baron,' Dickon told Johann. 'This is the Dock Watch, not the Palace Guard. These people don't just have copper badges, baron, they have copper heads.'

The sun was shafting down into the alley. It was almost overhead. The morning was gone. Shadows were thin and things not meant to be seen were in full view.

'And put that knife in a bag, Elsaesser. Maybe the scryer can get something from it.'

They came out of the alley. Dickon pulled out a pipe and a tobacco pouch. He lit up and inhaled a suck of thick, foul smoke. He did not offer Johann a chew.

Carts were trundling by, mainly carrying barrels to the street's famous hostelries. Life was going on. Across the way, three young women were soliciting passersby. The watchmen took no notice, so Johann assumed they had met their payments to the Luitpoldstrasse Station this month. He wondered how much it would cost to get the watch to be unwatchful while a murder was being committed. Not too much, he supposed.

'Skipper,' asked one of the sailors, 'can we go now? We were supposed to rejoin our ship just after dawn. Things will go bad for us if we're any later. Captain Cendenai is a hard woman.'

Dickon looked at the man and he shrank visibly.

'No you cannot go, sailor boy. I stopped that crowd ripping you apart because I don't want you dead until I'm completely sure you didn't cut old Margi up, you understand?'

The other sailor was heavily bruised about the face and holding his stomach. He was standing in a pool of his own vomit and still heaving occasionally, even though there was nothing left inside to come up.

'Bloody amazing isn't it, baron? This fellow is so used to the rolling waves that he gets seasick on dry land.'

Nobody bothered to laugh.

'What do these men have to do with the killing, captain?'

'Who bloody knows? They were on leave last night and were responsible for a bit of a disturbance down at the Sullen Knight. Incidentally, if you ever want a good punch-up that's the inn to drink in. A couple of our officers broke them up and administered a street sentence–'

'What's that?'

Dickon grinned. 'That's when the cells are too full to bother with idiots like this, and you give them a couple of headaches with the clubs, then leave them somewhere where people won't trip over them. They invariably wake up with a few lumps and a newfound respect for the Emperor's laws.'

'Damn the Dock Watch,' said the less-sick sailor. 'Bastards all!'

The officer holding the sailor stuck an elbow in the man's ribs, chuckling. The seaman bent double, feeling an old wound flare up.

'Find them a cell,' said Dickon, 'and give them some breakfast…'

The sick sailor finally brought something else up, a thin gruel laced with blood.

'…then keep them for some more questioning. Oh and find a herbalist for the puking champion.'

The sailors were dragged off, protesting feebly.

'They're all scum round here, baron. You see what I have to deal with.'

Johann thought he had seen enough to judge Dickon's methods. He was a watchman of the old school. Faced with a crime and no obvious culprit, his inclination was to haul in someone obscure and helpless and hit them until a confession came out. That looked tidy on the court books, but didn't do much about the actual problem. And it wouldn't work on the Beast. Looking at Margarethe Ruttmann, Johann knew that the Beast was a man who enjoyed his nightwork and he wasn't going to stop unless someone stopped him.

'Ulric,' said Dickon, 'but I could do with a cup of tea.'

Dickon walked over to the bench and grabbed by the ears the two officers who had beaten up the sailors. They must have been around at the same time as the Beast, but evidently they couldn't remember seeing anything or anyone more suspicious than usual. They yelped like dogs as Dickon wrung a report out of them.

'Useless scum,' Dickon spat.

'Sorry, captain,' said one of the coppers. Dickon slapped him with his open hand.

'You're mucking out the cells for a month, Joost.'

Johann looked around, wondering if any of these officers were capable of doing a job which required more than brute force and stupidity.

Most of the Dock Watch had a familiar look, with heavily-ridged brows, bruised knuckles and three days' beard. Big, hard arm muscles from hefting the club and big, soft stomachs from hefting the tankard. Two of the older men were laughing and joking in an attempt to impress the others with their hard-heartedness, trying to remember whether they had ever purchased temporary use of the deceased's body.

'Tell you what, Thommy,' said one, 'I don't fancy her much now.'

'Shut up, you ghoul bastards,' said Elsaesser. 'This was a person, not a lump of meat.'

'Not been on this watch long have you, son?' said Thommy. 'You'll learn.'

The young officer turned away in disgust and got back on his knees, looking closely at the ground.

There was a puff and the torch above the door of the Mattheus II was alight. The hostelry must have some sort of gas lighting, or a tame wizard in the tap-room. The landlord came out with a tray of free ale for the officers. Dickon got his first. 'It's not tea,' the captain said, 'but it'll do.' Only Elsaesser wasn't interested.

Johann stood by the young officer and watched him work. Elsaesser was sorting through the scraps of rubbish that had been strewn around during the Beast's work. There was a lot of it. He picked up each item, examined it, and put it back in its place.

'Is this your first?' Johann asked.

'No,' said Elsaesser. 'Third. I've been on the watch for a month. I missed the first four.'

'You're not from Altdorf?'

Elsaesser turned a piece of broken beermug over, looked at a maker's mark, and put the shard back.

'No, baron. I'm from the Reikwald Forest originally.'

'You're here from the Forest Rangers?'

'No, just out of the University.'

Elsaesser cast a cursory look at some waxed paper, an old food-wrapper.

'You have a degree?'

'Law. With a little military history and alchemy thrown in.'

The officer picked up a long strip of green material and held it up to the light. There was mud and blood on it.

'Then what are you doing on the Dock Watch? The service doesn't seem exactly suited to scholarship?'

'I *asked* for it, baron. They always need men.'

'You asked for the Dock Watch? But–'

'It's the crookedest watch in the city? I know. But the docks are where the Beast works. And I want to see the Beast caught.'

Elsaesser was a good man, obviously.

The officer stood up, brushing off his knees. He draped the piece of cloth over his hand and looked at Johann.

'What is it, Elsaesser?'

The officer's open face showed puzzlement.

'Look,' he said, holding the scrap against Johann's shoulder.

It was green, exactly the shade of his own cloak.

Johann took the cloth and felt the nap of the velvet. It was familiar.

Johann looked at Elsaesser and they both felt the world changing. Johann gripped the velvet strip and tried to feel something from it. He was no scryer, but he could not help trying. It didn't take a seer to draw a conclusion from green velvet.

'Yefimovich is right,' Johann said. 'The Beast is a courtier.'

Elsaesser shook his head. 'We don't know that. This could have been in the alley for days.'

'No, it's fresh. Look at this edge. It's been torn recently. And it's bloody.'

Johann held the strip up. It was a thin triangle, with two ragged edges and a hem. It came from the trailing edge of a garment. He looked at the hem. It was stitched with gold thread, and the velvet was a little worn where it would have scraped the ground.

Dickon was with them. 'What's this?'

'Green velvet, captain,' Elsaesser said. 'Like the baron's cloak.'

Dickon raised an eyebrow and laughed. 'So we have our man, eh?'

Johann explained, 'Green velvet cloaks are worn by tradition at the palace. By electors, courtiers, ambassadors, ministers. Even members of the Imperial family.'

For the first time, Dickon looked upset. He clamped his pipe between his teeth.

'You're saying the Beast is from the court? Merciful Shallya, that'd be worth a boatload of trouble.'

'It could as easily be a tailor or a servant,' said Elsaesser. 'Or a thief who's stolen the cloak, or someone who wants us to think that the Beast is a courtier.'

'It's not just the velvet, captain,' Johann said. 'It's the gold thread. That's expensive.'

Dickon was thinking it through, balancing justice against his career. Johann could imagine his rat's mind struggling through the maze of conclusions. The captain of the Dock Watch knew that there would be little thanks for anyone who proved that the Beast was an aristocrat. An altered of the warpstone, yes, or, better still, someone usefully unimportant and disgusting. Someone everyone could hate without complication. But a courtier, an ambassador, a minister... That would be too much trouble. A watchman who arrested and convicted a nobleman might win a medal, but he would never again be advanced in the service, he would never again have the trust of his betters.

'Good work, Elsaesser,' the captain snapped, snatching the
scrap from Johann and scrunching it into a ball. 'You've seen
through this trick. The Beast is trying to stir up trouble. With
Yefimovich spreading sedition throughout the city, the murderer is sending us on a false path. But we're not fooled. The
Dock Watch isn't that stupid.'

Dickon tossed the velvet in the air and it landed on the
Mattheus II torch.

'Captain,' protested Johann. 'That's important evidence.'

The velvet burned and fell as ash.

'Nonsense, baron. It was just a false trail. The Beast is a
clever creature. We know that. He wants us chasing all over
the place, harassing important people, while he stays about
his bloody business. I mean, can you imagine a minister of
the Emperor chopping up harlots in a back alley?'

For some reason, Johann thought of Mikael Hasselstein.
And of the late Oswald von Konigswald.

'Or even, perhaps, an *elector*?'

Elsaesser looked at the black scraps on the cobblestones.
Dickon stamped on them, grinding them into nothing.
Johann watched him do it. He could not have stopped the
man, but he was also not sure he wanted to.

After all, he had several of these cloaks. And so did most
of the people he knew at the court. Leos von Liebewitz had
been wearing one this morning. The last time he had seen
Wolf, he had lent the boy one of his courtier's cloaks for an
Imperial function. He had made his brother a gift of it.

'There, that's that trouble dispensed with. Now, let us
hope that our scryer accomplishes something. Unless I miss
my guess, this is her right now.'

A watch coach drew up outside Bruno's and the door was
pulled open. A young woman dressed in red, her red hair
done up in a scarf, stepped out. She wore a simple hammer
symbol amulet. Dickon extended his hand to her.

'Captain Dickon of the Dock Watch,' he said.

The woman looked at him, looked into the alley, looked
up at the sky, and collapsed in a faint.

'Sigmar's bloody hammer,' said Dickon.

V

IN HIS DREAM, Wolf was running through the forests. He was not quite an animal and resisted the urge to fall on all fours and propel himself with his hands as well as his feet. He was clothed and armoured, like a man, but he was also a wolf, with a wolf's teeth, a wolf's fur and a wolf's claws. He ran at the head of his pack, many of whom were also caught halfway between beast and human. Snow crunched under his feet as he dodged around the trees that stood tall and dark in his path. And ahead of him somewhere was his prey of the night. The pine trees smelled strong but his prey's scent was stronger. His snout was wet with his own saliva and he could already taste the copper and salt tang of the blood with which he would soon be filling his mouth and belly.

He sighted his prey and leaped, his strong hind-legs kicking against the hard-packed snow, his claws extended.

Something smaller than he cried and went down under him. His claws sliced into flesh.

The two moons were full in the night sky. As he rended his meat, he looked up and howled...

With the last of his howl still in his ears, Wolf awoke. He was damp with his own sweat and the thin sheet was sticky over his body. His thick coat of hair itched and his head swam with the fast fading remains of his elation.

He had had the dream again and felt nothing but shame.

Above him was the familiar lath and plaster ceiling of Trudi's room at the Wayfarer's Rest. He must have ended up here last night rather than returned to his apartment at the University. He wondered when he had last been at his college. Last night, he remembered someone saying that Professor Scheydt had been asking after him. And his brother, Johann.

Exhausted rather than refreshed by his sleep, he lay still in the narrow bed, feeling the warmth of Trudi, who was still sleeping soundly, her body pressed against his.

He tried to banish the dreams, but they would not go away. By day, he had no memory of the time he had spent with Cicatrice's Chaos Knights, although he had been able to draw out of Johann as much of the story as his brother knew.

For ten years, he had been under the influence of the scar-faced bandit king, and for ten years the warpstone had steadily worked its magic upon him, giving him a body and a mind to match his name. Only the sacrifice of Vukotich, the family's loyal servant, had restored Wolf von Mecklenberg to his original form. And while his form might have been changed back, there was still the question of what had happened to his mind.

He was twenty-nine years old and yet now, six years after his rescue, he seemed to be nineteen. At nights, his lost years crowded back in. But how much of his dreaming was memory and how much delirium?

At first, he had hidden away in the family estate, trying to cling to childhood, refusing to talk of any current matters, resisting Johann's attempts to tell him what had happened during his ten-year 'absence.' Then, he had tried to run away, to live wild in the woods, in the hope that he would find peace of spirit. Two chance meetings had given him examples to follow and he had returned to the von Mecklenberg estates and then travelled to Altdorf to enrol in the University.

The first had been with a nobleman whose face was tattooed with the mask of a beast. His name was Wolf too, Wolf von Neuwald, and he had lost a brother to Chaos. He had lived through many hardships and become an adventurer, a one-time associate of the hero, Konrad. Wolf met this other Wolf in a country inn and gradually each had drawn the other's story out. Wolf was confused by the other Wolf's cynicism and thought him cruel and hard, but he also admired the man's persistence in playing out the hand of cards fate had dealt him. Born a rich man, he was reduced to poverty; raised for the church, he was a wandering mercenary, callously certain that his next job might mean his death. From him, Wolf had learned acceptance.

The second encounter had been in Marienburg, where Wolf wanted to spend one summer learning his way around boats and the sea. Johann had arranged a position for him as midshipman with a trading boat on a regular route between the port and Norsca. Erik was a Norseman and, like the other Wolf, a mercenary. They had met on the docks and been drawn to one another at once, by a kinship they could hardly speak of. Both of them were, to some extent, shunned by their fellows and they both had a touch of Chaos in them.

For Erik, things were worse. Whereas Wolf had to live with having been a monster, the Norseman lived with the fear of constantly becoming one. The call of the moons was strong in him, but he had fought it successfully so far. Wolf dreaded hearing the news that Erik had succumbed to his wolfishness, for if the giant warrior didn't have the strength to resist, then how could he hope to deal with his inner daemon? The last he had heard, though, Erik had been still human.

It had been easier for Johann, who had caught up on his ten years' absence in a few short months and taken on the rights and responsibilities of an elector of the Empire. For Wolf, progress would always be much slower. And he would always need crutches.

Lately, he had taken to chewing weirdroot. It was easily available around the colleges of the University, or on the Street of a Hundred Taverns, and the dreams it brought were not of bestiality and violence.

Last night, Wolf thought, he must have gone through several roots. He tried to remember...

He and Trudi had gone underground, into the old dwarf tunnels, to a raucous party. There had been music and dancing and coloured lanterns. Wolf had been invited by Otho Waernicke, the Chancellor of the League of Karl-Franz, to a celebration of some mainly forgotten hero. The League was the oldest, most distinguished student fraternity at the University and – as an elector's brother – he was due to be admitted as soon as he had passed his first exams. If he passed his first exams, rather. However, if someone as party-obsessed as Otho had scraped through the academic requirements, there was no reason Wolf should fail. Wolf remembered dancing with Trudi, their bodies moving together to the noise of a band of elven minstrels. Then, things got vague...

He reached out to his bedside table and found his root pouch. It was full, whereas it had been nearly empty yesterday. He must have visited one of his usual suppliers, Philippe at Bruno's Brewhouse or Mack Ruger at the Breasts of Myrmidia.

Sitting up, he took a root from the bag and examined it. It had been cut in half with a blade and the wound had already dried over.

Trudi stirred and flopped an arm over his body.

He had met her during his first week in the city and they had been together ever since. He had known women before – and who knows what he had done during his wandering years – but Trudi was his first proper girlfriend. She was a serving maid at the Wayfarer's Rest and although no virgin priestess, she was not as loose as most you could pick up along the street.

She was young, of course, and illiterate. Sometimes, she asked him to teach her her letters, but mostly she was disdainful of any learning. Books had nothing to do with life, she usually said. Wolf, who had not spread a book open in months, had to agree with her.

He lay back and let Trudi edge herself over him, pressing him down with her body.

'I didn't feel you get into bed,' she said. 'You must have been very late…'

He did not want to tell her that he could not remember himself.

She chortled, 'But I knew when you woke me up…'

She pressed her hips against him, gently rocking, and ran her fingers through his chest hair, making little curls.

Wolf's body was responding to the girl. He tipped her chin up and kissed her, tasting the nightfilm on her teeth.

'You, you're insatiable,' she said.

She brushed her hair back out of her eyes and blinked.

'Just let me wake up. Ulric, but it must be past lunchtime.'

His mouth was dry. He snapped the half-root in two and offered her a piece. She waved it away and he popped them both into his mouth, chewing hard.

She stroked his sides, then bent down and pressed her face to his chest. As she nibbled around his neck, he stroked her long, fair hair.

He felt the dreams seep into his mind and chewed harder. The room expanded and his mind shrank.

He held up his hand and, for a moment, saw a clawed paw, tearing at Trudi's head, taking off her ear and half her face.

He froze and looked again.

'What is it, Wolf?'

His hand was normal. Her head was unhurt.

She kissed his mouth and he pushed a lump of rootpulp against her tongue. Accepting it, she swallowed and their dreams melted together.

They lost their perception of time but continued, slowly, to explore each other.

Finally, Trudi straightened up and took hold of her shift. She pulled it up over her head and shook out her hair, so it rested on her shoulders.

She put her hands on his chest and moved, gently.

He closed his eyes and touched her, moving from her shoulders, down across her breasts…

Something felt strange. He opened his eyes and looked. Trudi was lost in the moment, her eyes open but unseeing.

His hand had found four lines on her body, starting in one armpit, crossing her ribs and tapering off on her stomach. They were shallow cuts, already scabbed.

He tried to match his fingers to the marks, but they were too widely-spread. He managed to touch all four, but only by straining his knuckles.

He traced the lines, feeling Trudi shudder with something between pleasure and pain. Her stomach was ticklish, so when he touched her there, she laughed.

'Wolf,' she said, 'last night, you were a beast.'

VI

'THERE,' SAID A voice, 'she's awake.'

Rosanna awoke to the stench of tobacco in her nostrils. It stung and she shook her head. Her scarf was gone and her hair was loose.

She had been back in the village in her dream, choking on the thick smoke of a spring clearance fire, hearing the sap hissing as green branches were eaten by the flames. Her father had been there, and her mother and sisters. She had been standing on her own, the rest of her family joined with the rest of the villagers as they sampled mulled wine to keep away the chill. Amid the sibilances of the fire, she heard voices hissing 'witch' and remembered the punishments formerly inflicted upon gifted little girls. Her grandfather's aunt, the last in the family to have her scrying talent, had been burned by one of the inquisitions. Rosanna only survived because the Cult of Sigmar had put her under the seal of protection as soon as their village cleric had reported her gift. From the earliest, she had been raised to be sent to the Temple in Altdorf to serve the cult. Her cold hands were bleeding from her long hours with rough needles, pretending that she might have a future as a seamstress. She knew from their thoughts that her family would be as relieved to see her go as the rest of the village. She knew all their secrets. The thick smoke was wafted around her by the strong wind and her eyes watered. The smoke thinned and her dream was over. She was back in Altdorf.

Someone was holding a smoking pipe under her nose.

'Take that thing away,' another voice said. 'You'll poison her.'

She sat up on the cobblestones and hugged herself. There were three men around her, two officers of the watch and a distinguished-looking gentleman in the green cloak of a courtier. One of the watchmen, the captain in ordinary clothes, was waving the pipe.

Dickon, she remembered, of the Dock Watch. He had introduced himself before it overwhelmed her.

It. The fear.

'You must have had a shock,' said the courtier. 'Did you scry anything?'

She tried to remember. There was just a blackness, with flashes of red. It made her head ache. She thought there were eyes in the dark, but she couldn't tell if they were human or animal.

'Useless,' muttered the captain. 'They've sent me an imbecile.'

'No,' said the courtier, 'I don't think so. Sister, may I help you up?'

He offered his arm and she accepted.

On a plain of bleached bones and cast-off armour, men and monsters were fighting. She felt the cold wind and parried a blow. She was facing a hulking creature with a shaggy mane and finger-length teeth.

The courtier got her onto her feet and she walked a few experimental steps. She shook the vision out of her head. She was too used to them to take too much notice. Her ankles were weak, but otherwise she was all right.

'I'm not a sister, sir,' she said, 'I'm a miss. Rosanna Ophuls.'

'Baron Johann von Mecklenberg, at your service. But I understood you were sent from the Cathedral of Ulric.'

'Yes, but I am not a cleric, just a scryer. I was born with a gift, but that doesn't make me any more spiritual than the next woman. Sorry.'

The baron bowed his head slightly. Rosanna had seen him, she realized, at a state affair in the cathedral. He had flanked the Emperor himself. He was an elector. She would have to mind her manners. She remembered a story she had heard about him and thought she understood the scene she had picked up.

'Miss Ophuls,' said the watchman who had not spoken, 'did you see anything?'

'This is Elsaesser,' said the baron. 'He's one of the smarter people on the Dock Watch.'

Captain Dickon snorted and put his pipe in his mouth. Rosanna did not have to be a scryer to imagine his attitudes. The watchman thought that Baron von Mecklenberg was an interfering dilettante, and young Elsaesser a naive hothead who would soon learn better.

Elsaesser shook her hand and she got the impression of tall trees and heady air.

'The Reikwald,' she said.

Elsaesser was impressed.

'Don't be. It's just a party trick.'

'When you arrived,' said the baron, 'did you scry anything?'

She thought back beyond the blackness of her fainting spell. She remembered opening the coach door and setting her foot on the cobbles. Then there were flashes of red in the dark. She heard the ghost of a scream and received the image of someone in a long, voluminous garment, bent over a shrieking animal, working away inside it. No, it was not an animal. It was – had been – a woman.

'It was horrible.'

'Did you see the Beast?'

She nodded: yes.

'What did he look like?' asked the baron.

'Long... green... coat,' she said.

'A coat?' He held her elbow. She saw his cloak rippling and was fascinated by the gold stitching amid the velvet.

'Long… green…'

'This is pointless,' said Dickon. 'She's on the same false trail.'

'No,' she said, 'not a coat…'

'A cloak?' Elsaesser asked.

'Like this one?' said the baron.

'Yes… no… maybe.'

'Wonderful,' snapped Dickon. 'Yes, no or maybe. That narrows our options enormously.'

'Give the girl a chance.'

The watchman looked sullen and coughed out a brown cloud. 'Yes, baron. Although it's my guess that she couldn't scry a rainshower if the sky were full of clouds.'

Rosanna was annoyed by the captain. She pretended to be unsteady and put her hand out to balance herself. She placed her palm on Dickon's chest and let her mind reach out to him.

'Ahh, captain, you are impatient, I see. You would like to be back at home with your wife and children.'

'You are mistaken, Miss Ophuls,' Elsaesser said. 'The captain has a wife but, I believe, no children.'

Dickon looked dark and shifty.

'Oh, I'm sorry. I had such a clear impression. It happens sometimes. I see now that your wife is childless.'

'That's right,' Dickon said, 'not that it's any of your business.'

'But you do have children. Two of them. A boy and a girl. August and Anneliese. Four and two. And there's a woman, too. What is her name?'

'The captain's wife is called Helga, Miss Ophuls,' said Elsaesser. Rosanna wondered whether the young watchman were really as naive as he seemed, or whether he was enjoying his superior's embarrassment.

'Helga, eh? I must be badly mistaken. The name I'm picking up is…'

'I think we've wasted enough time,' said Dickon.

'…Fifi.'

Elsaesser tried not to smirk and Dickon took a keen interest in the cobblestones, pulling his cap down low.

'If you'd come this way, Miss Ophuls,' said the baron. She consented and took his arm again. Dickon stayed away, making sure not to touch her.

Rosanna was afraid of what she would have to do now. She had volunteered for this job out of a sense of duty. The Cult of Sigmar had spent a lot of money educating her, a poor barefoot seamstress from the Grey Mountains, even though she had no intention of becoming an initiate. She owed the Cathedral the use of her gifts. And the Cathedral owed a debt to the city of Altdorf, which it had succoured for three thousand years. So, with debt piled upon debt, she would have to step into the alley between the two inns and die again...

The baron helped her, as if he were assisting a very old duchess out of a carriage and escorting her to a ball. He led her to the alley, the watchmen keeping pace like train-holding servants.

'Everybody back,' said Dickon. 'She has to go in alone.'

Officers emerged from the alley and stood in the street.

Rosanna could see a form lying under a blanket and could see red patches on the blanket itself.

The first time, when she was a little girl, she had been asked to kiss her dead grandmother's forehead before the funeral. She had felt her lungs fill up with thick liquid and had coughed until her throat bled. By then, her parents were used to little Rosie's 'feelings' and understood only too well. She stayed away from graveyards after that but death was impossible to avoid. Lying in a bed at an inn, with her first boyfriend, she had experienced in succession the last moments of three people who had died in the bed: an old man with a fading heart, a young hunter with most of his chest shot away in an accident and an unwanted child stifled with a pillow by a mother barely in her teens. It was not a sensation she would ever get used to.

'This is your first time with the Beast?' asked the baron.

'Yes.'

'We've never called in a scryer before,' said the captain. 'It's a new approach.'

'What do you know about the murders?'

'That the Beast kills women, tears them apart.'

She was picking up the baron's own beast again. He was called Wolf. She smelled his breath, saw the steam rising from his pelt.

'You think you can go through with this?'

She took a deep breath. 'Yes, baron, I think I can. I believe it's important.'

'Good girl.'

'The first thing,' said Elsaesser, 'is to make sure that this is like the others. You understand?'

Rosanna wasn't sure.

'Many people die, many are murdered. Especially in the alleys off the Street of a Hundred Taverns. This woman might have killed a man herself, a few years ago. He could have friends or relations who see the Beast as a way of evening the score without attracting attention. Or it could be a monkey-see-monkey-do madman.'

'I don't understand.'

Elsaesser was patient. 'Violence is like a plague, it spreads without reason. The Beast could have inspired an imitator. It happens with most killings like these.'

'I see. What should I look for?'

Elsaesser blushed, obviously embarrassed. 'Well... ah... first, you should see whether she was... ah... molested, um, before or after...'

'He means was she raped, Miss Ophuls,' put in Dickon.

Rosanna remembered being led to a stone suspected to have been used as an altar in the Geheiminisnacht rites of a Chaos cult. Literally dozens of sacrifices had been raped in that place and she had felt for every one of them. Afterwards, their throats had been cut and the cultists had drunk their blood.

'Were the others?' she asked.

'We don't think so. The thing with sex crimes as vicious as these is that they are usually instead of rather than as well as, if you get my meaning.'

'Clearly.'

'These madmen usually turn out to be impotent, or inadequate. Mama's boys, most of them.'

The woman in the alley was getting no deader, but Rosanna could feel the residues fading fast.

'And be sure that we are dealing with a human,' said the baron. 'I'm still not convinced that the Beast is not an actual beast, or an altered.'

'So far,' said Elsaesser, 'the wounds have been consistent with some sort of hooked weapon. But it could also have been a set of claws.'

'Does the killer eat his victims?'

Elsaesser looked shocked. 'No, miss. We don't think so. It's hard to tell, but we think she's all there.'

'Well, that's something to be going on with.'

The baron and Elsaesser stood back. Rosanna tottered a little, but didn't feel faint any more. The Beast was gone, leaving only a memory behind. A memory couldn't hurt her.

She stepped across the entrance stone of the alley and the direct sunlight was blocked. The noises of the street were faint in her ears. She could have been distant from everyone, rather than a few steps away.

She walked in a little way and came to the blanket.

Bright blood seemed to run under her shoes in a river, washing into the street. Cries echoed between the walls and there was a dreadful rending sound, as a body was torn apart.

Her heart grew cold.

She felt an ache in her joints and the sting of gin in her throat. One of her eyes wasn't seeing properly. There was someone in the alley with her. Someone tall, in a long coat or cloak. She saw a flash of green and the glare of mad eyes. Then, something sharp went into her stomach.

She staggered back, breaking the contact.

Now, she was standing over the bloody work, watching shoulders heave. She saw a woman's white face. She was old, one-eyed. Her hair was stringy. Blood splashed across her face.

She was the Beast, but she knew nothing. She felt a tangle of impulses driving her, felt the desire to kill. Her cloak flapped around her as she tore away the skin and the flesh. Her mind contained just one idea. She must kill.

She broke the contact again. She had learned nothing. Her knees and ankles were going. The baron was there to catch her and to pull her out of the alley.

'There she goes again,' complained Dickon. 'Useless, useless.'

The baron unlaced her collar and let some air in.

'Well?' asked Elsaesser.

'I felt both of them,' she said. 'The woman had one eye.'

'And the Beast?' asked the baron.

She concentrated. 'The Beast is…'

She tried to find the words.

'The Beast is two people.'

Dickon thumped a fist into his palm. 'The sailors,' he exclaimed. 'I knew it! The sailors.'

'No,' said Rosanna, 'you don't understand. The Beast is two people, but with only one body.'

'This is insane.'

'No, captain,' said the baron. 'I think I see what Miss Ophuls means. The Beast is an ordinary person most of the time, as sane and rational as you or I…'

Rosanna nodded.

'…but sometimes, when the mood or whatever takes him, he is something else, a Beast.'

'Is the Beast a werewolf?' asked Elsaesser.

Rosanna wondered. In the dark, she had seen nothing but the eyes.

'Yes… no… maybe…'

'The same old tune, eh?'

The baron turned on the watchman. 'Captain, I'll thank you to leave this woman alone. She is obviously trying her best and I hardly think you are helping her.'

Dickon was chastened.

Elsaesser had darted into the alley and come out with something.

'Here,' he said, 'try this…'

He handed her a small bag.

'What is it?'

'It's Margi Ruttmann's knife.'

'Who?'

'Margi Ruttmann... her... in the alley.'

'Oh, yes... of course...'

She had not picked up the woman's name. That happened quite often.

'She may have tried to defend herself. She may have cut the Beast.'

She pulled the drawstring loose and let the bag fall. She turned the knife around in her hand, feeling the hilt.

'If he were wounded in a specific way, we could look for a man with that wound. It would be something to go on.'

She gripped the knifehandle and held the blade up.

Her cheek stung as the blade slipped in, piercing her eye. Half her vision went red and then black.

She was shaking.

She pinned him down and slid the blade into him, ignoring his screeches.

'Rikki,' Rosanna said. 'She killed someone called Rikki.'

Dickon snorted again. 'Well, that's that old case closed. At least we've accomplished something here.'

'Try holding it by the blade,' Elsaesser suggested.

Rosanna considered and then flipped the knife over, catching it in her fingers. It was sharp but she didn't cut herself.

'Excuse me,' she said, holding the knife up. She positioned the point against the bridge of her nose and then tilted the blade up, resting its flat against her forehead. It was cold as an icicle.

'This helps sometimes.'

Elsaesser and the baron looked on, radiating encouragement. They were both, she realized, interested in her.

The blade leaped in the dark and the point sank into heavy cloth. The blade was pulled away. The cloth tore. The ripping sound was extended for longer than was possible. Amplified, she heard it tearing forever.

'Well?' someone asked.

'Green velvet,' she said.

Elsaesser and the baron looked at each other, their hearts sinking.

'Green velvet,' she said again, 'like the baron's cloak.'

VII

DIEN CH'ING BOWED low, in the Celestial fashion, prostrating himself and touching his forehead to the flagstones. They were cold.

'My humble and unworthy self is honoured to be graciously admitted into your estimable presence, noble sir.'

The ambassador knew that Hasselstein had no patience with Cathayan courtesy, but conducted himself impeccably anyway. That was important. His mask must not slip.

'Get up, ambassador,' he said, 'you make yourself ridiculous.'

Dien Ch'ing stood, wiping non-existent dust from his robes. The palace floors were as clean as a virgin's conscience.

The Emperor's confessor was not wearing his lector's hood. He was dressed like any other courtier, in fine white linen and a green velvet cloak. Out of his habit, he did not look especially ascetic.

'Nevertheless, noble sir, I am pleased to be granted this audience.'

Hasselstein was obviously distracted. Dien Ch'ing assumed that the man had actually forgotten their appointment. He was unprepared for their discussions and that made him irritable. He was too much the smooth courtier to give offence to the representative of the Monkey King, but he had other, more pressing business, and he would prefer to be seeing to it. That was interesting. The cause of the Lord Tsien-Tsin could be assisted by such distractions.

Besides, it was just as well. Dien Ch'ing wondered how generous the welcome would be if Hasselstein and his Emperor knew that he did not, in fact, serve the Monkey King and that the real ambassador, despatched two years ago from far Cathay, was resting with his throat cut in an unmarked grave somewhere in the Dark Lands. He assumed that things would be very different indeed.

'Has the Emperor found the time to consider the Monkey King's petition, noble sir?'

Some memory of the matter surfaced in Hasselstein's mind and he dredged the facts together. Behind him, rolled up in tubes, were all the petitions. Dien Ch'ing could see his perfect forgery stuffed in with the others.

'Your proposed expedition to the Dark Lands, eh?'

Dien Ch'ing touched his thumb to his forehead and bowed again.

'Even so, noble sir.'

Hasselstein was playing with the papers on his desk, pretending to be busy. It was not like the man. Dien Ch'ing understood the Emperor's confessor to be a skilled politician, not a distracted curmudgeon. There was something seriously amiss at the court of Karl-Franz.

'It is being considered. The undertaking would be costly and difficult to put together. I'm sure you understand.'

'Indeed, noble sir. That is why the Monkey King proposes a joint venture. The Lord of the East should shake hands with the Emperor of the West. And the encroachments of evil grow greater every day. The time is right for a full-scale campaign.'

'Um,' said Hasselstein, 'possibly.'

Dien Ch'ing smiled inside, but let nothing show. He must be humble, he must be patient. One does not ascend the

Pagoda of Tsien-Tsin at a single leap. One must take the steps individually and pause for rest and reflection at each level. The plan for this trap had been laid years earlier, in the Dark Lands, and there would be no haste in springing it. Dien Ch'ing remembered how haste could spoil a recipe, and did not intend to fail his master a second time.

'You will pardon me, noble sir, for daring to express an intuition, but is there perhaps some pressing matter which occupies your thoughts?'

'What?' said Hasselstein.

'In Western parlance, what is wrong?'

'Oh, that...' Hasselstein almost smiled. 'You're sharp, Dien Ch'ing, aren't you? You "noble sir" and "unworthy humble self" a lot, but you don't miss much.'

Hasselstein shifted his papers again. They were conferring in the antechamber to one of the waiting halls of the palace. From their alcove, they could see de la Rougierre, the Bretonnian ambassador, waving his plumed hat and trying to attract the attention of a pretty maidservant. And that idler Leos von Liebewitz was swishing his cloak and fingering his sword, waiting for someone.

'A few hundred years ago,' Hasselstein began, 'no one was allowed in to the palace without a mask. The Empress Magritta forbade anyone to enter her presence without what she called "their true face" on.'

The maidservant was walking away, leaving de la Rougierre to stump off in a snit. The Bretonnian was a dwarf and fancied himself as a ladies' man. He was the subject of many amusing stories, mostly obscene. The stunted popinjay's assignment to the court was obviously a subtle Bretonnian insult to the Emperor and yet no one was willing to make any complaint. The situation was amusingly absurd.

'And you feel that nothing has changed?'

Hasselstein fingered his chin. 'So many masks, Dien Ch'ing. And who is to say whether the mask or the face tells the truth.'

Leos was joined by his sister, the Countess Emmanuelle, and de la Rougierre came back, his hat off and scraping the

floor again, trying for another conquest. Leos's gloved hand
went to his swordhilt.

'There was a disturbance outside the palace today.'

'Yes, Dien Ch'ing. It was Yefimovich, the fire-breather...'

Dien Ch'ing knew Yefimovich. He knew what lay underneath the Kislevite's mask. Hasselstein would be surprised if
he ever saw that particular true face in all its fiery splendour.

'I have heard he is agitating the citizenry against the privileges of the aristocracy. In Cathay, such impudence would
be rewarded in a civilized manner. The miscreant would be
stretched out between four willow trees, with fine nooses of
catgut around his ankles, wrists, neck and testicles, and left
to hang until he changed his opinions. We are a reasonable
people.'

Hasselstein laughed, bitterly. 'Indeed, Dien Ch'ing. I wish
we could serve Yefimovich in the Celestial fashion. But,
under the House of the Second Wilhelm, the people have
their rights. It's the law.'

Dien Ch'ing knew that was a joke. Like the Monkey King,
Karl-Franz might talk endlessly about the rights of his people, but he would rescind them in a moment if it meant
bringing a cream horn to his table a few seconds faster or
adding three gold pieces to his treasury.

'Of course, noble sir, what the fire-breather alleges is
absurd. Some are born to rule and others to be ruled. That
is the eternal truth.'

Leos and Emmanuelle were laughing at some joke of de la
Rougierre's. Powdered buffoons, all of them. Parading their
fine silks and their exquisite manners, weighed down by
their lineage, made stupid by generations of in-breeding.
The von Liebewitzes were like porcelain dolls, wrapped
from birth to death in a cocoon of spun cotton. It would be
so easy, so amusing, to snap their arms and legs off and then
to crush their tiny, painted heads to powder. As they argued
over the correct way to fold a napkin, children sold themselves in the streets outside. No wonder Yefimovich's
speech-making found such an eager audience.

'That's it, exactly,' said Hasselstein. 'The Emperor rules by
the sufferance of the gods and of the electoral college.'

Countess Emmanuelle was laughing like a girl. It was a trained laugh, polite and pretty, and nothing to do with an honest emotion.

'I have heard of an experiment tried some years ago in a few of the Tilean city states. Democracy, or some such nonsense. The rule of the people. A failure, I believe.'

'The people!' Hasselstein thumped the table, making his inkwells jump. 'Sigmar knows our Emperors have not always been fit to rule – this Empire has withstood Boris the Incompetent and Bloody Beatrice the Monumentally Cruel, after all – but the people! That mob outside our gates, howling for blood! They can hardly even feed themselves, or wipe themselves off after a visit to the privy. Could they ever rule anything?'

De la Rougierre was fussing around the Countess Emmanuelle's skirts, trying to touch her legs while pretending to demonstrate some dance step. If he did not show some caution, the dwarf would find himself spitted by Leos's deadly blade. And serve him well.

'And yet, heroes have come from among the people, have they not? The man Konrad, of whom all the minstrels sing, is he not a peasant? And Sierck, who saved the Emperor's life a few years ago, was a mere actor, I believe. Sigmar himself was hardly born to the green velvet, as it were. Many men of genius have risen through their own merits. Minister Tybalt is the son of a grocer, is he not? And the Cults of Sigmar and Ulric are well-remembered for the humble-born servants who performed such great feats. You yourself, I assume, have no especially notable antecedents...'

Dien Ch'ing was taunting Hasselstein, so subtly the man would never realize it. 'Well,' the cleric said, 'actually, my eldest brother is a margrave. Our family is very old. I dropped the "von" from my name when I entered the temple.'

'Ahh, so Yefimovich's taunts are personal?'

'He does not single me out for especial contempt. He hates all aristocrats.'

'A foolish man, not to know how the world is ordered.'

'A foolish man, yes, but also a dangerous one.'

'Surely not. You have the palace guard, the militia, the watch.'

'You are right, Dien Ch'ing. The Empire has nothing to fear from Yevgeny Yefimovich.'

The Celestial smiled and bowed. Hasselstein had spoken half a truth. By himself, Yefimovich was no real threat; but, in partnership with Dien Ch'ing, and with the blessings of the Lord Tsien-Tsin, Yefimovich could do more than spread fire.

An Empire always rests unsteady on its foundations. Plans were well-laid and already coming into operation. It was up to Dien Ch'ing to take advantage of any circumstances that arose. He had cast the yarrow sticks this morning and believed he saw a useful catspaw in the near future, a creature who could seed a panic which might spread throughout the city and perhaps topple a throne or two.

'Tell me, noble sir,' Dien Ch'ing asked Hasselstein, 'what do you know about this fellow they call the Beast?'

A cloud passed over the cleric's face. For a long while, he didn't say anything.

Then he began to tell Dien Ch'ing the whole story.

PART TWO
FOG

I

HE WAS ENTITLED to the use of one of the luxurious coaches the palace put at the disposal of the electors, or of the most important ambassadors. When he was down at the stables picking his horses, he saw footmen in the von Liebewitz livery harnessing a couple of magnificent animals to one of the electoral coaches and he took a moment to examine the gold filigree-encrusted monstrosity. It looked like a giant decorated egg, with jewelled lanterns, painted panels depicting the life of Sigmar and enough glitter to light a street. Obviously the Countess Emmanuelle was off to another of her balls this evening. Back in Nuln, she was the foremost hostess in the Empire; during her sojourn in Altdorf, she was trying to even things up by being the most expensive guest in the capital. The whisper was that the countess always went to these functions escorted by Leos, but that he came back alone, leaving his sister in the arms of her amour-of-the-moment.

Johann wondered which lucky noble house would have to lay down the red carpet and slow-bake the quail tonight. There was a ball at the house of the von Tassenincks, he knew. His invitation had been delivered a few days ago, but, even if he did not have other urgent business, he would not have been happy to attend. The parvenu elector, called in on a compromise to replace the dead and disgraced Oswald von Konigswald, had been trying to impress the city with his style and grace, but Grand Prince Hals and his sullen heir Hergard were simply clowns, straining too hard to apply their tongues to the bottom of the Emperor, and Johann always thought the college had made a bad decision granting a seat to the von Tassenincks. There had been a dreadful scandal involving the Grand Prince's mad nephew a few years earlier. In fact, that incident had given Johann the inspiration for tonight's adventure.

He could have taken out the twin to the von Liebewitz carriage, but opted instead for a plain black coach. Rather than bother with five footmen to ride on top and carry the torches, he chose only Louis, his usual driver. A few extra crowns would be useful to the man, whose wife was expecting their thirteenth or fourteenth. All sons. Louis joked that he would soon be able to field a football team, with substitutes and line-keepers. The coachman was dependable and could keep his mouth shut. His loyalty was to who bribed him first, not who bribed him most.

With a good, strong, ugly horse between the shafts, the coach slipped anonymously through the palace gates, rumbled past the Temple of Sigmar and took a turn towards the river, crossing at one of the trade bridges. Then they were in the Street of a Hundred Taverns. It was well-placed, with the University and its environs to the left and the docks to the right. Even with the Beast at work, there were students and workmen enough to keep the beer and wine flowing. Of course, the streetwalkers and tavern girls were wandering about in gangs of five or six – all, presumably, with daggers tied to their thighs and blackjacks hanging from their girdles – but perhaps they did more business that way. Last night, Margarethe Ruttmann would have been one of them. Now, she was in several separate piles at the Temple of Morr, beyond even the reach of the watch's pet necromancers.

He wondered if Wolf were back at his rooms within the University buildings yet. He had asked a few days ago, but the bursar at Wolf's college said the student hadn't been seen for over a week. Then Johann wondered what the University life was like. He had had a place open for him at the University – all the von Mecklenbergs had been educated there, for centuries – but Cicatrice's raid had changed the course of his life. It was literally a miracle of Sigmar that Wolf was getting a second chance. While Johann's contemporaries had been learning dead languages and studying the outcome of battles on maps, he had been in the forests somewhere, learning how to stay alive.

The last time he had been driven up this street, the street girls had pressed close to the coach whenever it slowed down, explaining the services they offered, citing unrealistically low prices and championing their own abilities. Now they hung back, talking only to faces they knew. The black coach must look faintly sinister, Johann supposed. The word out on the street was that the Beast was an aristocrat from across the river. Green velvet would not be a popular fashion here for a while, even if bright gold was never quite out of favour. Dickon might have burned that scrap of evidence from the alley, but the story was already out.

The most fantastic rumour was that the Beast was Prince Luitpold's insane twin brother, reared in secrecy since birth and let out at night to prevent him preying on the palace's important and wealthy guests. This afternoon, an old woman in the crowd had described the Phantom Prince as having hair down to his waist and talon-like fingernails. Apparently, he ate only raw meat and howled at the moon.

The coach had to stop because of a disturbance. It was outside the Sullen Knight, where men were shouting and scuffling. Johann noticed that there was a thin carpet of mist covering the cobbles. An Altdorf fog was coming down.

His first impression was that a bunch of students and a gang of dockers were working up for a major fight.

Two of Dickon's Dock Watch were strolling by on the other side of the street, unconcerned. That, apparently, was typical. There were women at the upper windows of the taverns, egging their men on.

A broad-shouldered youth wearing the cap of one of the University's fraternal societies was haranguing a group of roughly-dressed loafers. The student's friends were trying to calm him down, but the loafers were already throwing punches, and more students were appearing from somewhere.

'Nobody mixes it with the League of Karl-Franz!' shouted the trouble-maker, waving a clay stein with an embossed coat of arms.

One of the loafers spat.

'Spit on the League, will you?' roared the student. 'You'll earn yourself a bloody nose like that.'

Johann noticed that the loafers all had a cloth emblem patched to their breasts. It was a docker's hook. Most of them had real hooks dangling from their broad leather belts.

He had heard of the Hooks. They were one of the gangs that tried to run the waterfront, ensuring that their friends were suitably employed on the docks, tithing a percentage from everyone's pay. They were usually feuding with a similar faction, the Fish. During the Beast crisis, some of them were even pretending to be a Citizens' Vigilance Committee, although Johann understood that was just another excuse for beating people up. Now, they seemed ready to take on the League of Karl-Franz.

The students were singing now, a song which involved a great deal of beer drinking and stein clashing. It sounded defiant.

'Louis,' said Johann, 'isn't there a way around this?'

The coachman shook his head.

'A pity.'

Caps were flying into the air and someone was throwing vegetables. A rotten cabbage exploded against the coach door.

This was a nuisance.

Johann saw a figure hurrying through the crowds, coat collar turned up, and recognized him.

He opened the door and shouted out, 'Elsaesser. Over here.'

The young watchman heard and darted through the students towards the coach. More trays of beer had been brought out onto the street and the League of Karl-Franz were getting rowdier.

Elsaesser climbed into the coach, wiping a pulped tomato from his jacket. Tendrils of mist trailed in with him, dissipating swiftly. The watchman was out of uniform and off-duty. Johann had arranged to meet the officer at the Black Bat, but luckily their routes had crossed before that particular inn. The coach wouldn't be able to get through until the fight was over. There were other vehicles stalled in the road, including a cart piled high with beer barrels and a flashy gig in which a well-dressed young man was escorting two fluttery young ladies.

'Baron Mecklenberg,' the young officer said, 'good evening.'

'Von Mecklenberg, actually.'

'I'm sorry. I have a problem with titles.'

'You sound like a follower of Yevgeny Yefimovich.'

Elsaesser looked sheepish but stuck his neck out. 'The man has some sound ideas, baron. I don't trust or like him, but he is a genuine reaction to problems that are not going to go away.'

Johann was impressed with Elsaesser's bravery. Not every young watchman would dare to come so close to sedition in conversation with an elector of the Empire.

'At the University, I signed the petition against the dismissal of Professor Brustellin.'

'Funnily enough, so did I.'

Elsaesser looked at the baron with a new respect. 'I shouldn't have quibbled about my name,' Johann admitted. 'I've spent too much of my life away from palaces and estates to have many noble illusions about the aristocracy, in the Empire or elsewhere. In fifty years, Brustellin's book will be recognized as the masterwork of philosophy it is.'

The Professor had published a volume entitled *An Anatomy of Society* that had been banned upon the orders of the Emperor. He had likened the Empire to a human body and drawn a parallel between the aristocracy and a bone-sapping cancer.

'But now he's an outlaw.'

'All the best people are. Sigmar was an outlaw.'

Elsaesser made the sign of the hammer.

'Well,' said Johann, 'did you find out where our man is?'

Elsaesser grinned. 'Oh yes. Nobody wanted to tell me, but I found an old sergeant who wanted drinks money for this evening. I have to say we're not talking about a popular individual here.'

'You're telling me. I mentioned his name to Mikael Hasselstein and got an icy blast of disapproval.'

'Still, I think you're right. He's the man for the job.'

The student leader was drunk enough to be bold. Or stupid. He strolled through the melee and found the biggest, meanest-looking member of the Hooks and poured the dregs of his stein over the man's head. Then he gave a swift punch with a blocky fist and broke the appalled Hook's nose.

A cheer went up from his comrades and from the women on the upper storeys on the left side of the road. The student turned round and raised his hands in triumph, accepting the applause, and a club came down on his head, denting his cap and probably concaving his skull. He was lucky not to find a hook spearing into his kidney.

Elsaesser was nervous.

'That's Otho Waernicke, Grand Duke of Somewhere-or-Other,' he said of the downed student. 'He's an absolute cretin. The League of Karl-Franz are always burning down some dormitory or other, or bothering the novices at the nunnery of Shallya. If their degrees weren't bought and paid for by their daddies before they enrolled, they would never graduate from the University.'

'You weren't a member then?'

'No, you have to have a lineage for that. I was an "inky".'

'What?'

'That's what the Leaguers call students who actually study. Inkies. It was supposed to be an insult, but we became rather

proud of it. We formed a League of our own in the end and
always swept the debating contest.'

'I bet they hammered you at boxing, duelling and drinking, though–'

'Oh yes, and pox-catching, dying young and long-distance
vomiting. It must be a hard life, being born to the green velvet.'

A chill passed over Johann's heart. 'Yes, a hard life...'

He was thinking of Wolf.

'I'm sorry, baron, I meant no slur.'

The Hooks were laying into the Leaguers, mainly using
their fists and steins. There was blood on the cobbles, but
the hooks weren't out. Yet. The women on the upper storeys
were betting with each other and a little man was running
around making odds and taking credit notes.

Otho Waernicke was sleeping it out, but his friends were
putting up enough resistance to do him credit.

Johann took out a document and handed it to Elsaesser.
The watchman noted the seal and was impressed.

'You spoke with the Emperor then?'

'Ah, no,' Johann admitted, 'but I spoke with young
Luitpold and I did borrow the Imperial seal.'

'So, what does this say?'

'Nothing. It's just a blank sheet of paper inside. No one
will dare break the seal. So we have approval to bring our
man out of retirement...'

'Isn't this dangerous?' Elsaesser asked.

'I don't think so. I do have influence with Karl-Franz. I
should think that the Emperor outranks Dickon of the Dock
Watch.'

Elsaesser's eyes were round and his face pale. 'But, ah, I...'

Johann saw what the officer was worried about. 'I shall
make sure that you do not suffer, Elsaesser. This is all my
responsibility. Your future is assured.'

'I'm glad to hear it. Dickon transferred me from the Beast
case to the vagrancy squad. As of tomorrow, I'm supposed to
walk up and down this street harassing tarts and pimps. If
they're on the streets, they must be destitute, and that's a
crime so I'm supposed to fine them three pfennigs on the

spot. Dickon gets half the take at the end of the month and the rest is parcelled out to the other watchmen.'

'What if they really are destitute and don't have three pfennigs?'

'Then I'm supposed to thump them with my club. That's how justice works on the docks.'

Johann made a fist inside his suede glove and pressed his signet ring to his chin. 'When the Beast is caught, I shall make sure that things change at the Dock Watch. You have my word on it.'

'Thank you, baron.' Elsaesser did not sound convinced.

The fight was dying down, inconclusively. Most of the battlers had gone back to their inns, or been carried off to apothecaries, and only the hardiest, toughest and stupidest were still exchanging punches and kicks. An old woman was checking patches of blood in the cracks between cobbles, looking for gold teeth.

Louis was able to drive on and the coach continued. The last of the brawlers got out of its way.

Johann saw that Otho Waernicke was sitting up and singing now.

Elsaesser gave Louis the directions to the warehouse of the Reik and Talabec Trading Company. Their man should still be at work, to judge by what Elsaesser had learned about his current situation.

'It was the only thing he could get when he was kicked out of the watch,' the officer explained. 'He's a glorified stock-keeper, really.'

The coach turned off the Street of a Hundred Taverns and started threading down through the odd byways of the docks.

'Just one thing puzzles me,' Johann said. 'Have you found out why they call him "Filthy Harald"?'

II

It was a slow night at the Wayfarer's Rest, so Wolf and Trudi headed, arm in arm, up the street for some livelier entertainment. They had stayed in bed, mainly dozing, until nearly nightfall. Like most students, Wolf was used to keeping vampire's hours. He felt better with the rising of the moons, more alive. He was hungry and not just for food.

There was a thin mist rising around their ankles, bubbling slightly. Wolf recognized the makings of a proper Altdorf fog and was glad all the taverns in this area of the city were on the same, well-lit thoroughfare. An Altdorf fog crept off the two rivers once every few months or so and descended upon the city for a couple of days. The citizens were used to it and had long contrived good reasons for staying in their hearth-warmed homes for the duration, but to Wolf it was still almost exciting, almost glamorous...

Anything could happen in an Altdorf fog, as if the city instantly became engulfed in a giant weirdroot dream. Lovers could meet for a few hours and then be separated forever. Certain creatures which usually kept to the sewers and backrooms would come out for a few nights on the streets, masked by the thick, grey clouds. There were many stories of adventures in an Altdorf fog, or jokes about romantic entanglements. At the Vargr Breughel Memorial Playhouse, Detlef Sierck was appearing in *A Farce of the Fog*, based on one of the oldest of the jokes, and Wolf had taken Trudi a few nights ago. They had laughed continually at the fools' parade of lecherous husbands, ravenous mistresses, ardent lovers, innocent wives, vulgar midwives, comic watchmen and absurd clerics, and marvelled at the fog effects contrived on the stage.

Tonight, the fog did not seem quite as jolly as it had in the play. It rose fast and hung thick in the air. It was impossible to see from one side of the street to the other. Even the inn lanterns were shrouded, Trudi was shivering under her shawl and not saying much. Wolf knew what she was thinking about. The girl couldn't read the posters, but she had heard the rumours. And there was a new poster up, unmistakable even to the illiterate, with a caricature of a bestial face – indistinct and yet unmistakable – over a pledge of a substantial reward.

The fog was all around them now and the innkeepers were all out lighting extra torches and laying in for a siege. Those hardy drinkers prepared to venture out in any weather would keep all the taverns in business for the next few days and the landlords wanted to be sure their patrons could find their way to their establishments.

'Halt,' said a voice. 'You there…'

Wolf turned to look and realized that he was the one who was being asked to halt. A tall, wide figure was coming through the fog at him. He did not wear the helmet and badge of a copper – not that that would necessarily have made Wolf feel safer, what with all the stories he had heard about the Dock Watch – and so Wolf surreptitiously slipped his arm from around Trudi's and rested his hand on the pommel of his dagger.

He had some gold in his purse and a pouch of weirdroot slung under his jacket in the small of his back. He did not want to lose either.

'Let's have a look at you.'

A lantern was held up and shone in his eyes. Trudi flinched and pressed close to him. Wolf could still not see the man's face, but in the light he saw the docker's hook hanging from his belt and the embroidered symbol on his overcoat.

'Student, are you?'

Wolf nodded. It was best not to provoke trouble.

'Pleased to meet you, sonny-boy...'

The Hook's tone was mocking, unpleasant. Wolf guessed from his voice that he was a youngish man himself, still in his twenties. Sometimes, Wolf did feel his age, did feel too old for all this...

'This your girlfriend?'

Trudi tried to hide behind him, like a night-animal getting behind a rock.

'Pretty one, isn't she? Students get all the pretty ones. Not like us honest working men.'

Wolf could see the Hook wore a Citizens' Vigilance arm-band. He was one of the unofficial patrolmen the waterfront faction had put out on the street while the Beast was loose.

'Still, that'll change come the Revolution...'

Obviously, this vigilante was a disciple of Yevgeny Yefimovich.

The Hook reached out and stroked Trudi's hair. Wolf made fists and felt his sharp nails digging into the meat of his hands.

'How about a little sample?'

Wolf could smell gin on the Hook's breath. None of these vigilantes were taking seriously their mission to protect the locals. The CV was just an excuse for more bullying.

'Excuse me,' Wolf said, in protest.

The Hook chuckled. Wolf realized now there were others in the fog. The vigilantes never went around on their own. He could make out the shapes. Even more, he could distin-guish the smells. He still had some of the senses he had developed during his time with the Chaos Knights, espe-cially after dark, especially when the moons were full, especially in the fog.

The Hook leered, greenish teeth shining in his shadowed face, and leant forwards. His features appeared, horridly distorted, in the lantern's beam and he poked out his tongue.

'Raaaahh!'

Trudi swallowed a scream and her fingers dug into Wolf's shoulder.

'You should be careful who you go with, love,' the Hook said, 'or the Beast'll get you!'

Trudi spoke, slowly and quietly, to Wolf. 'Make... them... go... away...'

The girl didn't like the Hooks. She hadn't told him much about her life before they met, but he had picked up bits and pieces. She had been with the Fish for a time, passed from man to man, and had had friends killed in the Waterfront War. Some of her clothes still had the stitches in the fish shape where the insignia had been ripped off. She was out of the gang life, but still remembered some of the bad times. She had a few scars, where they didn't show.

Wolf did not want a fight. He was as afraid of what he might do to the Hooks as what harm they might do him.

'They say the Beast is from over the river,' the Hook began, conversationally. 'Yefimovich says the killer is a palace lackey or a rich merchant. Obviously, the monster comes from the overprivileged classes.'

Wolf realized he was wearing his best clothes. He might look like a beggar by the standards of the court, but he was still a pampered prince to these men.

'Me, I reckon different. The Beast is rich scum, sure as Sigmar's mighty hammer. But I think he's from this side of the river. I think he's from the University. I think he's a bloody student.'

The Hook's lantern made a little bubble of visibility in the fog. Wolf and Trudi and the Hook were in it, and his comrades were on the edges, lurking like deep sea predators. Wolf did not know where on the street they were and how close he might be to a friendly inn.

'Let them go, Brandauer,' said one of the other vigilantes. 'They're just kids.'

Under other circumstances, Wolf would have taken objection to that.

'Need to be taught a lesson,' Brandauer said.

'This isn't catching us the Beast,' said the more conscientious vigilante.

Brandauer grumbled, but let his lantern fall from their faces.

'Watch yourselves,' he said, turning away. Wolf could have put a dagger between his shoulderblades with a single, easy move. He knew precisely where to strike if he wanted to pierce the heart. Or the liver. Or the kidneys. He had learned his anatomy in a forest university, cutting and hacking with a short sword.

But that had been another life, another person. That had been a beast, not a man.

The Hooks were gone. Even their lanternlight was obscured in the fog.

Wolf realized he had been sweating. Trudi relaxed her grip.

He wondered about the Beast. He did not like to think of the murderer, stalking through the night as he had through the forests. The thing that made him afraid was that he could understand the madman, know the pleasures he experienced in his alleyway hunting expeditions. Perhaps the Beast was a Chaos Knight, as he had been. Some alterations were easy to conceal with a mask or a cloak. And some were impossible to detect at a glance. In Cicatrice's company there had been knights who appeared to be children or old men, but who were frenzied berserkers in battle, stronger than the armour-skinned, axe-handed giants. It was unnervingly easy to imagine the Beast as someone like that. An old beggar, a lost child, a street woman. Any face could be a mask.

Wolf and Trudi walked towards the faint luminescence of the tavern lights. Reading a few signs, he knew exactly where he was. There was the Drunken Bastard, the hostelry that catered exclusively to the miserable, solitary drinker. And the Crooked Spear, well-known as the pick-up place for young men who preferred the company of their own sex. And the Crescent Moon, which attracted the unquiet dead, they said.

None of them were exactly promising. Alone among so many illuminated signs, the Crescent Moon's ironwork symbol hung in darkness. Its patrons did not need torches and lanterns to find their way.

Suddenly a pulse of desire throbbed in his brain. He needed to chew the root. Sometimes, the urge hit him at the oddest times: during lectures, in polite conversation, on long coach trips, in bed with Trudi. If it ever became a problem, he would deal with it...

His mouth went dry and the fog swirled inside his head. He saw sparks like fireflies, dancing before his eyes...

...but it was not a problem.

'Wolf?'

Trudi held him tight, again.

'It'll be all right,' he mumbled, reaching round under his coat for the pouch. Trudi let him go and stood apart a little, her outline blurring in the fog.

Wolf shook a fresh root into his hand and took his knife to it. He slivered off a slice and took it onto his tongue, relishing the sting as the juice seeped out.

'That's better,' he said, putting the root back and concealing his pouch again. 'That's a lot better.'

Someone came out of the Crescent Moon: a slender girl in a long cloak. She turned up her collar and walked with confidence, dodging out of the way of a drunk stumbling blind through the fog. Even through the fog, Wolf could see the red tint in her eyes and knew why she could see in the murk. She was whistling an old Bretonnian tune. Wolf envied this creature for whom the night and fog held no terrors. The man she had avoided made the sign of Sigmar as she passed and continued, stumbling faster towards the Drunken Bastard, hand in his purse dredging for coins.

The girl came close and stopped. She smiled, her teeth sharp pearls, and looked with curiosity at Wolf.

'Do I know you?' the vampire asked. She spoke Reikspiel with a faint, attractive Bretonnian accent.

Wolf would have remembered. She was lovely, fascinating. She looked perhaps sixteen, but there was no way to judge her age.

'I don't think so.'

'Genevieve,' she said, extending a slim, cold hand to be kissed. 'Genevieve Dieudonné.'

Trudi did not like the girl. She had problems with dead people. It was one of the prejudices of her class.

'I've heard of you,' Wolf said.

The vampire's smiling face closed a little. Her hand became a little colder.

'You have met my brother, Johann. We look quite like each other.'

'Johann is a common name.'

'Johann von Mecklenberg, the Elector of Sudenland.'

Genevieve smiled again. 'Ah yes, not such a common person.'

'Wolf,' he said, 'and this is Trudi.'

'Hello, Trudi,' the vampire said.

Wolf could not be sure whether Genevieve was trying to put Trudi at her ease, or slyly enjoying the girl's discomfiture.

The juice was beginning to affect him. He stared at Genevieve's face, seeing strange things in it. Sometimes portraits grow faint with age and flake to reveal other pictures that have been painted over. Genevieve's girl's face was like that, with another face underlying it: an old, predatory face, with needle teeth, hollow cheeks and eyes burning like red lamps.

'I don't care much for the court, I'm afraid,' the vampire said. 'Too many bad memories. Perhaps I'll see you again at the theatre.'

Terror gripped Wolf as he felt his brain seizing up. He was losing touch with the functions of his body. His face was frozen and he was retaining the mask of courtesy, exchanging politenesses with the ancient girl. But he felt as if Wolf were shrinking inside his body and someone else gaining the ascendant.

The fog was pressing in, driving his consciousness down into the depths of his person.

'Watch yourself in the fog,' Genevieve said, slipping into it. 'There are hunters about.'

He heard her walk away, her shoes slapping tinily on the cobbles. Her smell – sweet with an undertaste of blood – lingered a few moments and was dispersed in the fog.

Genevieve, he had heard, had come to live with what she was. Like the other Wolf and Eric, she did not fear the beast inside. Wolf felt an urge to run after her, to talk with her further. There was something he should learn from the vampire.

The fog grew thicker, clinging to his clothes. Even Trudi was hard to see. He breathed in the cold, tasting weirdroot as the air rushed over his tongue. The dreams were in his blood by now.

There were shapes in the fog. He could see them now. They called to him.

'Wolf?'

Trudi seemed a long way in the distance, shouting to him as if he were at the top of the highest mountain in the Empire.

There were colours in the grey fog. And music.

His feet were uncomfortable, confined in their heavy boots, the toenails pressed into flesh, the toes constricted. Pain and strength mingled in his limbs.

'Wolf?'

He was Wolf and he was not Wolf. The taste of the blood was still in the air.

The girl tugged at his sleeve. A burst of anger exploded inside him.

Hissing, he turned on the girl, his sharp-fingered hand lashing out…

III

'I THINK THAT'S why they call him Filthy Harald,' someone said.

He turned around, throwing-knife in his hand. Two men had come into the warehouse, one in his early thirties, the other ten years younger. They didn't make him feel sick on sight, so they were probably all right.

'You have shit on your boots, sir,' said the older man. He wore his green velvet cloak as if born to it. A courtier.

He shrugged and sheathed his knife. He saw no threat from the two newcomers.

'I was just beating it out of someone,' he snarled.

The gentleman in velvet and the off-duty watchman looked at each other and shrugged.

He let them hang for a moment, then explained, 'Someone has to clear out the sewer inlets when they get blocked. It's part of my contract with the Reik and Talabec.'

He wiped his boots on a rough mat. He would have to sluice them off properly later.

The gentleman looked a little upset. But he didn't wrinkle his nose in distaste. He was rich and probably titled, but he

was not queasy about messy realities. Harald knew that this
was not a typical court popinjay. If it came to a fight, the
courtier would take quite a bit of killing.

'Well,' said Harald, 'what can I do for you?'

'We have a commission,' said the aristocrat.

Harald didn't say anything. He took a wet rag from a
hook on the wall and wiped the last of the dirt from his
boots.

'This is Baron Johann von Mecklenberg, the Elector of
Sudenland,' said the officer.

Harald didn't bow and scrape. It wasn't his style.

'How is Dickon?' he asked.

'What?'

'Dickon. Is he still captain of the Dock Watch?'

The youth was astounded.

'You've got the copper smell, boy. It can't be mistaken.'

'I'm Helmut Elsaesser. And I am from the Dock Watch.'

Harald didn't like the feeling that he was being called
upon to demonstrate his skills, like a conjurer at a children's
party.

'You have sharp eyes, thief-taker,' said the baron.

Harald nodded, agreeing with him.

'Dickon is still captain.'

'I'm sure he's the best money can buy.'

The boy laughed. He was all right.

The baron looked around the warehouse. Goods were
piled up, with chalk marks on the boxes to indicate their
eventual destination. Room and board came with the job. A
cot in a cupboard and three company meals a day. You
could call it a life.

'You used to be with the watch?'

'Yes, baron. Used to be.'

Harald's boots would pass. He looked up at his visitors.
They had brought a little of the fog with them. Outside, it
would be cold, difficult. Ideal weather for cutpurses, pimps,
pickpockets and ruffians. Bad weather for coppers.

'I understand you resigned.'

Harald spat out a short laugh.

'That's what you heard.'

Elsaesser was passing a document from hand to hand.

'They say you were the best copper in Altdorf.'

'I'd heard that too.'

'But not recently.'

Harald sat down. A pot of tea was stewing on the small table.

'I'm in the mercantile business now. I've retired to make my fortune.'

'By unblocking sewers?'

'And catching pilferers, and stock-taking and sweeping the place out if I have to.'

Without being asked, the baron sat down at the table. Elsaesser stayed upright, like a dutiful footman. He was clutching his document as if it were a charm blessed of Verena. Harald saw the Imperial seal. He wasn't impressed. He'd seen it before.

'Quite a descent in the world.'

'You could look at it that way, baron. A man should make the best of his circumstances. Whatever they are.'

He had been with the Reik and Talabec Trading Company for three years now and he couldn't think of the first names of the merchants who employed him.

'I've heard stories about your resignation.'

'You can take your pick of them.'

'What's your story?'

Harald didn't see why he should go through all this again. But it was expected of him.

'I killed a man. Several, in fact. But one in particular.'

'Ulli von Tasseninck.'

Harald remembered. The weight of the knife in his hand. The arc of the throw. The satisfying thud of impact.

'You knew him, elector. I'm not surprised.'

'The nephew of Grand Prince Hals von Tasseninck, Elector of Ostland.'

'Yes, a distinguished family.'

The young man, a corpse already, taking five more steps then crumpling onto the flagstones. It had been a neat job. No blood spilled.

'And a powerful one.'

'Show me an elector who is not powerful. You should know.'

Harald poured himself a mug of tea. He did not offer any to his visitors.

'Couldn't you have used a little more tact? Ulli was head-strong, yes, but he was born to the green velvet.'

Harald felt his bile rising and gulped down tea to calm his stomach.

'Baron, I saw a naked man chasing a girl, with his cock in one hand and a meatcleaver in the other... Well, I guess I forgot to enquire as to his lineage–'

Ulli had left his green velvet courtier's cloak draped over a statue of Verena, presumably hoping to blind the goddess of justice. Harald had wiped his knife on the cloak and thrown the garment over the dead man.

'The girl was Ulli's property, was she not? A bonded slave?'

Harald shrugged. 'It was dark in that temple. I didn't see the brand of ownership burned into her back.'

The baron had no answer. Harald knew that the man approved of his actions. Most people approved of him. That didn't help much. What people – especially those in green velvet – thought, and what they did were two separate courses.

'She was thirteen years old,' Harald said, 'and your friend had been using her since she was eight.'

Dark points appeared in the baron's eyes. 'Ulli von Tasseninck was not my friend.'

'Did you know that the Grand Prince endowed a college in his name at the University? There's a statue of him out-side it, looking like a saint, brandishing the spear of learning. The Ulli von Tasseninck School of Religious Studies.'

A slash of a smile split the baron's neatly trimmed beard.

'Actually, the statue was damaged recently. Someone smashed its head and replaced it with a pumpkin lantern.'

'That's a crime.'

'You wouldn't know anything about it.'

'I hate crime.'

'I thought so.'

Steam rose from Harald's tea. He understood the baron a little better now. He was a good man, too.

They were all good men. A dying breed.

'What happened to the girl? You bought her, didn't you?'

Harald remembered. She could hardly speak and would hide under a table whenever anyone new came into the room. When he had asked her what her name was, she had not known what he had meant. When he had explained that her name was what everybody called her, she smiled and said, 'Bitch.'

'No, I freed her.'

'I understood that cost you a lot.'

'Everything I had. My house, my savings, my horse, everything. Even my job. That was Grand Prince Hals's price.'

The baron nodded.

'I kept something back, though,' Harald said. 'Most of the weapons came with the commission. They belong to the watch. But this,' he patted his knife, 'is mine, bought with my own crowns.'

'Fine workmanship. Magnin the steelsmith?'

Harald nodded.

'I have one of his swords.'

Harald took out the knife and looked at his face in the polished steel. His reflection curved with the blade.

'She's married,' Harald said. 'Ulli's plaything. She married a chandler and got fat. She has hundreds of babies.'

'All named after you?'

'No, none of them. We don't see each other. She has too many memories.'

He kissed his blade, feeling the stone cold hardness against his lips.

'So, you have a steel mistress?'

'You could call it that,' he said, slipping his knife away. 'But it's just a good tool.'

'You were married, weren't you?' It was the first thing Elsaesser had said in a while.

Harald's stomach boiled again.

'I was. My wife died.'

'I'm sorry to hear that,' said the baron. 'Plague?'

His gut felt as if lashworms were eating through it.

'Hooks,' he said. 'Or Fish. They never found out.'

'That was back during the Waterfront War,' Elsaesser explained to the baron. 'Just before it petered out. It was strange. One day, both gangs were at each other's throats. Then, the fighting stopped. The war chiefs of the Hooks and the Fish just disappeared.'

Harald remembered the faces looking up at him from under the water, disappearing as the weights on their boots pulled them down.

'Another unsolved case,' he said. 'Dickon has a barrelful of them.'

'I've met Dickon.'

'Then you know what kind of a copper he is. Money at the end of the week and anything for a quiet life.'

The baron held out his hand and Elsaesser put the document in it.

'This is an Imperial warrant, Mister Kleindeinst.'

The baron laid it carefully on the table, squaring the corners.

'For what?'

'For anything you say. Immediately, it's an order reconfirming you in your old position.'

'Dickon will love that.'

'You won't be under Dickon. You'll report to me and I'm answerable only to the Emperor.'

Harald's stomach was calming down but there was a tightness in his belly replacing the ache. He could almost taste the desire. This warehouse was a grave and he could feel the earth shifting as he struggled out of it.

'Then, these are sealed orders giving you the authority to go anywhere, question anyone, do anything…'

There was a great deal of darkness in the baron's eyes. Harald felt as if he were looking into a knife-mirror again.

'And, finally, this is a warrant of arrest for a certain criminal,' said Elsaesser.

'A warrant of arrest,' explained the baron, 'or, if necessary, a warrant of execution.'

Harald picked up the document and sniffed it.

'This isn't real, is it?'

'No,' said the baron, 'but that will be our secret.'

'Boy,' Harald said to Elsaesser. 'Get a chair and sit down. Do you want tea?'

Elsaesser brought two cups from a shelf. Harald poured drinks for his visitors.

'I suppose I had better enjoy this,' he said, drinking again. 'This was the only perk of the job, imported tea from Kislev. And I don't work here any more.'

The document was in his shirt pocket, above his heart.

'I brought this,' Elsaesser said, pulling out a small, cloth-wrapped packet. 'It was in a desk at the Luitpoldstrasse Station.'

He unwrapped the object and let it fall on the table. The copper badge hadn't changed. It bore the watch code number for the Luitpoldstrasse District, 317, and his own service serial number, 89. Harald picked it up and felt it in his hand. His stomach wasn't bothering him now. It was as if he had regained the use of a crippled limb. He slipped the badge into his pocket.

'What do you know about the Beast?' asked the baron.

'Seven,' Harald said, imagining them laid out in a row. 'Seven so far.'

'And there will be more.'

'Yes. He can't stop. A womanslayer is the worst kind of criminal there is.'

'Can you catch him?'

The baron was serious now. Harald felt the weight of the badge in his pocket. For a small scrap of metal, it felt awfully heavy.

'You know,' he said, putting his boot up on the table, 'this is why they call me "Filthy Harald".'

The baron looked at Elsaesser, puzzled.

'I don't understand.'

'Every filthy job, baron. That's when people come to me. That's what I get. Every filthy job.'

IV

SHE HAD MISSED the main service at the temple, but attended a late evening ceremony. There were no pews. Worshippers at the Temple of Sigmar were expected to stand up, or to kneel on the hard stones. After her day, she decided on kneeling, although that meant a chill seeped into her knees and crept up through her body. Contact with the ground brought her closer to the god anyway, as she picked up the residue of the many devout prayers that had been offered in this small chapel. There were ignoble, ungodly thoughts too – even ignoble, ungodly prayers – but Rosanna was used to weeding them out and allowing herself to sink into the centuries of pious converse with the patron deity of the Empire.

They had kept her down at the Luitpoldstrasse Station well into the evening, sorting through odd items of clothing left over from the victims. And bits of irrelevant rubbish found lying around at the scenes of the killings. She was not a necromancer; she could not communicate with the dead and quiz them about their last moments. She was a psychometrist, picking up images and impressions from inanimate objects, usually strong emotions that had been associated with people who had been in contact with the things she scried from.

It had been a ghastly task, living through seven deaths, and all she had picked up was a tangle of confusion and spilled blood. She thought the Beast was a madman with a knife, but could not rule out the persistent suggestion that he was an altered creature. Through the pain, she only had the vaguest impressions of staring eyes. And she kept seeing green velvet.

But almost as bad as the shocking detritus left by violent death were the aching impressions she picked up of the lives the women had lived before their murders. Hunger, cold, poverty, lifelong abuse, joyless love. One woman had had maybe seventeen children, none surviving. Another had been introduced to weirdroot in infancy by her father, and had not spent a day outside her dreams for the rest of her life. The Beast would eventually go from the docks, but the misery would remain, unchanged.

She prayed to Sigmar, trying to cleanse herself of the deaths of seven women. In the centre of the octagonal chapel, looking up at the stylised image of the warhammer above the altar, she tried to reach out to the god who had been a man. Sometimes, her gift brought her epiphanies. But she was never sure of them, never sure that she had not merely tapped into the shared delusions of three thousand years of devout souls rather than reached the gods themselves.

Most people did not see enough, but Rosanna Ophuls frequently saw too much. It was worse, ultimately, than seeing nothing.

The graveyard shift cleric concluded the service and she stood up. Her only fellow communicants were an old woman who attended every service available at the Temple, from the earliest in the morning to the latest at night, and Tilo, a distracted-looking novice with ink on his fingers and a terrible stutter. She rubbed her knees and tried to get some warmth into them.

'R-R-R-Ro...'

'Yes,' she said, not waiting for him to finish.

He was going to ask her out to a coffee house. She could pick it up from his mind. His forehead was bright red and his hair, even in his early twenties, was thinning. His scalp glowed scarlet.

She felt kindly towards him.

'I'm sorry, Tilo. I've been summoned by the Lector.'

'Muh-muh-muh…'

Maybe some other time?

'Maybe, Tilo.'

His lips twitched in a smile.

'Excuse me.'

She stepped past him, through the doorway of the chapel. Tilo seemed to stumble slightly and pressed against her.

Inside her brain, a bubble of Tilo's mind exploded.

…she was looking down at herself, naked and tied to a bed, flames licking upwards from her flesh. Her face was painted and she was grinning like an empty-eyed weirdroot imbecile. Her breasts and hips were as exaggerated as those of dwarf goddess carvings. She was covered in a thin film of some perfumed oil and it was burning without pain. Her body rippled as she writhed against her bonds, lifting her back off the bed in an arch, invisible clouds of warmth and musk radiating from her hot centre. She was begging for something, words dribbling out of her mouth…

She pushed away from the novice, breaking the contact.

In his eyes, she read his horror.

'You saw,' he said, not stuttering, 'you *saw!*'

He ran away, his robe flapping about his legs.

There was a fountain outside the chapel. She pushed her face into the jet of water and tried to wash Tilo out of her.

'I am not a pretty girl,' she told herself, lying. 'What other people see is not me.'

She rubbed cold water into her face. She never wore rouge, tried to cover her long, red hair with a scarf. She did not lead men like Tilo on. And yet, wherever she went, she could feel men's eyes following her. All women experienced much the same thing, she supposed, but not all women could feel what she felt, could feel the dirty tendrils of men's desires slinking into her mind.

'Rosanna,' a voice said.

She stood up, her face dripping. The front of her dress was wet and clung.

Siemen Ruhaak, an initiate of the Order of the Torch, stood in the corridor, his hood up. The Order of the Torch was the cult's administrative arm. Ruhaak was always fetching people for audiences. The novices were afraid of him, because he always appeared when they were due for a scolding. Rosanna always felt slightly sorry for him, seeing the doubts that writhed beneath his sternness. If the Lector, Mikael Hasselstein, was a Knight of the Cult of Sigmar, then Siemen Ruhaak was his squire.

'Am I late?' she asked.

Ruhaak shook his head. 'I was just coming for you.'

'Is the Lector ready to see me?'

'Yes. He has just returned from a palace function. I would appreciate it if you did not disturb him overmuch. He seems distracted. He has so many things to consider.'

Rosanna couldn't quite understand. She couldn't even scry what Ruhaak was getting at. Something vague was troubling the man and he didn't even know what it was.

Ruhaak knew more about her than Tilo. As they walked through the passages towards the Lector's office, she noticed that he was careful not to touch her. He even held the sleeves of his robe tightly against his side to avoid a casual, accidental brushing.

There were two kinds of men: those who wanted her and those who were afraid of her.

Outside the Lector's office, two Knights of the Fiery Heart stood to attention, in full armour. Hasselstein did not usually bother with such precautions, but in a crisis he almost always called for the cult's military wing. For a powerful man – in Altdorf, Hasselstein was second only to the Grand Theogonist Yorri XV in the hierarchy of the cult – the Lector was remarkably easy to spook.

The knights stood aside and Ruhaak opened the door for her. She bowed her head as she entered the office. The door was closed behind her and she was with Mikael Hasselstein, the Emperor's confessor. Ruhaak had not come in with her.

She had talked with Hasselstein before, but never alone. Mostly, she saw him in the distance as he was about the business of the cult and of the Empire. Usually, he was getting into or out of a carriage, holding up his expensive robes. She knew he was convinced that Mornan Tybalt, the Master of the Imperial Counting House, was his deadly rival and was always embroiled in scheme and counter-scheme to gain the most favour with Karl-Franz. Hasselstein spent more time at the palace than the Temple and spoke eloquently about the need for the cult to remain at the centre of the court's political life. Sigmar had a hammer but the Lector fought with a quill and a ledger.

She looked up.

The Lector was lying on a couch with his boots off. He wore his cleric's robes, but open like a coat. Underneath, he was in a courtier's finery. He looked a little ill. The office was large but cluttered. There was an indifferent portrait of the Emperor up on one wall, given pride of place. An antique screen in the Nipponese style, decorated with images of Sigmar wielding his hammer, was set up before the slit windows. The room was lit with a single candelabrum. Rosanna got the impression that the Lector had just extinguished most of the lamps to save his eyes from hurt. The desk was piled high with books and papers, and an array of seals was set out on the blotter, neatly ordered by size and function of etiquette.

Hasselstein fixed her with his eyes and sat up.

'Ophuls,' he snapped, 'stay where you are.'

She stood as stiff as the knights sentry outside.

'There's a stool behind you,' Hasselstein said. 'Sit down.'

She did so, demurely tucking her dress around her legs. It was a low, wooden footstool and made her feel like a child.

'That's better,' he said, breathing again. If Ruhaak was cautious about touching a scryer, then Mikael Hasselstein was terrified. As the Emperor's confessor, she supposed, he carried a lot of things in his head that he could, even if threatened with torture, share with no one but his god.

'Ophuls,' he said. 'Rosanna, isn't it?'

'Yes, lector.'

Hasselstein stood up and began pacing the room in his stockinged feet, describing a half-circle around her. Even without contact, she could feel the storm of concerns surrounding his head. They crackled in the air like lightning. Ruhaak was right the Lector had a lot on his mind.

'Child, you've been with the Temple for some years?'

She nodded.

'You are a good and faithful servant of Sigmar. I have only excellent reports of you.'

He poured himself a glass of Estalian sherry. The Lector was not known for his asceticism. A cold bird sat in a dish on the floor by the couch, its ribs exposed and its legs twisted off. Rosanna remembered that she had not had time to eat today.

The chicken had led a happy life, pecking at corn, scratching around in the straw. It had been the special pet of the farmer's daughter. But the farmer's daughter had not been fond enough of it to neglect a profit. One day, she had gathered the bird up in her arms and neatly strangled it. Rosanna had sampled plenty of animal lives like that. She was a vegetarian.

Hasselstein stood still, sipping his sherry.

Uppermost in his thoughts was a woman. Rosanna scried a flurry of skirts, a lingering trace of perfume and the warm press of a body. So far as she knew, Hasselstein had no official mistresses. She pulled her invisible feelers back in and let them lie like her hands, folded in her lap.

Hasselstein drank more of the liquor. He was tired.

'You have been down at the docks today?'

'Yes, Father Wallraff sent me to help the watch.'

'Wallraff, eh? A man with initiative. Good for him.'

Rosanna had the impression that the Lector did not want to reward the father for his initiative. She would not have been surprised to learn that the sharp young cleric had suddenly been assigned to missionary duty beyond the Sea of Claws.

'I've been trying to help in this case of the Beast.'

Hasselstein drained his glass. 'The murderer, yes. I have heard of him.'

Rosanna could not help herself. The impressions pouring from Hasselstein were too strong to ignore. There was the laughter of a woman and the sticky taste of sweat. The Lector did not think like Tilo, constructing fantasies for the night. He was not imagining, he was remembering. She scried bodies pressed together in a hurry, lovemaking with a hard edge, blood and bruises in with the kisses and caresses. There was also a great darkness, as if the cleric were trying to blot out part of his memory.

'A bad business. What have you learned?'

Rosanna forced herself to ignore the pictures in Hasselstein's mind.

'Little, I'm afraid. The murderer is a man, I think. A human being, that is. Or of some closely related race.'

Hasselstein's face knit. Anger burned like a halo around him.

'I had imagined from the savagery associated with the slayings that we were dealing with a monster of Chaos.'

'I don't think so. The Beast is twisted in mind, not in body. At least, that is my impression. It's not very clear. There is something strange about the murderer, physically. I've scried that much from the scraps the watch have kept. I keep feeling that something important is just within my grasp, but that I cannot pick it out from the confusion.'

'You are young,' Hasselstein said, 'your gifts are not fully trained yet.'

'Perhaps the cult would care to assign someone with more control. There is always Hannelore Zischler or Beate Hettich.'

The Lector thought for a moment and then made a decision. 'No, Rosanna. You must have your chance. Bringing in another scryer would confuse matters. Besides, the others are not in Altdorf. These murders show no sign of pausing to allow us to send for Zischler or Hettich. The Beast must be caught soon.'

'Yes.'

'Can you tell me *anything* more about the murderer?'

Rosanna wasn't sure whether to mention it, but, 'It's not something I scried, but before I arrived the watch found some important evidence that was destroyed.'

Hasselstein was keenly interested.

'Yes,' he said, impatiently, 'what was it?'

'A scrap of green velvet, lector. Like the courtiers wear.'

Hasselstein made a fist and his glass shattered in it. Rosanna flinched as his rage filled the room.

His face was set and inexpressive, but his mind was in a turmoil.

He took out a handkerchief and bound his cuts.

'Rosanna, have you taken any vows? I know you're not a novice, but you are attached to the cult?'

'I have pledged allegiance and obedience.'

'Obedience? Good. The cult must come before anything, you understand? This is a precarious time for the Empire and only we have the best interests of the Empire as our first concern.'

Hasselstein had said as much during his private sermons to the Temple staff. Father Wallraff had been amusing about the speech, asking her if she could think of a time in history which had not been a precarious one for the Empire.

'Whatever you learn about the Beast, you must bring first to me. If I am not available, confer with Ruhaak. This is vitally important.'

'I... I understand.'

'Be sure you do. We have the Order of the Fiery Heart, remember. Anything the watch can do, our own Templars can do better. I do not trust the watchmen. Too many criminals have escaped from them.'

Rosanna did understand. The Dock Watch, as she had seen, were greedy bullies. If the Beast was a rich man, he would find it easy to purchase his freedom. She could not be responsible for that.

'And we must have secrecy. This may not be a story it would be useful for many people to know about.'

Hasselstein was thinking of his woman again. She was crying out in passion as they coupled.

Didn't anyone in this Temple think of anything else?

'I understand.'

'We are a wealthy order, Rosanna. I see no reason why you should not profit from your labours in this case.'

Rosanna could not have been more shocked if the Lector had slapped her.

'Should you acquit yourself to my satisfaction, I believe I can authorize a healthy pension. Enough to set you up in any corner of the Empire, in any business you might choose. You would have a substantial dowry should you prefer hunting a husband to hunting a murderer. Should you be tired of your own name and family history, a new background could be contrived for you.'

This was an astonishing suggestion.

'What I mean is that this is such an important matter to me – to the Cult of Sigmar – that your performance is of the most immediate interest to me. Serve us well and there is little you might desire that is not within my gift.'

Rosanna bowed her head. Her scarf was slipping from her hair.

Forgetting himself, Hasselstein advanced and extended his hand in a familiar gesture, as if to lay the cleric's healing touch upon a supplicant. It was the traditional way of ending a confession, symbolising the priest's assumption of the sins of the communicant.

A fraction of an inch away from her hair, which was rising slightly to meet the charge of his body, Hasselstein's hand froze.

In his mind, he was pleasuring a woman in a dark, cramped space, a cupboard or a small room. Her knees were braced and she was gripping a chairback to stay unsteadily upright. They both grunted as he ground inside her and the odour of sex hung in the air like an Altdorf fog. Her skirts and his robe were disarrayed, bunched between them, and his hands were in her clothes, fastened like leeches to her body. His face was in the woman's hair. It was red, like Rosanna's. But then it was blonde and silk-fine. As the couple peaked, she turned her head to look into his face, to lick hungrily at his chin. Looking through his eyes, she saw her own face again, but rippling like the surface of a disturbed pond. Hasselstein's desires were superimposed upon his memories. Rosanna saw her eyes changing colour, from green to blue, and her features shifting. The face distorted and became several other faces. One of them, she was sure, belonged to Margarethe

Ruttmann, the Beast's last victim. And others, just beyond her recognition, seemed similarly familiar.

The Lector snatched his hand away and rubbed it against his robe.

'You have my blessing,' he said. 'Now, go...'

V

THE GIRL RUNS *through the fog, but the Beast is faster than anything in the city. It doesn't know whether it runs on two legs or four, but its claws strike sparks from the cobbles. The girl is limping, her ankle turned on some loose stone. She is sobbing, knowing what comes next.*

She is already marked, the scratches across her face are still bleeding.

There aren't cobbles under their feet any more. Wooden planks shift and rumble as they run down the jetty.

They are on the docks. The old, disused docks. There is nobody else around. They are alone together. The Beast is pleased.

The boy-shell holds back, allowing the girl a few moments to make a move. She finds a ladder and climbs down from the wharf, towards the shingles of the riverbank.

The Beast dispels the boy-shell and grabs the wooden posts that stick up beyond the ladder.

Below, the girl is climbing. She has sunk into the fog, but it can hear her mewling and the beating of her heart. It can smell her fear.

The Beast knows her. It knows her name: Trudi.

The fog is wonderful. It feels like part of the Beast, as if its breath were solidifying in the air around it. The Beast was born for the fog and feels comfortable in it. The fog is its friend, like the crooked alleyways are its friend, and the tangle of piles under the docks, and the night that falls as thick as velvet upon the city.

The ladder is old and rotted through. A rung snaps and the girl falls. The Beast hears her sob as she lands badly, the wind knocked out of her.

Somewhere out on the river, a foghorn sounds. Two barges pass dangerously close to one another. The Beast hears the night watches swearing at each other. They are very far away.

Not bothering with the ladder, the Beast leaps. The river is low at this time of night, so it falls in shallow water, its knees and ankles bending as its bulk is forced into a crouch.

It feels pebbles under its feet and hands, and fragments of clay pipes thrown away by sailors and dockers for centuries. Sometimes seashells are shifted this far inland, scraped from the hulls of the ocean-going ships that sail down the Reik from Marienburg.

The Beast stands on two legs, slicing its claws through the air. The boy-shell is lost in the fog, lost forever…

The girl is near, huddled up against a thick, wooden post, trying to still her breathing.

The Beast lopes towards her, shingles crunching under it.

It tries to say her name, as it has tried to say the others. The word will not come from its mouth. Its jaw doesn't work as it should.

The Beast finds the girl…

…and the girl screams.

VI

DIEN CH'ING REFLECTED that he was not as young as he had formerly been. His face was still as smooth as new vellum and his hair had been white since childhood. Few could guess his age, but he knew. Sixty-five. He had been serving the Lord Tsien-Tsin – Tzeentch, as the Master was called in this barbarous land – all his life. There had been rewards. Continued strength, health and vitality were among them. Tsien-Tsin, Lord of the Fifteen Devils, repaid faithful service with longevity. Ch'ing could reasonably expect to live to a very great age, far greater than that enjoyed by even the most venerable of his ancestors.

His life had taken him across the face of the Known World many times. He had visited each of the continents, had amassed and squandered fortunes, had seen his enemies suffer and perish, had tasted the delights afforded only to the initiates of his proscribed cult. And still, he felt, he was only a few tiers up the pagoda. He had served the Invisible Empire for the length of his days. It was time, he believed, that a little more of the greater purpose of Tsien-Tsin were revealed to him.

Tonight, he would meet with his immediate superior and perhaps a little more would be explained.

He had slipped out of the quarters allotted to him in the palace and taken advantage of the fog to travel unseen across the city. It was a skill he had cultivated for many years. In a sense, the helpful fog spoiled the trick. Any fool could skulk and hide in fog, but only an adept of Ch'ing's stature could pass unnoticed through a crowded city at the height of mid-day on a clear, cloudless day.

Using the key that had been delivered to him, he let himself into one of the rooms at the back of the Holy Hammer of Sigmar on the Street of a Hundred Taverns. It was not the rowdiest, most decadent of the many hostelries in the vicinity. Indeed, it was one of the quietest, best-ordered and neatest, as befitted a private club open only to the most desperate thieves and professional murderers in the city. Only those with a key were admitted and securing a key was more difficult than gaining an audience with the Emperor.

In the darkness of the passage, Ch'ing could hear a conversation being conducted in the tap-room.

'I say it gives the business a bad name,' claimed a man with a Tilean lilt to his voice.

'I agree with you, Ettore,' said a more cultivated, suave-sounding man, 'but what can we do? The matter is in the hands of Sigmar and, of course, the Dock Watch.'

There was some laughter. Ch'ing smiled. So this was what murderers sounded like when they were relaxing.

'The Beast is just a butcher,' said Ettore. 'He gives murderers a bad name.'

'You strangled your last wife with her nightcap, I believe.'

'That was a personal matter.'

'And then you took a red-hot poker to your children.'

'They were disobedient. Besides, your hands are hardly clean, my friend Quex.'

'I don't deny that,' purred the suave murderer, 'but I have never killed without being paid for it.'

'I say we should trap the Beast ourselves,' a third, gruff-voiced, assassin said.

'What?' spluttered Ettore. 'Us, help the Dock Watch?'

'They've been poking around too much since the Beast started killing tarts. They're not catching him, but they are harassing us. When was the last time old Dickon actually caught anyone?'

Nobody knew.

'Well, he pulled in Fagnar Brisz today and a couple of coppers roughed up Schatten.'

'That's terrible. They'll be refusing bribes next.'

'Brisz is an animal,' said Quex, 'little better than the Beast. His use of the bandsaw on the Widow von Praunheim was simply unnecessary and distasteful.'

'Well, Quex, if the Beast keeps it up, you can debate etiquette with Brisz in Mundsen Keep.'

'The Beast is an amateur, gentlemen, and amateurs always get caught. Or disappear without trace.'

'I say good luck to him and let's have another drink.'

'A fine idea, my man.'

A hand clamped down over Ch'ing's shoulder and he twisted, his hands up, ready to defend himself.

He favoured the crane-style, arms out for balance, feet kicking like the lightning-fast pecks of the bird's deadly beak.

'Careful,' said a familiar voice. 'The corridor is narrow, you'll break your wrists.'

Ch'ing relaxed and bowed. In the darkness, Yefimovich's eyes glowed like hot coals.

'It is good to see you, my friend,' the High Priest of Tzeentch said. 'How long has it been since we first met?'

'More than thirty years. Not since Zhufbar.'

'Ah yes, a failure. I still regret it. We were out of favour after that.'

'Quite so.' The marks on Ch'ing's arms, where the daemon sting had appeared, still pained him.

'The man died, you know. In the north, on the Great Battlefield at the Top of the World.'

Ch'ing bowed in gratitude for the news. 'I'm pleased to learn of that.'

'And the vampire woman... well, you must know of her subsequent history. She lives in this city.'

'Genevieve Dieudonné. Our personal business is not over. But she must wait for the while. After all, neither of us is getting any older.'

Yefimovich laughed. 'I have a room upstairs. Come on.'

They climbed to the first floor, in the pitch dark. Yefimovich glowed slightly, a red undertone to his skin.

'Where is your familiar?' Ch'ing asked.

'Respighi? Don't let him hear you call him a familiar. He thinks he's an acolyte. He is out in the fog somewhere, doing my work.'

'Give him my most pleasant wishes.'

'I'll be sure to.'

Inside the room, the agitator lit a lamp. He had a cot and a table, and more books than the palace library. There were many copies of his own seditious pamphlets, tied up in bundles: *Sons of the Soil, Arise!*, *Casting Asunder the Chains*, *You and Your Betters* and *Come the Revolution*.

Ch'ing picked up a book. It was new and neatly-bound, but had no title embossed on the spine.

'This is my most popular work,' Yefimovich said. 'It's called *Beasts in Green Velvet*. It is an analysis of the misdeeds of the ruling classes. It will inflame the peasantry of the Empire, with its stories of men, women and children trampled under the iron heel of privilege.'

The High Priest sounded pleased with himself. Ch'ing cast his eye over a few lines. The book was like a gazeteer of the first families of the Empire, with a list of their crimes down through the centuries. This page was about the Kreishmier family of Ferlangen. He had never heard of them, but they seemed to be a long line of petty tyrants, hanging, branding, torturing, raping, robbing and enslaving the local peasantry as the whim took them.

'All cunning lies, I trust?'

'Oh no, that's the clever part. This is all true. These people allege that, as disciples of the proscribed cults, we serve evil. And yet, look at all their works and accomplishments...'

Baron Otto Kreishmier, since deceased, had once hanged twenty-seven of his tenant farmers between sun-up and sun-down on the Feast of Mitterfruhl to collect on a wager with his sister.

Ch'ing set down the papers. 'Things are not ordered very differently in Cathay. The Monkey King sits in his Eternal Gardens boasting of his youthful exploits, while his ministers rob him blind and use the people as chattels. And, as you know, Kislev suffers under an absolute monarch.'

The High Priest's eyes grew. 'Yes, but only in the Empire are the people told they are free even as they are being wrapped in chains. Our kings and tsars do not claim to be anything other than tyrants. Karl-Franz is an elective ruler, and a precarious one at that. This will shake him a little...'

Yefimovich tapped a pile of papers. The ink was still wet. 'Tomorrow, this pamphlet will be on the streets. The Empire is a tinderbox...'

Yefimovich took his lower eyelids between his thumbs and forefingers.

'...a tinderbox waiting for a flame.'

He pulled his skin and his face came off in one piece. It dangled, a dead mask.

Knowing what to expect, Ch'ing averted his gaze.

'That's better,' said the High Priest. 'Now my skin can breathe again.'

Ch'ing turned around and looked into the true face of his comrade in Chaos.

Yefimovich was thoroughly human in his features, but they were as transparent as moulded glass. Under his face-shaped bubble of skin raged an eternal fire. Ch'ing could see the lines of his skull, but rather than being covered with flesh and muscle they were clothed in forever-burning fire. No heat came from him, but the flames still writhed.

'You know, there are people in this city who think I am a fire-breather.'

VII

SHE WOKE UP and instantly forgot her dream…

…but her heart still beat at ramming speed and the terror was still upon her. She shivered in her own sweat. The echo of her cry was still dying in the small, stone-walled cell.

Rosanna sat up, the last blanket falling away from her. She had been writhing in her sleep and almost all the bedclothes had been thrown off her cot.

Outside the slit window of her cell, where the moons should have been, was a wedge of grey. A night-candle burned on her writing desk, casting a small pool of light upon the piles of books jumbled there. She always needed a flame in the dark. It was her last connection with childhood.

She hugged herself, until the trembling subsided.

Sometimes, she was gripped with raptures in the night. But mostly, her dreams were terrible. It was a part of the gift to which she could never become used.

As always when the horror was squirted directly into her mind, she wished she had been born fat, stupid and normal like her sisters. She would have married a hunter or a woodcutter, and dropped five children by now. The only

thing to disturb her nights would have been her husband's
snoring.

She disentangled herself from the last of the blankets and
walked across the tiny cell – the flagstones were shockingly
cold under her bare feet – to the stand where there was a
basin of fresh water.

Although not a cleric or a novice, she was still under the
strict regime of the Temple. There was no mirror for her van-
ity. Just now, she was grateful for the absence. She did not
think she could look into her own face without remembering too much...

She slipped her hands into the cold water and was fully
awake. Her heartrate had slowed to normal. She splashed
water on her face and rubbed away the sweat and sleep.

...parts of her dream came back to her...

She pressed her fists against her eyes, trying to keep the
dream away.

*...she was running through the fog and there was someone –
something – coming after her. She could hear its rasping breath
and fancied the clatter of its claws on cobbles. The smell of dead
fish was all around her. She was running on wooden boards now,
desperate to get to the end of a quay. A ladder stood out in the fog.
If she reached it, she might be safe...*

She knelt, letting the dream that was not a dream come
back.

*...she climbed down quickly, her long skirts caught and tore on
some neglected nail. Looking up, she could see the silhouette on
the lip of the jetty, its eyes shining. Green velvet. Sharp teeth.
Claws. It was unmistakably the Beast. Her face still stung from
the rakemarks. She was afraid, but not just for herself...*

Rosanna was confused. As so often in her intuitive visions,
identities were scrambled. She could not make out any
names. The girl she was dreaming she was worked in a hostel called the Wayfarer's Rest and had brothers called Jochim
and Gustav, but her own name did not swim in her head
with these other scraps. The thing that followed her had the
faces of many men she had known, but Rosanna could not
sort out which was the real aspect of the Beast and which the
confused overlay of memories. There was a name uppermost

in the girl's mind as she ran. Wolf. Wolf was the girl's lover.
But the face that went with the name was mixed up with the
dark blur of the Beast. The scryer tried to separate the two,
and could not. There was an idealized Wolf, but she guessed
he existed only in the girl's imagination: this noble, hand-
some, kindly face resembled that of the Baron Johann von
Mecklenberg. That was another layer, prompting her to wonder just what the elector's interest in these crimes was. In the
girl's mind, Wolf's face was constantly changing.

…the Beast caught her, and her body was opened…

Rosanna fought the dream. Despite her duty to learn, she
kicked against the vision. She did not want to know any
more, but the momentum was too great. She was forced to
dream through until the end, until the complete darkness
descended.

…after an eternity of pain, she died.

The dream shut off and Rosanna was herself again, the
other girl gone from her mind as if she had never been there.

Rosanna did not believe in any of the gods. Not even
Sigmar. No gods could allow such things.

The dead girl had known her attacker and yet not been
sure of his identity. Like the others, she had died in a state
of panic and confusion. The rustle of velvet was as strong
with this girl as it had been with Margarethe Ruttmann.
Green velvet.

Reliving the dream had made her void her bladder. She
took off her wet nightdress and washed herself thoroughly,
as if trying to wipe away any trace of her contact with the
dead girl.

It was quiet outside. Beyond the fog, the sun would be rising soon. The work of the day would begin.

Rosanna returned to her cot and pulled the blankets over
herself. She curled up small and wrapped the bedclothes
tight around her, like a prickly cocoon.

What she had dreamed had happened. And it had happened tonight, probably at exactly the moment she first
dreamed it. This murder was distinct from the seven others.

Somewhere out there, undiscovered, was an eighth corpse.

PART THREE
DUEL

I

As THE BELLS of the Temple of Sigmar sounded the hour of seven, the sun rose over Altdorf. The city, however, remained in the dark under its blanket of fog.

The lamplighters stayed in their beds late, knowing that they would not be needed to extinguish the city's street-torches until the fog lifted. Later, the Imperial Militia would kindle the traditional fogfire in Konigsplatz and, across the river, the Temple would open its refectory for those stranded away from their homes by the weather.

Along the city's miles of riverfront, lanterns would be strung to guide the ferrymen and the bargees. The business of trade must continue, even if the fog slowed the riverboats and barges to a crawl.

Meanwhile, with the tax collectors blundering about in the murk, the influx of contraband into the city would increase tenfold. With harvest produce just due to flow into the docks, some rapid and illegal profits would be made and the Fish would make thankful offerings to Manann, God of the Seas, for sending the fog and enabling them to circumvent the revenue men.

At the palace, a victory procession arranged in honour of the heroes of the Empire who had recently defended Averland from the goblin hordes was quietly cancelled. Karl-Franz did not care much for the fog and had a superstitious dread of venturing out into it. His great-grandfather, Matthias IV, had gone out among his people in the fog, using the gloom as a disguise so he might learn their true feelings about their Emperor, and had disappeared without a trace. Even a century later, white-bearded vagrants were turning up regularly, claiming to be the rightful Emperor.

The fog having descended the evening before, a notice had gone up in the barracks across the square from the palace and a platoon of the Imperial Militia had been routinely seconded to the city watch to help out with the extra duties required. Later, this traditional measure – practiced in every fog – would be the cause of controversy and confusion, and not a little spilled blood.

The fog spilled over the high walls of the city, but tended to dissipate into thin streamers of mist in the surrounding forests. The city was a bowl, cupping the thick grey and brown broth to itself. The fog came off the Reik and the Talabec, shrouding at first the docks and the waterfront. But by this morning it had spread to every quarter.

The fog affected everyone, from the Emperor in his palace and the Grand Theogonist in the Temple to the boatmen and workmen of the docks, the students and professors of the University, the gamblers and harlots of the Street of a Hundred Taverns, the Hooks and the Fish and a dozen other lesser factions, the toll-keepers of the bridges, the merchants of the north-eastern business quarter, the beggars and paupers of the East End, the staunch servants of the Law and the furtive worshippers of the Dark Powers, and the actors and artists of Temple Street. Some hated the damp, clinging curtain that permeated everything; but some loved the fog, and ventured out in search of the possibilities it offered.

It was a good time for crime and a better one for intrigue.

SCHYGULLA, THE DOCK manager, was an old Hook and Per Buttgereit's cousin was with the Fish. So, without ever having been involved in either faction, the apprentice was caught up in their pointless, continuing struggle.

He had wanted to be a student, but he couldn't master his letters. His father had told him that 'apprenticeship is a wonderful opportunity,' and signed him up for five years of shit work on the docks at a minimum rate of pay. His father, at forty-eight, was still apprenticed to Lilienthal the stone-mason. He still talked about the opportunities that would open up to him when he finished his training, just in time to drop dead from a heart attack after thirty-five years of hefting huge blocks of granite and making pots of tea.

Buttgereit was supposed to turn up at the Beloved of Manann dock before everyone else and get the kettle boil-ing. Then, he was to wait for Schygulla to think of something crappy for him to do. Usually, it was scraping something off something, or sorting out the good fish due to go on sale across the river in the Marketplatz from the bad fish due for a fast turnover into soup in the East End. Today, of course, it was stringing lanterns underneath the docks. If a task involved going where the smell was worst, Schygulla always assigned Buttgereit.

The lanterns – slow-burning candles surrounded by pol-ished reflectors in tin cages – were easy to break and any damage would have to come out of his apprentice's wage. He had carried them carefully down to the end of the dock and was having to take them down two at a time.

'This ladder is rotted through,' he complained to himself. 'Someone will probably take a nasty fall and be swept away.'

There were fifteen lanterns and fifteen spots along the dock, above the high watermark, where they were supposed to go.

Probing his way through the fog, Buttgereit could hear Schygulla laughing with some of his old cronies. They were relating stories about the lascivious Elector of Nuln and her elite cadre of strapping guardsmen. To the Countess Emmanuelle von Liebewitz, they said, remaining faithful to a true love meant not going to bed with more than ten men at the same time. The old men, thrown out of the Hooks long ago, all laughed meanly at that one. The countess was rumoured to be so vain of her beauty that she had a summerhouse constructed only of mirrors and insisted that her female servants always wear masks so that she might shine all the more by comparison.

Buttgereit took the rungs one at a time, barely able to see his feet, and afraid that a slat would break. When he put a foot into the water, he knew that he was at about the right place. The river would cover the shingles at this hour in the morning. He pulled his wet shoe out and shook it. There was a rope strung from the ladder to the pilings that supported the dock. It was supposed to mark high-water but it had sagged a little and looped under the surface. The first lanternhook was on the ladder, just above the rope.

He had seen the Countess Emmanuelle at a river procession once and she hadn't looked especially decadent. She was undoubtedly the most beautiful woman in the Empire, though. She reminded him a bit of his mother, only with more facepaint and expensive clothes. Admittedly, she had had several young men – some no older than Buttgereit – in the ceremonial barge with her and they had all been gussied up in tight uniforms with lots of braid and polished leather. Some of them wore as much paint as she did. Buttgereit had hated them all personally. Their job seemed far more rewarding than making tea and scraping barnacles.

'Hurry up, fishface!' Schygulla shouted down at him. 'The Reik and Talabec have all their lamps strung and are unloading already. We'll lose trade if you don't stop dreaming and get to work.'

Buttgereit grumbled under his breath and, holding onto the ladder with his left hand, hung the first lantern from the hook, which was just by his knees. With the second lantern dangling from his teeth, he let himself down two rungs and crouched, still trying to keep out of the water. This would be just the time for the ladder to fall apart and drop him into the scummy waters of the Reik.

Schygulla was a fiend for palace gossip. Now he was repeating unthinkable stories about the Countess Emmanuelle's brother, Leos. According to the dock manager, the viscount had been spoiled for all women by the ravages of his sister and sought solace with the Countess's cast-off male lovers. Buttgereit would have liked to see the old fool tell that story to the Viscount Leos's face. The man was reputedly the most deadly duellist in the Empire and he would make a fine carving job of Schygulla's face. Of course, those born to the green velvet didn't deign to match swords with over-the-hill dock ruffians, but it made a pretty picture.

'I said hurry up, not play with yourself!' shouted Schygulla. He said something about Buttgereit that the apprentice couldn't hear and the cronies barked with laughter.

Bastards, all.

Buttgereit applied his tinderbox flame to the wick of the first lantern. Light grew and he could see a little better.

Beyond the rungs of the ladder was a dark space. There were criss-cross wooden pilings, reinforced with rusted iron stays and cables, rooting the Beloved of Manann quay in the shingles of the riverbank and anchoring it in the stone walls of the docks.

Water lapped at the pilings and fog swirled in the enclosed space. There was something floating in the water, wrapped up in cloth, caught by one of the cables.

Buttgereit couldn't make out what the lump was. Then, he saw the threads of blood in the water.

'Buttgereit,' shouted Schygulla, 'what in Sigmar's name are you doing?'

The apprentice's stomach was roiling.

He wanted to call up to the manager, but he was afraid that if he opened his mouth to speak his breakfast would burst out.

The floating lump was shifting in the water, being dragged towards him.

'Buttgereit, I'll take my hook to you!'

There was a face just under the surface of the river. The empty eyesockets stared up at him, bloody tears pulled away by the current.

Finally he found his voice and yelled.

II

IT WAS EASY to lose track of the time in the fog. Shortly after dawn, Genevieve Dieudonné entered the quarters she shared with Detlef Sierck on Temple Street, just across from the Vargr Breughel Memorial Playhouse, where the actor-playwright was still appearing in *A Farce of the Fog*. The six hundred and sixty-seven year old girl pulled off her cloak and hung it on the back of the door. She admired it. A gift from the future Emperor Luitpold, who had something of a crush on her, it was a splendid garment of green velvet. If she were to visit the palace more often, she would fit in easily.

She thought of Oswald, the corrupt calculating machine in green velvet. She turned her back on the cloak.

Tendrils of fog had come in with her. Satiated from her night's feeding, she felt the somnolence that came upon her every few weeks. She would sleep for several days and awake replenished.

But she did not want to retire just yet. Her blood was still flowing and she could still taste what she had taken…

In the next room, Detlef was sleeping. He kept late hours himself, dining after his performance, but they had not been together last night. Genevieve could not remember the last time they had actually slept together, rather than find a mutually convenient time for love making. The human and the vampire cycles were too different.

There were pictures of Detlef up on the walls, posters showing him in his greatest role: as Lowenstein in *The Treachery of Oswald*, as Baron Trister in *The Desolate Prisoner of Karak-Kadrin*, as Guillaume in *Barbenoire: The Bastard of Bretonnia*, as Ottokar in *The Loves of Ottokar and Myrmidia* and as the Daemon Prince in *Strange Flower*.

They had been together for four years now, since their experiences at the fortress of Drachenfels. The years had been good, but they had been kinder to her than to him. Detlef's weight had increased and he had put on so many old-man make-ups to play the great roles that he seemed much older than his actual age. She, however, was unchanging. Her mind was old, but her blood was still young.

An unthought tear, a bubble of red, appeared in her eye and trickled down her cheek. She wiped it away with the back of her hand and licked it clean, relishing the tang.

After so many years, she ought to be used to transience. Everybody changed. Even her.

There was a great deal of clumping about inside and Detlef stumbled in, his nightshirt ballooning over his stomach, his hair and moustaches in a mess. He did not bid her good morning.

'The house was half-empty last night,' he said. 'There was too much fog outside the theatre for our farce to have much appeal.'

'Attendance has been falling off for weeks, my dear.'

'You're right, Gené. We are nearing the end of our run.'

Genevieve caught his meaning, and sadly agreed.

'Where were you last night?' he asked, wearily.

'Feeding,' she said, remembering...

MRS BIERBICHLER, HELMUT Elsaesser's landlady, had practically adopted him, claiming that a young man so far away from his birthplace would tend to neglect himself and that a woman should step in and sort things out for him. His landlady was childless herself, but several of her friends had young female relatives and chance meetings were forever being contrived. To be fair, Elsaesser quite liked the Widow Flickenschildt's niece, Ingrid, whose blonde braids reached nearly to her knees when uncoiled, and had arranged to see the girl again one night next week. However, it was hard not to resent such smothering care and attention.

'Eat, eat,' his landlady told him, piling yet another plate of oatcakes onto the table, 'or you'll grow thin and die.'

Elsaesser's protests were hopeless. Mrs Bierbichler ladled syrup onto the cakes and slipped the plate in front of him.

He took his knife and fork to the food. When, full-mouthed, he nodded his approval, she let slip that this was a Flickenschildt family recipe she was trying out.

Elsaesser was surrounded by women who wanted him to hurry up and get married. He felt as if he were the victim of a huge conspiracy. The cakes were good though.

'Hot coffee,' Mrs Bierbichler said, pouring some into a bucket-size container. 'It will settle your stomach and keep you warm. If you eat too fast, you could get indigestion and die.'

Elsaesser took a swig. The coffee was strong, black and bitter. Mrs Bierbichler did not believe in sugar or cream in coffee. She said that made you fat, and if you were too fat you could die.

'You shouldn't go out in a fog. You could catch a chill and die.'

Swallowing coffee-soaked cakes, Elsaesser replied, 'It's my job, Mrs B. It's a duty.'

'Well, it should be some other man's duty. Someone less vulnerable to nasty colds.'

'It's important.' Elsaesser was serious. 'The Beast must be caught.'

Mrs Bierbichler raised her hands to the gods. 'The Beast! Ach, he only cuts down girls who are no good. Why should you run after such women, when there are lovely girls I could name so much closer to home, so much nicer for you. Such good cooks! Such hips for child-bearing! You could catch a disease and die, you know, from girls who are no good.'

'Nobody deserves the Beast,' he said, slowly, feeling his resolve build.

Since the first murder, Elsaesser had been following the crimes. His last few weeks at the University had rushed past, as he passed his exams with the expected ease, but he had spent more time thinking about the Beast than of his future. He could have had a position with any watch in the city, but he had insisted on the docks. His professors had been appalled but he had insisted. In his head, he knew all the victims intimately, their names, their lives, the circumstances of their death: Rosa, Miriam, Helga, Monika, Gislind, Tanja, Margarethe. To get Professor Scheydt to approve his posting to the Dock Watch, he had told the man that Rosa May, the first victim, had been his mistress. He had never met the girl, but he needed to give the pragmatic professor a reason for his need to catch the Beast. Scheydt, a cleric of the law, could understand revenge better than he could justice.

Elsaesser told himself he wanted the Beast brought in to serve the cause of justice, but sometimes he was not sure. Sometimes he wondered why he burned with the need to stop these particular murders. People died by violence throughout the city, throughout the Empire, every day, but Elsaesser only took the Beast personally. The facts of the case would creep into his dreams and he would find himself surrounded by the images and impressions he had of the women's last hours. He knew all the women, all the victims. But also, after these months of intensive study, he knew the Beast.

The murderer was becoming more active: the first three killings had taken place over four months, the last four had been within the last five weeks. In the madman's mind, something was coming to the boil. Four out of the seven victims had died during fogs or on nights when the fog seemed to threaten to appear. Some maniacs killed by the moon, but the Beast was stimulated by the fog.

'No,' said Elsaesser, 'nobody deserves the Beast.'

He shoved his plate away and got up. His uniform coat was hanging from its stand, the copper badge new-polished.

He slipped it on and felt better. Merely by becoming a watchman, he was doing something.

Mrs Bierbichler came for him with a long scarf and wrapped it around his neck, muffling his chest and face.

'You must wrap up warm. If the cold gets into your lungs, you could die.'

Mrs Bierbichler knew a lot of ways that you could die.

THE LONG TABLE in the dining hall rattled as Otho Waernicke thumped it, sending plates and cups jumping into the air.

'Bow, you heathens,' he shouted.

There was a massed moaning from the soreheads and hangovers who had crawled down to this late breakfast, unshaven, bleary-eyed and mainly bruised. Last night, the League had been in three serious fights and an assortment of minor scraps.

The chaplain, startled, continued to offer up thanks to Ulric for the new day, albeit with a more attentive audience.

Otho thumped the table again and roared for the steward.

His head hurt. A lot. Some time last night, he had offered to drink a dwarf under the table and asked his opponent to name the poison. This morning, he had woken up under the table with a dwarf snoring in his ear. They had gone on from Alte Geheerentode brandy to gin laced with gunpowder. If he belched, Otho could kill a man at fifty paces.

There was some squealing and shouting from the vestibule as last night's whores were kicked out into the street with a few extra pfennigs for their trouble. The League's hall was sacred to Ulric and the Emperor, and it was traditional to eject all women between the chaplain's morning thanksgiving and nightfall.

Otho's chest and legs hurt too. He couldn't remember where the bruises had come from. There was a long scrape up his side that made him think of a docker's hook.

The thanks given, and the women out of the building, the chaplain turned around the bust of Ulric that stood on the great mantelpiece. Ever since the League had been founded, the eyes of its patron deity had been turned to the wall between nightfall and thanksgiving, so the god would not have to look upon the trespasses of his youthful, high-spirited worshippers.

With the eyes of Ulric on them, the students of the League became models of gentlemanliness, moderation and propriety.

At least until nightfall…

INSIDE THE MAN-SHELL, *the Beast rested. Last night's work had been satisfying and momentarily succoured the creature. But it was becoming hungrier sooner. It had ventured out two nights in a row. Tonight, it might make it three…*

III

WHEN JOHANN AWOKE, his chambers in the palace were eerily quiet. Suites were kept open in the west wing for any of the electors whose business might bring them to the city. He occupied his with only a few servants, while down the passageway was quartered the huge retinue required by the Countess Emmanuelle von Liebewitz and her brother. Usually, he was awakened by the flurry of activities required by the countess-elector's levée. Today he slept well past that.

He dressed himself but called in Martin, his valet secretary, to trim his beard. Afterwards, as he ate a breakfast of fruit and cheese, he went through the day's communiqués. There was a long letter from Eidsvik, his steward back in Sudenland, reporting on the harvests and requesting his approval for certain charitable gestures. The von Mecklenberg estates had done well enough this year not to need to draw on the tithe of farm goods it was entitled to collect from the outlying farms and Eidsvik suggested contributing the offerings to the poor. Johann decided to go along with it and dictated a brief assent to be sent off along with a document granting the steward power of attorney for a further two months while he concluded his 'business' in Altdorf.

Then there was a note in precise script from Professor Scheydt at the University, setting out simply Wolf's attendance record for the past few terms and hinting in more complex terms that Johann's brother could only remain enrolled on his course if he were to attend more lectures or pay larger bribes. Johann had no immediate answer. He could not bring himself to think of Wolf in connection with the murders in the docks, but he could also not forget the wolf-faced giant he had faced at the top of the world. Could innocent blood really wash away such a monster forever? Before Harald Kleindeinst found the Beast, Johann would have to find Wolf.

There was a notice of the cancellation of the victory parade and a circular of the Emperor's orders for the day. The Imperial Militia were to take up their 'fog positions' to perform 'fog duties.' Johann, still relatively new to the capital city, didn't know what that meant, but Martin explained that it was a traditional measure. Even the palace guard would find employment in the fog. Under the circumstances, Johann thought that putting more armed men on the streets was a compromised blessing. Finally there was an invitation to a private party at the Matthias II, to be hosted by the Bretonnian ambassador, de la Rougierre. Johann was about to crumple that card and throw it away, when he remembered that Margarethe Ruttmann had died next to the Matthias II. What was de la Rougierre's connection with the place? And who else was included in the invitation? Martin did not know. He decided to put off a decision. It might perhaps be a sound idea to attend this party. There were people who said that the Beast was a dwarf.

Today, Johann wanted to seek an audience with the Emperor, to discuss the Beast. He had been doing too much in Karl-Franz's name without having strictly gained the right to use it. Before this went any further, he wanted official approval.

There was a commotion and Luitpold exploded into the room in a flurry of velvet.

'Uncle Johann,' he said, 'come quickly–'

'What is it?'

'Von Liebewitz is fighting a duel in the gymnasium. To the death.'

SIEMEN RUHAAK MADE Rosanna wait until Hasselstein had finished his breakfast. She stood outside the Lector's chambers, fidgeting. If she was wrong, she would look foolish. But she was not wrong.

On her way to Hasselstein's office, she had seen Tilo, emerging guiltily from the confessional. She wondered how much he had told his cleric about her and his feelings. Impure thoughts were as much sin as impure deeds. But that didn't make people any more comfortable around someone who could genuinely judge them by their thoughts.

She still felt the dead girl's wounds.

Rosanna was not even the first to have an audience with the Lector. Hasselstein's door opened and Adrian Hoven, the cleric-captain of the Templars, stepped out. He was wearing his breastplate and helmet, as if prepared to dash off on some military venture for the greater glory of Sigmar. Hoven took no notice of her and barged past. She recognized a packet of sealed orders in his mind, concealed even from her prying thoughts and understood that he had been charged with some secret, urgent task.

'Enter,' decreed Hasselstein.

She stepped into his chambers and found him dressed exactly as he had been last night. He had either slept in his clothes, or not at all. A breakfast tray was abandoned on the floor and he was drinking tea from a monogrammed mug.

'Lector,' she said, without formalities. 'The Beast has killed again. I saw it in a dream.'

Hasselstein choked and spilt tea down his shirt.

As HE DRESSED, she prepared for her sleep. In the fog, the heavy curtains weren't necessary, but she drew them all the same.

Watching Geneviève, Detlef Sierck was conscious of the difference, apparent and real, between their ages. Another sonnet was forming in his mind. When she was asleep, he would set it down. He had been writing sonnets almost since the beginning, since the play in the fortress, but he had not shared them with her, had not sought to publish them. The plays were for everybody, but the poetry was private. When the time was right, he would have the whole cycle printed and bound up for her. He had a title: *To My Unchanging Lady.*

Pulling on his trousers, he was aware that he would need a new wardrobe soon, unless he lost some weight. He was prepared to do anything to become healthy and slim, except take exercise, eat less, go to bed early or give up wine.

Detlef sat with her as she lay on the bed, waiting for the deep sleep to come, to give her a little of the death she had staved off for so long. They talked, not the high-flown talk of new lovers, but the intimate, ordinary talk of an old married couple. However, lately, people who did not know Genevieve was a vampire had begun to mistake her for his daughter.

There were always actresses to tempt him and Genevieve did not tap him overmuch for fear of bleeding him dry. So they both had to pursue outside interests, but they were very special to each other. Without Genevieve, he might never have built his genius into a real career. He could easily have spent his life boasting of the theatre he would one day create without actually doing anything.

'The farce is played out,' he was saying, 'our audiences don't want to laugh any more. It's the Beast. He has brought horror to the city and the people can't shake it off even for the length of a play.'

Genevieve nodded, comfortable in her near-doze, and murmured agreement. She was at her most child-like when she slept.

'I shall close *A Farce of the Fog* at the end of the month and present something else.'

'Horror,' Genevieve said, almost under her breath.

'Yes, that's a good idea. If they can't laugh, perhaps they can still scream. We have done Drachenfels to death, but there is still the story of the Wittgenstein family and its monster. Or of the horrid fate of the von Diehl brothers. Either of those would make a play that would curdle the spine and shiver the blood...'

Genevieve mumbled.

'You know what I mean, Gené.'

Detlef thought some more. 'Of course, those are stories of monsters and daemons. Perhaps the Beast requires something a little closer to home, a little more intimate in its horror.'

Genevieve's eyes were closed, but she could still hear him.

'The Beast suggests the story of a man who is outwardly a mild, devout, conscientious individual, but inwardly a fiend thirsting for blood... no offence, Gené. Some citizens say our murderer is a beastman or a daemon, but my informants in the watch tell me they are definitely looking for a human culprit. There's that old Kislevite play by V. I. Tiodorov, *The Strange Case of Dr Zhiekhill and Mr Chaida.* It is the story of a humble, respectable cleric of Shallya who samples the forbidden potion and becomes a raging, animalistic libertine. It's dross, of course, but I can prepare a loose translation, with some improvements. Some major improvements.'

The vampire was asleep but Detlef was seized by his idea.

'Of course, the transformation scenes will require all my stagecraft. I want a scene to make people forget the Beast, to make them confront their real horrors, the horrors that come from inside. It will be a masterpiece of the macabre. The critics will quake and foul their britches, women will faint all over the house and strong men will be reduced to abject terror. It will be wonderful. Gené, my darling, this will frighten even you...'

IV

GRAF VOLKER VON Tuchtenhagen looked less arrogant this morning.

'Surely, there is some other way we can settle this?'

He had obviously been dragged from his drunken bed by his second and could barely remember the grave offence he had given the family of von Liebewitz.

Leos slashed the air with his rapier. It felt like an extension of his body. Bassanio Bassarde had once jested that it was the only sexual organ the viscount possessed. The noted Marienburg wit was dead now, his windpipe laid open by an elegant manoeuvre.

'We are all gentlemen here,' von Tuchtenhagen blathered as his seconds stripped his jacket. 'No offence was meant.'

Leos said nothing. He had risen early, untired after his late night in the fog, and taken his usual run around the palace grounds. Men who neglected their bodies were fools.

'Whatever it was that I said, I retract.'

Leos stood, arms loose, ready. That calm that always came upon him before combat was like a cloak. He never felt more alive.

'Ambassador,' he said to Dien Ch'ing, the Celestial who had consented to serve as referee, 'convey to my honoured opponent my apologies…'

Von Tuchtenhagen sighed with relief, stepping forwards.

'…this is no longer a personal matter. It gives me great regret to kill him…'

Von Tuchtenhagen froze, his flabby face a mask of fear. Tears were trickling from the corners of his eyes. He was unprepared. The sleep was still in his eyes, the stubble on his face. Leos rubbed his own smooth, beardless chin with the back of his hand.

'…but this is a matter of the honour of a lady.'

Last night, at the von Tasseninck ball, Leos had overheard von Tuchtenhagen discussing the Countess Emmanuelle with a cleric of Ranald. The graf had suggested that Leos's sister resembled a rabbit, not in appearance but in conduct.

'And of my family.'

The Celestial nodded gravely. He did not need to relay the message.

'Leos, I have money,' said his opponent. 'This need not happen…'

A cold fury burned in the viscount's breast. The suggestion was unworthy even of von Tuchtenhagen. The family were new to the register, elevated by Matthias IV a short century ago and still striving to obscure the memory of the merchants and tradespeople they had been. Von Liebewitzes had fought alongside Sigmar at the birth of the Empire.

Leos brought up his foil, bent at the knees and hung his left hand in the air.

'You have accepted the terms of this combat,' Dien Ch'ing said in his high, musical voice. 'This is a matter between gentleman and no other may intervene.'

Von Tuchtenhagen brought up his shaking sword and Dien Ch'ing held its point against Leos's weapon.

'The duellists shall fight until the matter is settled.'

'First blood?' Von Tuchtenhagen suggested, a flare of hope in his tone. Leos shook his head, impatient to get on with it.

'The victor shall be the gentleman left alive at the end of the duel.'

Dien Ch'ing took a handkerchief from his sleeve. It was silk, embroidered with dragons.

When the silk touched the polished wooden floor, the duel would commence.

The Celestial's hand went up.

Countess Emmanuelle von Liebewitz, elector, lady mayoress and Chancellor of the University of Nuln, examined her face minutely in the ornate mirror and plucked a stray hair from her arched eyebrows.

'There,' she said, 'perfect.'

Yevgeny Yefimovich was getting tired of wearing his hood. He had sent Respighi out late last night to get him a new face, but his servant had not yet returned.

In his upstairs rooms at the Holy Hammer of Sigmar, he addressed his most fervent followers in the Revolutionary Movement. Prince Kloszowski, the radical poet, lolled as usual, a cigarette dangling from his lips, his beard a studied mess. Stieglitz, a former mercenary who had served with Vastarien's Vanquishers, was fingering the stump where his left arm had been and groaning softly, as was his habit. The man's face was a mass of scars, the result of a few too many brushes with the aristocratic oppressor. Professor Brustellin, recently forced to resign in disgrace from the University, was polishing his round eyeglasses and drinking steadily from his ever-present, never-emptied silver bottle. And Ulrike Blumenschein, the angel of the masses, was combing out her long, tangled hair before a mirror. Between them, these people would bring down an Emperor. They believed this would usher in an age of justice for the common people, but Yefimovich knew it would lead only to a power vacuum which would allow for the triumph of Tzeentch.

'We must seize the opportunity,' he told them, 'and exploit it for all we can–'

'But what proof is there,' put in Brustellin, 'that the Beast is of the hated classes?'

Yefimovich explained patiently, 'None, of course. It was destroyed by the lackeys of the Emperor.'

'Proof that has been destroyed is the best kind,' said Kloszowski, with a sardonic smile, 'one never has to produce it.'

'Remember, Dickon of the Dock Watch was seen to burn something at the site of the last killing,' Yefimovich said. 'That was our proof.'

'The Ashes of Shame,' declared Kloszowski. 'That shall be the title of my next work. I'll have it written, copied and distributed by nightfall. It'll be sung in every tavern, to a dozen different tunes, by this time tomorrow.'

Brustellin, disenchanted with words, sneered, 'More poems, just what the revolution needs!'

The poet was angered. 'Clothhead academic! My poems do more for the cause than your dusty tracts. Poetry is for the people, not for ink-blotched scholars and dried-up prunes of clerics.'

'I was flogged, you know,' said Brustellin, loosening his cravat, preparing to bare his back to exhibit yet again the marks left by the punishment that had preceded his expulsion. 'Twenty years of teaching and that young dolt Scheydt had me flogged and thrown into the streets.'

He was down to his shirt and everyone was telling him not to go further. They had all seen a sight too much of Brustellin's ravaged back.

'You were flogged and Stieglitz here was mutilated and crippled,' spat Kloszowski. 'But only I have been hanged by the hated classes...'

Dramatically, with a practiced movement, the poet pulled his scarf away to reveal the burn. The rope had been rotten and snapped itself instead of Kloszowski's neck. He had written several poems about the experience. 'I was face to face with the gods,' he claimed, 'and they were working men like ourselves. Not a plutocrat or popinjay in the lot of them.'

Brustellin muttered something about the arrogance of princes. Kloszowski stamped his feet like a child in a temper tantrum. He hated to be reminded of his noble origins, although he was reluctant to drop the title from his name.

'You cannot argue that I have not suffered with my working brothers, professor. My soul has been dragged through the dirt with the best of them.'

Yefimovich spread his hands and the revolutionaries stopped arguing.

'The Beast is the best thing to happen to this city since the thumb tax, my friends,' he said. 'For once, the people are angry with their masters. That anger is our strength.'

'It's a shame that the Beast has killed only worthless drabs,' said Ulrike. 'The people would be more inflamed if he were to prey on decent, humble womenfolk. A good mother, or a precious daughter. Maybe a priestess of Verena.'

'That can be arranged, my dear,' Yefimovich said. 'People are putting every crime in the city off on the Beast. If a few deaths would prove politically useful, we have people who can take care of them.'

Ulrike nodded, pleased that her idea had been taken up.

These people all had their reasons. Stieglitz had seen too much injustice, Brustellin had thought it through and reasoned that the rule of the Emperor was wrong, and Kloszowski thought the revolution sounded romantic, but Ulrike Blumenschein roused the rabble because she was mad. That made her the only one in the group who could pose a threat to Yefimovich. The mad often have insights that a sane person would not. If he were swept away, she would become the figurehead of the movement and, her hair trailing and eyes shining, would lead them all to be happily slaughtered by the Imperial Guard outside the gates of the palace.

'Be ready to move at a moment's notice,' he said. 'The day is coming soon.'

Kloszowski clapped, tobacco ash falling onto his loose shirt. He pulled on his workingman's coat and hat – Yefimovich was sure he had spent an afternoon rubbing his clothes between two stones to get that authentically proletarian tattered look – and left the room. Yefimovich nodded and the bent professor and the one-armed mercenary went after him. They all had their orders for the day. By nightfall, the city would be rumbling with dissent. The fog helped. It made everyone angry. Yefimovich fancied that he could deliver a speech blaming the Emperor for the fog and everyone would believe him.

Ulrike was the last to go. She had taken to lingering around him lately. Being an Angel of the Revolution was a lonely job. Eventually she followed the others, on her way to the underground chambers where her trained scribes copied out the movement's pamphlets and poems, and she posed for inspirational pictures to be distributed on cards and posters.

Yefimovich only had to wait a few minutes before a rat-like scratching at the window told him that Respighi was back.

He unlatched the window and his assistant crawled in. Respighi was an extraordinary mix of races. His father, it was said, had been a dwarf trollslayer and his mother a human woman under the influence of warpstone. He could usually pass for a dwarf if he wore loose pantaloons to cover his tail, although his face was pushing out recently, becoming more rodentlike. With his boots off he could climb walls and with his tail out he could hang from the ceiling. The creature loved Tzeentch as much as he hated his long-lost father.

For the moment, he was the high priest's servant and it was his job to find Yefimovich the skins which concealed his true nature from the world.

Respighi laid a pouch on the table.

'How fresh is it?'

The altered shrugged and whistled. 'Some time late last night. I've been on the dodge. Lots of watchmen out.'

Yefimovich knew Respighi had just got lost in the fog. It didn't matter. It would be fresh enough.

Yefimovich doffed his hood and enjoyed the slight flinch Respighi gave as he saw the high priest's face of fire. Then he pulled the new face out of the pouch and pressed it over his own.

His flesh tingled as the magic worked, binding the stolen skin to his own. When it was fixed, he wiped the traces of blood away from around his still-burning eyes and licked his new lips. He tasted rouge.

'What did you get me, Respighi? A man's face or a woman's?'

The altered shrugged. 'Who knows? It was foggy.'

Yefimovich felt his face. The mask was shifting, settling on to his old features. His skin was smooth, unstubbled.

'I can tell you one thing,' Respighi muttered. 'It's human.'

DICKON HAD KNOWN Schygulla for years. The dock manager had been a war chief in the Hooks long before Willy Pick's day, when the watchman had been walking the waterfront with his eyes closed and his hand out. They had stroked and threatened each other many times, and the Beloved of Manann still sent him cases of wine and sweetmeats every festival day. The company brought in more goods and paid less excise than any other crew on the docks.

When the body was discovered, Schygulla had sent a runner not to Dickon's family house but to the rooms of his mistress. The Hooks knew him too well, he reflected as Francoise 'Fifi' Messaen berated him for having her early morning despoiled by the interloper. The great Detlef Sierck had kicked Fifi out of his repertory company for being 'a talentless slut,' but the actor-manager had been wrong: Fifi was a girl of many talents, most of them horizontal. After a night with her, Dickon needed to go home to his wife and get some rest and a cup of tea. But today that wasn't going to happen.

The runner had guided him through the fog to the wharf, where the Beast's leavings had been dragged up and gathered together on a sheet of soaked canvas. This one was worse than the others.

'Merciful Shallya,' Dickon swore.

A young man was sobbing at one corner of the dock. Schygulla looked at him with contempt and spat. 'That's Buttgereit,' he said. 'He found the thing.'

Dickon understood why Schygulla called the corpse a thing. It was hard to imagine that it had ever been alive, much less a woman.

'Do you know her?' he asked the dock manager.

Schygulla looked disgusted. 'Are you kidding me, captain?

Her own true love wouldn't recognize her after a night with our Beast.'

It was true.

The fog was getting into his bones. It would be time soon for Dickon to go into the back room at the Luitpoldstrasse Station and take his savings out from the hollowed statue of Verena. He had been supplementing his salary very well and should have enough to take Fifi and the children and retire to the country, somewhere far away from Hooks and Fish and smugglers and slashers.

'Let's get some coppers down here and clear this up, captain,' Schygulla said. 'I'm losing business.'

Dickon agreed.

V

THE GYMNASIUM DOORS opened and a huge man strode in, his heavy bootsteps like bass drumbeats.

Dien Ch'ing paused, his arm still upraised. His kerchief fluttered but remained in his grip, hanging.

This was all absurd, but amusing. Only trousered barbarians could bind themselves with so many rules in such a simple matter as murder.

Graf Volker pulled his sword away and barked with panicky laughter. Viscount Leos stayed cool, his weapon still at the ready.

'Hold,' said von Tuchtenhagen. 'I invoke the rules of chivalry.'

Leos straightened up and let his sword rest by his side. He was a chilly character and strange for a Westerner. Ch'ing wondered if the beardless young aristocrat had any Cathay in his blood. There was certainly something subtle in his eyes.

'I am unable to fight and so I request that my champion, Toten Ungenhauer, stand in for me.'

Leos did not seem concerned. Von Tuchtenhagen's champion was a full foot and a half taller than the youth and had a chest as big as a barrel. He wore a tunic emblazoned with the von Tuchtenhagen arms. It left his massive arms bare.

At the Second Siege of Praag, Ch'ing had seen Gotrek Gurnisson, the dwarf Trollslayer, in action, wielding a two-edged axe against a horde of beastmen. Toten Ungenhauer was proportioned like Gotrek, but nearly twice his size. Leos von Liebewitz was rumoured to be the greatest duellist in the Empire, but surely he could not stand against such a monster.

Ungenhauer stepped into his master's place and took a sword. It looked like a knitting needle in his ham-sized fist. Ch'ing assumed he would throw it away and simply wrench the viscount's head off, ignoring any feeble cuts he might sustain in getting past Leos's foil. That would not be against the rules of chivalry.

Although it was not strictly according to the code, spectators were filing in to the chamber and taking seats. A knot of von Tuchtenhagen creditors who had hoped to see the Graf Volker shredded were leaving in disappointment, but other courtiers were settling in. Ch'ing saw Johann von Mecklenberg and the future Emperor sitting high up, near the back of the hall. Hergard von Tasseninck, who had been present when the original insult was delivered, was there with his mistress. And, veiled, Marquess Sidonie of Marienburg, whose husband Bassanio had been efficiently despatched by Viscount Leos late last year in a similar duel. The most notable absence was that of the Countess Emmanuelle, who supposedly didn't care for the sight of blood.

Von Tuchtenhagen had overcome his fear and was excitedly walking back and forth, chortling to himself and to the audience, working himself up.

'Von Liebewitz,' he said, 'I should like to elaborate upon my comments of the last night. Your sister, I understand, spreads her legs for servants and sailors…'

The audience gasped. Leos seemed unmoved.

'If it were dark enough, she would take a dwarf or a halfling into her bed. Or an altered… if he were freakish in the right direction…'

Leos brought up his sword slowly and placed its point

against Ungenhauer's outstretched blade. The giant grinned, displaying gaps in his teeth.

'I believe it would take a beast to pleasure her to her full satisfaction,' von Tuchtenhagen spat, 'an absolute beast!'

Ch'ing raised the kerchief and let it flutter to the floor.

The swords clashed and parted with a resounding *chink!*

KARL-FRANZ I OF the House of the Second Wilhelm, Protector of the Empire, Defier of the Dark, Emperor Himself and the Son of Emperors, poured sugar into his coffee. He was mildly surprised that his son had not turned up yet for their hour together. It was part of the palace ritual. Karl-Franz would quiz Luitpold on his lessons and try to impart some of the wisdom he had acquired in his years of office. Still, it was not the first time the future Emperor had found some distraction elsewhere. He yawned. These days, nothing ever seemed to happen...

THERE WAS A '317' worked into the headstone above the door. On the docks, there was a joke that the sign signified the average number of bribes the Dock Watch accepted in any given week. The watchmen at the Luitpoldstrasse Station admitted him without question. The older ones recognized him and the youngsters had heard of him.

Elsaesser said good morning and he nodded to the young officer.

He found Economou, a sergeant he remembered, and enjoyed the burst of rage and fear in the man's face.

'What...?!'

Harald curled his lip and held up his fist.

A couple of bullies came up behind Economou.

'Joost,' Harald said, 'Thommy. Have you missed me?'

A slow grin spread over the sergeant's face. 'You're trespassing, Kleindeinst. You two, strip your tabards and eject this intruder from the station.'

The bullies enthusiastically pulled off their apron-like garments, embroidered with the emblems of the city and of the Dock Watch and rolled up their sleeves.

'I've looked forward to this for a long time, Kleindeinst,'

said Joost. 'It took me years to work off the black mark you put on my record.'

'Yes,' agreed Thommy, unconsciously massaging his once-broken collar bone. 'It's a delight to see you again, especially now you're a civilian...'

Harald held up his fist and uncurled his fingers, letting the officers see his badge.

Economou's jaw hit his chainmail choker.

'You came back?'

Harald let a slow smile spread. 'Yes, sergeant. I came back.'

Joost and Thommy hustled back into their tabards and backed off.

'Find me a desk, sergeant. And get me what you've got so far on the Beast.'

Economou hurried away. Joost and Thommy crammed into the door, trying to follow him.

Harald miaowed at the retreating watchmen.

'I beg your pardon,' said Elsaesser.

'Pussies,' Harald explained. 'Just a pair of pussies.'

The young officer nodded. 'Oh.'

The double doors pushed inwards and a pocket of fog belched into the station. A man stepped out of it, gasping. It was a messenger and he had run a long way carrying a fog lantern.

He put the dripping lamp down and got his breath back.

'There's been another one,' he gasped, 'down at the docks. Another killing.'

'The Beast,' said Elsaesser.

The messenger said, 'Yes.'

'Come on, boy,' Harald told the younger man, 'let's go goose Dickon and get this investigation underway.'

ETIENNE EDOUARD VILLECHAIZE, Comte de la Rougierre, the ambassador from Charles de la Tete d'Or III of Bretonnia, inflated his chest like a peacock as he prepared to explain, for the millionth time, that yes, he was a dwarf and yes, did also hold high office in one of the kingdoms of men.

'My parents were hostages for life, Gropius,' he told the dancing master. 'I was raised in the household of one of the

king's ministers. My brothers were content to become jug-
glers and jesters. I have always felt a higher calling...'

He twirled his waxed moustaches and waved his puffed
sleeve at the man, allowing a shower of lace to flutter around
his arm. The auditorium of the Flamingo Club, a private theatre located on the wrong side of Temple Street, was small,
but still encouraged de la Rougierre's flair for the dramatic
gesture.

'I have repudiated my dwarfish name and taken that of my
noble benefactor. My body may be that of a dwarf, but my
soul is Bretonnian to the core. I am the best of both races,
strength and style.'

'Pardon my ignorance,' beseeched Gropius, 'but I was not
aware that there was any great population of dwarfs in
Bretonnia–'

'If there were, do you think they would have allowed my
parents to be hostages for life. You are a very stupid man and
I decline to explain further. I am not a freak to be gaped at
and petted. I am a powerful individual in my own right and
my abilities are of the highest. I must uphold the honour of
King Charles wherever I go.'

The dancing master was properly cowed. He applied a
taper to the lights that fronted the stage.

'Your prowess is indeed legendary,' he admitted, his aston-
ishment overcome and his natural inclination to fawning
and toadying returning. 'We have heard of your many...
um... conquests.'

De la Rougierre strutted, hand on hip, dismissing the subject with a wave. He took his seat.

'And those stories about the Countess Emmanuelle,' he
licked his lips, 'are they–'

'Please, I insist! There is a reputation at stake here...'

...namely, his own, should it come out that the countess
had persistently refused his advances.

'...there are matters a de la Rougierre does not discuss
with a tradesman.'

The dancing master bowed and let the subject drop.

'Now,' the ambassador said, 'bring on your finest.'

'Uh, certainly, your excellency.'

Gropius snapped his fingers and said, 'Miele.' A pert, petite girl stepped out from behind the curtains and stood on the tiny stage. She simpered and danced a few steps.

'Enough,' said de la Rougierre. 'Show me another.'

Her face fallen, Miele slouched off, trailing her fur boa.

'This is Tessa Ahlquist,' Gropius explained.

A slender dancer with long, ladylike legs – adequately displayed by an immodest costume – replaced the first girl. The ambassador was more interested, but quickly tired and had her dismissed. Tessa Ahlquist stormed off in a flurry of feathers.

Angry, de la Rougierre turned on the dancing master. 'I thought I made my instructions quite clear. This is a very special function and I have very special requirements.'

Gropius paid attention, nodding like an imbecile.

'I want a big woman, you understand. Big!'

Gropius chewed his moustache. 'Ah, of course, your excellency. I understand perfectly. You want a dancer of stature.'

'Why yes, that's it exactly. Stature! The girl should be heroically proportioned, you understand. Heroically.'

A ratty smile spread across the dancing master's face.

'Milizia,' he shouted, 'would you come out and dance for the gentleman!'

The next girl appeared…

…and de la Rougierre fancied that he was again in love.

VI

IT WAS THE most incredible thing Luitpold had ever witnessed. And it was over in seconds.

He was just about to intervene, invoking the ancient rights of the Imperial family to save his fencing teacher, when Johann laid a hand on his arm and shook his head. The elector was right. Leos von Liebewitz would never forgive him if he were robbed of his honour that way. The viscount would rather die.

Luitpold had imagined that the duellists would step back, take the measure of each other and then join in combat. That was what he had been taught to expect.

Instead, they stepped forwards. Ungenhauer, the von Tuchtenhagen servitor who was rumoured at court to be affected by the warpstone, lunged for Leos, his arms out...

Leos seemed to move casually, as he half-bent out of the champion's way. He just touched Ungenhauer's neck with his foil, then danced out of his reach, coming around behind the man.

A gigantic gusher of blood came from Ungenhauer's throat, spraying the floor in a circle as he turned. Dien

Ch'ing raised the skirts of his robe and scuttled away from the mess, but Graf Volker had his boots ruined and one of the seconds got a faceful, forcing him to retire, choking, against the wall.

A roar began in Ungenhauer's chest but it came out of the new mouth in his neck, not the old one in his face.

He raised his hands, as if in triumph, and collapsed to his knees. The whole gymnasium shook.

Leos picked up Dien Ch'ing's silk and wiped off the point of his sword.

Ungenhauer toppled forwards and tiles broke under his face.

There was a moment of incredulous silence and then the applause started.

Leos was indifferent. He was busy wrapping his weapon and handing it to his second. Graf Volker was on his knees praying to Sigmar.

The Celestial raised his hand for quiet and was rewarded.

'By the rules of chivalry, honour is restored. The life of Graf Volker von Tuchtenhagen is the property of Viscount Leos von Liebewitz, to be disposed of as he sees fit...'

Von Tuchtenhagen was crawling towards the viscount, incoherently begging for forgiveness. Doglike, he licked Leos's boots.

'Call for a cleric,' Leos told Dien Ch'ing, 'and a barber. I will not kill a man who is unshriven, much less unshaven.'

'IT IS CONFIRMED, Lector,' said Ruhaak. 'A messenger has brought the news from the docks.'

Mikael Hasselstein was preoccupied. His junior repeated what he had just said. It sank in. He rolled the facts around his mind and worried at them.

'I did not doubt it, Siemen. Miss Ophuls has an extraordinary gift.'

He could not keep his thoughts on the murders. Last night had been a bad one. At the von Tassenynck ball, Yelle had been threatening to break it off, had been insistent. It had taken all his persuasion and all his skills to bring her round. That, and a quick coupling in an antechamber, made all the more exciting by the possibility of imminent discovery. But his attachment was becoming a nuisance. It was affecting his work.

Ophuls sat in the corner, knowing everything and keeping it inside. Hasselstein resented the girl. How simple his life would be if he were able to read thoughts.

Yelle had changed him, he realized. Loving her was draining him, leeching time from his days that he could not afford to spare.

Ruhaak waited for orders. He was a fine instrument, but had no initiative. The Grand Theogonist had not been the same since his bastard Matthias was killed and the whole burden of the Cult of Sigmar had descended upon the shoulders of Mikael Hasselstein. Until now, they had been broad enough to stand it, but the strain was pressing him close to the ground.

Being the Emperor's confessor was a unique privilege, but the sins Karl-Franz worried and fretted over were so paltry, so insignificant. Hasselstein envied the Emperor his uncomplicated nature. He was a truly good man and truly unselfconscious about it. Not so the cleric who gave him absolution. If the Emperor could unload his sins on Mikael, who was there for Mikael?

Yelle was such a harlot, too. There had been other men even when things were good between them. Too many other men. He had even seen her making up to that grey-faced toad, Tybalt.

Hasselstein tried to look as if he were pondering the problem of the Beast, not wrestling with his own heartaches. Ruhaak was respectfully silent, but Ophuls was near to fidgeting. How much did the witch know?

Perhaps he should take the girl as his confessor. She could see his sins anyway, he was sure. They might as well formalise the relationship. No, she was a woman. She reminded him of Yelle. All women were harlots. Even the novices of the Sisterhood of Sigmar were always clustering around the Knights Templar, showing their ankles and bending over on any flimsy pretext. Vixens, harlots and temptresses, the lot of them. Sometimes, Hasselstein thought women were all creatures of Chaos, their bodies shaped by the warpstone to taunt men, their hearts those of daemons, their instincts essentially cruel.

If only Ophuls were a man, like Ruhaak or Adrian Hoven or Dien Ch'ing. Then they could use her gift together. But these witches were always women. In past centuries, the cult had branded them as creatures of Chaos and sought to burn them. That had been a waste. Even if uncontrollable, Rosanna Ophuls was of great use to the cult.

'Miss Ophuls,' he said, 'do you have any more bright thoughts?'

She was surprised to be consulted before Ruhaak and took a moment to put the words together.

'Nothing immediately, lector…'

But there was something. 'Yes?'

'Yesterday, at the site of the last killing, I met with Johann von Mecklenberg.'

'The Elector of Sudenland?'

'Yes. He was taking an interest in the Beast. I don't know why. He is a rare type. He was unconsciously screening his thoughts.'

Hasselstein thought about von Mecklenberg. He was a handsome young man, with just the right amount of roughness to take the boyishness out of his face. He was Yelle's type. Had they been lovers? He didn't know if they even really knew each other, but there was something furtive about the elector, something not quite right.

'Screening his thoughts? That suggests he has something to hide.'

'Not necessarily. I do not think he was deliberately trying to keep me out. Nor was I setting out to read him. I just noticed his mental shields and was curious.'

'You've done well, Miss Ophuls. This is interesting news.'

Rosanna Ophuls was a dangerous dog, Hasselstein thought. She could turn and snap at her master as easily as she could tear out the throat of an enemy. But she was a strong dog all the same.

'I shall send you to help the Dock Watch again,' he said. 'If von Mecklenberg shows up again, get close to him, find out what you can. This business keeps leading back to the palace.'

And Yelle, he added silently. But silence was still too loud. Ophuls wrinkled her brow, as if trying to catch a misheard name.

Hasselstein tried to shut up his mind tight.

Deliberately, he addressed Ruhaak. 'Simeon, get Adrian Hoven back. I want an escort ready to accompany Miss Ophuls and I want more men ready to put on the streets. The watch have had their chance and it is time that the Cult of Sigmar intervened. The Beast will be brought in under our banner.'

MILIZIA DANCED FOR the funny little creature, the dwarf who acted like a Bretonnian, until her breasts and belly were tired of jiggling.

De la Rougierre was clearly delighted with her perfor-mance and she knew how to take advantage of that. She leaned close and let him stare at her, his stubby fingers curl-ing his moustaches. She knew what she looked like from beyond the footlights. Melons in a sack. But some men made such a fuss.

Gropius was standing back, marking time with his long forefinger. There was no music, but she knew the pieces she danced to so well that she could do without it. She was accompanied only by the slapping of her bare feet on the stage, the discontented mumbles of the other girls and the strange little noises de la Rougierre kept making.

The ambassador was enchanted and his eyes followed her every movement. There was spittle in his beard.

Finally he could bear it no more and asked her to stop.

'My dear,' he said, 'you are truly a magnificent creature. Seldom have my eyes beheld such… such *ample* beauties…'

Backstage, Tessa, Miele and the others were complaining. Big, ridiculous Milizia, with her big ridiculous tits, was showing them up again. Usually, when she stepped on a stage, the customers thought that not all of her was real. However, after a few of the scarfs had come off, they changed their opinion and were astounded.

'...you will be richly rewarded,' the dwarf babbled, 'in gold crowns. I shall have a carriage call for you.'

She bowed gracefully and thanked him. Gropius pursed his lips, but nodded his approval. He would take a cut, of course. If this worked out, Milizia might look for new management, or even handle her career herself. Perhaps de la Rougierre might offer her a permanent position, as a dancer or as something else.

The ambassador walked out of the theatre, striding as if his legs were as long as Tessa's. Turning as he got to the door, he doffed his hat to her, scraping the floor with its feathers. Winking and kissing his fingers, he left.

Gropius looked up at her and told her to put her clothes on.

VII

SAM WARBLE WAS impressed.

He had taken the uncomfortable barge journey to Altdorf – a thing he was loth to do – only on the condition that he be paid in advance. He had asked for a higher fee even than usual, firstly because his employer could well afford it, and secondly because the commission had sounded deeply boring.

He had not expected to see Toten Ungenhauer killed. And to get a front row seat. Even if it meant dressing up as a footman and wearing a false beard, the entertainment was worth the price of admission.

He remembered when Ungenhauer was the chief enforcer for the Marienburg Fish. Warble visited his friends' graves whenever he could and that kept putting him in mind of the big thug-for-hire. The Marienburg Fish had tactfully expelled Ungenhauer when it became too much trouble to saw off his horns every month and keep pretending he was a real human being.

He looked around the gymnasium for his employer. Sure enough, the marquess was there, recognizable by the big nose that stuck out under her veil. He nodded subtly to her and she did everything but get up, bare her buttocks and blow him a kiss. Rich widows were all fools.

Von Tuchtenhagen was in one corner with a cleric of Verena, either delivering a lengthy and detailed confession or begging to be spirited out under the divine's robes. He had ignored the viscount's suggestion that he take advantage of some skilled barbering and meet the deity of his choice in a presentable manner. Warble sympathised with the man. When you were dead, nobody gave a plugged pfennig for hair-oil and perfume. You could ask Ungenhauer, even if you weren't going to get much of an answer.

It was well within the viscount's rights to kill the graf. Nobody was going to argue with that. There was also no question in Warble's mind that von Tuchtenhagen deserved to die. He had read Yefimovich's *Beasts in Green Velvet* and knew that enough of it was true to make him believe the anecdote told about Graf Volker, the three shepherdesses, the missing cufflink and the pit of quicklime.

Leos wasn't even being especially impatient. He had put away his gentleman's sword and selected a common garotte for the task.

Most of the audience had gone. This wasn't the show, this was a distasteful but inevitable aftermath.

Finally, even the cleric had had enough and left the grovelling von Tuchtenhagen to Leos.

The Celestial, whom Warble didn't like the look of, held the graf by the shoulders while Leos looped the garotte around his neck, making sure there was silk between the wire and the flesh. That was the privilege of a gentleman. Not to be touched by the thing that killed him.

Von Tuchtenhagen gave everyone a chance to see what he had eaten for breakfast.

Then, with a swift move, Leos yanked the noose tight and let the graf fall next to his champion.

Smiling, he stood back. The Celestial checked von Tuchtenhagen's pulse and breath. The green velvet scum was dead.

Everyone packed up and got ready to leave.

'You,' a full-size human servant said to him, 'shorty.'

Warble reached for his dagger but realized it was in his other pair of boots. He was dressed as a servant and servants in the palace weren't armed unless they wanted to be tortured as suspected assassins.

'Help me clear this mess up.'

Warble shrugged. Harald Kleindeinst wasn't the only one who got stuck with all the filthy jobs.

UNSEEN AND YET *aware, the Beast smelled blood and knew that it would prowl again tonight…*

'THIS IS ROSANNA Ophuls,' said Elsaesser. 'She's from the Temple.'

Harald acknowledged the girl's presence and hoped she wouldn't get in the way.

'Don't worry, I won't,' she said.

'Rosanna is a scryer.'

'So I see.'

The body had been dragged out of the water by a couple of Schygulla's dockhands, and laid out on a table in the warehouse of the Beloved of Manann. Dickon, still sulking about the return of Harald Kleindeinst, was busy shepherding official investigators through his ring of guards while keeping out trouble-makers. It was the most useful thing Harald could think of for him to do. It wasn't really demeaning enough, he reflected. Now he had some Imperial authority over his old captain, he wanted to settle a few old scores.

Revenge was an ignoble and fruitless pursuit, but he was just a weak-willed human being and couldn't be held responsible for his base impulses.

If he wanted suspects, this place was full of them. Schygulla, the manager, used to run with the Hooks. Most of his employees were familiar faces from Harald's pilferer-rousting days. But, come to that, few of them had as many unsolved crimes to their credit as the watchmen on this case. Walking through the crowd of bystanders, Harald had felt his stomach going again.

He looked at the eyeless, faceless corpse and knew he was-
n't after an ordinary criminal. The Hooks and the Fish often
mutilated their kills if they wanted to make a point to the
dead men's comrades, but even the gangs' berserkers didn't
do this sort of thing to women.

'Scryer,' he said, 'what can you tell me?'

The girl didn't want to touch the dead thing, but she laid
her hand on the flayed flesh of the victim's forehead.

'Wolf,' she said.

'A wolf did this?'

She shook her head. Her eyes closed and her whole body
shook. She turned her head on the axis of her neck, as if
straining for a sound or a scent.

'Wolf,' she said again. 'That's the word that was on her
mind.'

'Wolves don't usually hunt in the city,' he said, 'and they
usually eat at least part of their kill. An animal wouldn't
have rolled her off the jetty, but left her in case he wanted to
come back for another meal.'

'Not a wolf. *Wolf*. I think it's a name.'

She took her hand away and wiped it off on her dress. She
was not nervy about this business. She didn't want to stick
her fingers into human meat, but if it had to be done she
wasn't going to complain. Rosanna Ophuls was all right.

'There's a famous Wolf,' said Elsaesser. 'Wolfgang
Neuwald.'

'Neuwald? That's a familiar name. Ah, you mean
Wolfgang von Neuwald.'

'That's right, captain. He's in Ferring the Balladeer's songs
about the hero, Konrad. They say he wears a wolf's face tattooed over his own.'

'Hero? That's an interesting word, Elsaesser. I've met people who think Constant Drachenfels was a hero.'

'Neuwald… ah, *von* Neuwald's supposed to have killed
before. And he was from Altdorf originally.'

Harald shook his head. 'I know about Wolf von Neuwald,
watchman. I didn't like him, but slaughtering bawds wasn't
his style.'

'It's not an uncommon name,' said Elsaesser.

'T'll have every Wolf, Wolfgang, Wolfie, Wulfrum, Wolfgard and Wulfric pulled in and put to the torture,' snapped Dickon.

Harald, Rosanna and Elsaesser looked at the captain of the Dock Watch as if he were an idiot.

'You're an idiot, Dickon,' said Harald.

The captain looked as if he had an answer ready, but made himself forget all about it.

'Just because this woman died thinking of Wolf doesn't mean he was her killer. Most men I've seen die call for their mother, or their girl–'

'Brilliant, Kleindeinst,' sneered Dickon. 'So Wolf is the whore's mother?'

Rosanna was annoyed. 'She wasn't a whore, captain. She worked in the Wayfarer's Rest. She was a maid.'

Dickon huffed and walked away, taking out his pipe.

Harald looked at the corpse, examining every detail of every wound. He wanted to build up a picture of the kind of animal he was after. He wanted to know what made the Beast get hot, what gave the killer his pleasure. His stomach was filling with acid, but he could imagine the thing he was up against.

'I think you're right,' Rosanna said. 'Wolf was the girl's lover. I can make out a face. I think I'd recognize him.'

Harald broke out of his concentration on the corpse. He pulled the blanket over, tucking it gently around the dead girl.

'Can you draw?'

Rosanna started to ask him what he was talking about, then caught up with him.

'Yes. I could draw him.'

Harald took Schygulla by the ear and told him to get some paper and a pencil. The manager rummaged through a desk piled with ledgers and found some loose leaves.

Rosanna sat down and began to sketch.

'The runner should bring back the landlord of the Wayfarer's Rest soon,' said Elsaesser. 'Then we'll be able to get her name.'

'Really? If this were your girl, could you recognize her?'

Jack Yeovil

The boy was shocked. Just now, Elsaesser was in the dangerous stage. He got too involved with the job, but it was all still much like a game. If he survived the waterfront watch, he would learn. He might make a good copper.

Rosanna handed him the sketch. He looked at it.

'You've drawn Johann von Mecklenberg without a beard, scryer.'

She bit her lip. 'Yes, I know. I tried not to. The face I'm seeing isn't quite the baron, but it's very close.'

'This could be Baron von Mecklenberg as he was ten years ago, as a student,' said Elsaesser.

'Ten years ago, this girl would have been about seven,' said Rosanna.

Harald looked at her, not needing to ask a question. 'I can scry her age,' she said, 'but not her name. It's like fishing in the dark, you don't always get what would be most convenient.'

'Hmmmn.' Harald examined the girl's sketch. She was a good draughtswoman. He wondered about the Baron Johann. He still hadn't worked out what von Mecklenberg's interest in all this was. He instinctively trusted the man – which wasn't exactly his usual attitude to electors and aristocrats – and intended to stick by his first feeling. But there were questions he would have to find answers for.

'You've met the elector?' he asked Rosanna.

'Yesterday. When they found the last girl.'

'What did you make of him?'

She was surprised to be asked the question, but did not try to get out of answering. 'He's concerned. I don't think he's the Beast.'

'Neither do I,' chipped in Elsaesser. 'If he were, he would be stupid to set you to catch him.'

Harald thought about that. 'Unless he wanted to be caught…'

The warehouse door was opened and Dickon let a watchman in. He was dragging a bald, middle-aged man who had put a cloak and boots on over his nightshirt.

'This is Runze, of the Wayfarer's Rest.'

The landlord looked at the thing on the table. Harald

lifted the blanket.

'Sigmar's mighty hammer,' Runze swore, 'it's Trudi!'

The man turned, clutching his belly and was sick over Dickon.

'Pathetic,' Harald said to himself. 'Another weak stomach.'

'TRUDI?'

There was no answer.

Wolf turned over in the bed and found no one there. He was not at the University, or in the room at the Wayfarer's Rest.

'Trudi?'

He tried to remember the night before, but could not.

Water was dripping somewhere and the floor was shifting. He wondered if he were on a boat.

There were questions he would have to answer. Where was Trudi? Where was he? What had he done last night?

And why was he covered in blood?

PART FOUR
RIOT

I

WHEN IT WAS all over, there would be an Imperial inquiry, presided over airily by the Grand Theogonist Yorri. Whether the titular head of the Cult of Sigmar could possibly be impartial in the matter of the Great Fog Riots was a question that many asked but few answered to anyone's satisfaction.

However, when all the allegations and rumours were discounted and the more fabulous lies disproved, these facts were definitely ascertained.

Firstly, this particular fog was the thickest, heaviest, foulest, longest-lasting and most debilitating to descend upon the city within living memory. Since the term 'living memory' included that of Genevieve Dieudonné, 667, it was a simple matter to amend the statement to the effect that this was the worst the fog had ever been.

For the rest of their lives, weather bores who had happened to be in the city during the Great Fog would annoy their friends and relatives and any total strangers who could be trapped into paying attention with fantastic, but dull, tales of the fog's duration, quality, quantity and climatic peculiarity.

Secondly, at some time in the early afternoon, members of the revolutionary movement began to distribute a fresh pamphlet authored by Yevgeny Yefimovich, featuring the first publication of Prince Kloszowski's poem 'The Ashes of Shame,' in which it was alleged that the Beast was finding shelter within the palace of the Emperor. Among other things, this handbill claimed that Dickon of the Dock Watch, never an especially popular public figure, had found a green velvet cloak in the alley next to the murdered body of Margarethe Ruttmann, and that he had personally burned this piece of evidence. Yefimovich concluded his pamphlet with a call for all honest men to rise up against the hated oppressors and bring down the corrupt rule of Karl-Franz.

Thirdly, in a jurisdictional dispute typical of a city with more Imperial, religious, local and political factions than many nations, a surprising number of mutually hostile armed bands of men ventured out into the foggy streets, ostensibly to protect the citizens from the twinned dangers of the fog and the Beast. The watches were first reinforced by detachments of the Imperial Militia, augmented by the palace guard in the richer sections of the city. Meanwhile, under the command of Adrian Hoven, patrols of the Knights of the Order of the Fiery Heart combed the area of the palace and the Temple of Sigmar, tactlessly putting to the question many citizens lost in the fog.

In addition to these official forces, a group of Hooks under the command of Willy Pick, flying the spurious standard of a Citizens' Vigilance Committee, took up tactical stations on the city's bridges and casually terrorised passersby. And the League of Karl-Franz, vowing that a little weather was not going to halt their traditional Imminence of Winter wine-drinking contest, flowed in numbers from the colleges of the University towards the Street of a Hundred Taverns. Of course, the list of armed factions was swelled by many of Yefimovich's agitators, by a number of harlots who had decided it best that they carry weapons with the Beast at large, and by sundry fools and adventurers who thought this seemed like an interesting time to wander around in search of excitement.

Between them, these three factors set off the most serious outbreak of urban violence Altdorf had ever known.

The first clashes occurred in the early afternoon, when an inexperienced Imperial Militia lieutenant ignored the advice of the Dock watchmen he was detailed to assist and attempted to persuade a group from the Citizens' Vigilance Committee to abandon their positions at the north end of Three Toll Bridge connecting Temple Street in the west with Luitpoldstrasse in the east. No one was seriously injured, but the lieutenant was pitched into the slow-flowing Reik and had to struggle out of his armour to escape drowning. He learned a valuable lesson and peace was briefly restored.

Just as the temple bell was sounding the hour of three – in the afternoon, although the fog made it hard to distinguish from three in the night – Don Rodrigo Piquer de Ossorio Serrador Teixiheira, the seventeen year-old second son of an Estalian duke, was returning with a severe headache from the House of von Tasseninck, where he had succumbed to an excess of wine during the ball of the night before, to his quarters at the University, where he was endeavouring to master alchemy and siege engineering. Angry at having missed the duel everyone was discussing and feeling in need of the proverbial 'feather of the chicken that pecked you,' he rapped on the door of the One-Eyed Wolf, insisting that the landlord open up and serve him some sherry. The landlord wasn't at home, but the front bar of the hostelry was currently occupied by a chapter of the Fish, who were listening attentively while the one who could read was explaining the contents of 'The Ashes of Shame.'

Barging in, Teixiheira swished his green velvet cloak in a manner he considered quite stylish and requested, in somewhat belligerent tones, that he be served, insisting that his breeding demanded that these commoners do all within their power to oblige him. He was discovered hanging under the Old Emperor Bridge, his cloak having been cut into strips and used to fashion a crude but functional noose. Yorri's Commission decided that Teixiheira was the first official casualty of the riots.

By the hour of five, seventeen others had come to violent ends and the riots had not even really got underway yet. These souls lost their lives in simple skirmishes between individuals or groups of not more than three or four. Typical was the case of Ailbow Muggins, a halfling fruit and vegetable merchant, who mistook an approaching pair of Knights Templars for revenue men intent on discovering the load of contraband harvest goods he had just taken delivery of from a Fish. Muggins was surprised trying to pour powder and shot into the horn of his state-of-the-art flintlock pistol and died, not from the swordblow to his head, but because a spark struck from his hat buckle by the blade ignited the powder in his horn. Cleric-Sergeant Rainer Wim Herzog, who inflicted the stroke and lost an eye in the explosion, was later decorated by Cleric-Captain Hoven and commended for valour, if not in the field, then at least in the fog.

Yorri's Commission could not later account for the activities of Dien Ch'ing, the ambassador of the Monkey King, who apparently spent the day visiting several peculiar establishments scattered throughout the city, purchasing disparate elements that might well be connected with sorcery. Some criticism was also passed on Etienne Edouard Villechaize, Comte de la Rougierre, the ambassador of Charles de la Tete d'Or III, who was believed to have spent the afternoon and early evening at the Matthias II tavern in the company of Milizia Kubic, an exotic dancer of heroic proportions, and to have conducted himself in a manner unbecoming a diplomat of Bretonnia. The sworn testimony of Norbert Schlupmann, a keg-hand at the Matthias II, who spent the afternoon peering through a small hole bored in the ceiling of de la Rougierre's rented apartments, was examined closely by the Grand Theogonist and then placed in the great library of the Temple with many other proscribed works, its contents sealed forever from the public eye and ruled not germane to the investigation.

At some time in the afternoon, Harald Kleindeinst, while questioning the staff of the Wayfarer's Rest in an effort to piece together the last hours of Trudi Ursin's life, survived an assassination attempt and managed, after a very brief chase, to subdue Watchman Joost Rademakers, his would-be murderer. Unfortunately, Rademakers did not survive long enough to explain his motives for attempting the crime. At the time, however, Kleindeinst expressed the opinion that his fellow officer was acting upon the orders of an unnamed third member of the Dock Watch. An autopsy conducted in the Temple of Morr revealed that Rademakers expired due to complications following a crushed windpipe and that the thirty-six bone fractures sustained during his encounter with Kleindeinst were not necessarily contributory factors in his demise.

The corpse of Graf Volker von Tuchtenhagen, suitably cleaned up, was delivered from the palace to the house of the von Tassenincks, following the tradition that the responsibility for the body of a losing duellist devolves, if his family are unavailable, on the owners of the property where the original insult was delivered. Grand Prince Hals, never particularly close to the deceased, had the graf packed in precious ice and sealed up for shipping back to his estates in Averland, where, upon the delivery of the news, his mother would die of grief and his tenants would hold an unofficial and unauthorized three-day festival of merrymaking and licentiousness. Toten Ungenhauer was turned over to the local Temple of Morr, where a cursory examination revealed that he had indeed been drastically altered by warpstone. After scientific dissection, von Tuchtenhagen's champion would be disposed of in the same lime pit that would, after a respectful period, receive the unwanted, much-abused bodies of Margarethe Ruttmann and Trudi Ursin.

The first of the fires was set just after nightfall, at the house of Amadeus Wiesle, an unpopular moneylender active in the East End of the city. The Commission was never able to determine whether this fire was the responsibility of a citizen with a specific grievance against Wiesle or by an agitator in the thrall of Yevgeny Yefimovich, and the watch – given a list of the creditors evicted, abused, physically disabled, sold into servitude or executed thanks to their involvement with

the usurer – decided not to pursue the matter further. By
then, the watch had far more pressing affairs to consider.

If it had not been for the fog, word of the fire in the East
End might have spread faster and caused a panic. As it was,
there was a panic anyway, for a surfeit of other excellent reasons.

Although no one was yet aware of it, the Beast was awake
and was beginning to stalk its prey of the evening...

II

Harald Kleindeinst had arranged to meet them at the Wayfarer's Rest in the middle of the afternoon, but was late. Rosanna had the impression that the officer was the sort of man who kept to his word unless an immovable object got in his way. He had given her Helmut Elsaesser as an escort and told her to poke around Trudi Ursin's room, to see if she could pick up anything useful about the girl. So far, the investigation had been proceeding on the assumption that the Beast was a random murderer, striking merely as the opportunity presented itself. But it would be a lot easier to build up a case if the victims were selected according to a system, no matter how insane. Kleindeinst had had Elsaesser reassigned to the case and put him in charge of finding connections between the dead women. Obviously, the young officer had already been thinking along that course, since he had memorised a great deal of information about the Beast's previous victims: Rosa, Miriam, Helga, Monika, Gislind, Tanja, Margarethe. And now Trudi.

Elsaesser seemed to know them all intimately. Rosa, Monika and Gislind had worked for the same pimp, a Hook

named Maxie Schock, and Miriam and Margarethe, older
than the others, had at different times been involved with
Rikki Fleisch, the small-timer Margarethe had murdered.
Three blondes, two indeterminate brown, one black, one
redhead and one shaven with dragon tattoos. Six prostitutes,
one fortune-teller and, now, one hostel maid. Miriam, 57,
was the oldest and Gislind, 14, the youngest. They had all
worked in the same area, the rough sprawl around the Street
of a Hundred Taverns, and those with homes had lodged
within walking distance. The watch had already been
through over two hundred husbands, ex-husbands, children, boyfriends, 'protectors,' 'admirers,' customers,
associates, friends, enemies, acquaintances and neighbours.
A few people had cropped up in connection with more than
one of the women – there were jokes being told at the
Luitpoldstrasse Station about the appetite of that dwarfish
Bretonnian ambassador, de la Rougierre – but no one could
be tied in with all of them. The only thing the eight had in
common was their deaths, unmistakably the work of the
same hand.

Rosanna sat at the dressing table and looked into the
cracked but clean mirror, trying to see a dead girl's face as it
had been. She was trying to forget the red ruin she had seen
at the Beloved of Manann warehouse, the blood sucked
away by the water, greyish patches of skull showing through.
Elsaesser searched the room, apparently at random, looking
for things he had seen before. 'Helga had shoes like this,' he
said, going through a box in the wardrobe. He made a discovery. 'And most of them used this stuff.'

She looked over. He had found a cache of weirdroot. He
scraped one of the dried roots with his fingernail and
dabbed his tongue. 'This is snakeshit,' he said. 'Last year's
crop. Maybe older.'

Rosanna looked back at the mirror. Her face was cut in
half by the crack.

She touched the hairbrush and got the impression of
long, thick hair, crackling as it was combed out. From the
corpse, she hadn't been able to tell what the girl had looked
like when she was alive.

'Two people lived here,' said Elsaesser, holding up a maid-servant's apron and a man's jacket. 'See, I can scry too. It's called deduction.'

He seemed pleased with himself. That worried Rosanna a little. She wasn't sure why Elsaesser was so hot on the Beast. Partly, she saw, it was because he liked puzzles. The only thing she had caught from his mind was the feeling of his fingers working away at difficult knots, trying to get them loose. His hands were always restless. The whole process of tracking the killer excited him. He was like a first-time huntsman, exhilarated by the chase but not yet blooded, not yet forced to see a kill. And there was some other motive, something harder to define.

It was really much simpler when you did something you were told to. There were no motives to untangle and ponder. She was here because the Lector wanted her here. And, after yesterday's session with the leftovers of the victims, she was here because she wanted the Beast stopped.

Elsaesser dropped the apron on the bed and examined the jacket. It was obviously of a good cut. Trudi had had a rich boyfriend, or a light-fingered one with access to a tailor's shop.

'The League of Karl-Franz,' the officer said. 'Look.'

He tossed the jacket at her and she caught it. On the lapels was the Imperial seal, picked out in gold.

'The Leaguers all wear these things. I should have recognized it straight away.'

It was like holding an angry animal. The jacket struggled in her grip and she heard growling, spitting and snarling. Claws slashed, teeth were bared. There was snow underfoot and a trail of blood to follow. Yellow and red eyes shone and she realized they were her own, thrown back at her by the mirror.

'Trudi's boyfriend is a first-year, not fully inducted,' said Elsaesser. 'He'll be able to put on some extra braids if he passes his first exams.'

She dropped the garment.

'What's wrong?'

Rosanna could not stop shaking.

'Wolf,' she said.

Elsaesser was attentive, contrite. 'I'm sorry, I should never have just thrown the thing at you. I keep forgetting about your gift.'

'That's all right, it would have happened anyway. I can feel it in this whole room. It's strong, like a musk.'

'You should act more like a witch...'

She hated that word, but was willing to put up with it from the well-meaning young officer.

'...cover your clothes with symbols and emblems. Wave your hands and mutter hocus pocus.'

The gooseflesh under her sleeves subsided. Elsaesser stroked her hair, as if he were fifty years older rather than six years younger than her. He had none of the caution Mikael Hasselstein exhibited around her and that made her realize how few of the people she knew were willing casually to touch her in the way ordinary people did each other. She didn't even scry anything more from the officer, beyond a general attempt to soothe her after her nasty contact.

'I'm not a witch, or a sorceress. This isn't something I learned, it's something I was born with. It's like being double-jointed, or having a good singing voice.'

He was serious again. 'Is it Wolf?' he asked.

'I think so. Names are difficult, sometimes. There are odd things about him. He must be a student, but he feels older. He has been through a period of his life he barely remembers, but is constantly plagued by. He's not an altered, but he has undergone some... some transformation...'

Elsaesser was paying close attention.

Kunze, the landlord, had said that Trudi had a boyfriend who stayed with her sometimes. Aside from being a student and not short of the odd crown, he didn't know anything about the man. However, Kunze had described him as 'a hairy devil' even though, when pressed, he had admitted that the boy didn't wear a beard.

There was a knock at the door.

'Come in.'

A girl in an apron entered the room and curtsied. Rosanna felt the wave of fear coming off her. She had been crying.

'I'm Marte,' the girl said. 'Mr Kunze said you wanted to see me.'

'You were Trudi's friend?' Elsaesser asked.

Marte said, 'We worked alternate shifts, officer. She was a good girl and filled in when I was sick. I'm sick a lot.'

Rosanna noticed that the girl was a little lame and her skin colour was not good.

'Did you know her boyfriend?' she asked.

Marte's face twisted and Rosanna tried hard not to flinch. The maid had just switched from passive fear to active fear.

'Him,' she said, loathing in her voice, 'he was a bad one. An animal. He was sweet as sugar one minute, then a vicious beast. I don't know why she stuck with him. I'd never let a man use me as he used her. We bathed together, every week, and she always had some new bruise or scratch that he'd given her.'

The yellow and red eyes burned in her mind.

'Do you know his name?'

Marte was more angry than scared now. 'Did he do it? I always said he was a bad one.'

'His name?'

'Merciful Shallya, was he… was he *the Beast*?' Marte was on the point of fainting.

Elsaesser took her by the shoulders and held her up. 'What was his name?'

'Oh yes. His name. It was Wolf…'

Elsaesser and Rosanna looked at each other.

'Aristocracy, he was. He kept it quiet, but Trudi told me his brother was an elector…'

Inside her mind, something vague was coming into clear, hard focus. Rosanna remembered the sketch she had made for Captain Kleindeinst and the face that had kept trying to impose itself over the one in Trudi's mind.

'His name was Wolf von Mecklenberg.'

III

THE BARGE WAS empty. Wolf tried to remember coming aboard, but couldn't. The cabin door was splintered and he guessed that he had broken in.

He had slept in his clothes and woken up feeling grimy next to the skin.

He had gone out last night, with Trudi. There had been a thick fog. He remembered an argument.

But nothing else.

He wished Johann were here. Johann would know how to save him from the animal inside him. Johann had spent ten years tracking him, trying to rescue him from the Chaos knights.

Those had been bad years, but they were gone now. Gone forever.

He could remember some things. He could remember that day in the woods when he had got in the way of Johann's arrow.

His shoulder still hurt when it was damp, and sometimes bled. Now there was an ache between the bones, precisely where Johann's shaft had pierced.

That day, he had been snotty. He had been taunting his brother for his faint heart. As a boy, Johann had not been a natural killer. Wolf had been the huntsman in the family. He had lived for his time in the woods, loping along in the tracks of some stag or hog, his bow always ready. If it swam, flew, ran or burrowed, Wolf could kill it.

Now, he wished he had been more like Johann, instinctively turning away from murder.

His trophies were dusty and forgotten in some storeroom on the estate. And he wished he could get rid of his urge to kill.

It must have been easy for Cicatrice to work on him. The seed of Chaos had always been there, nestling in his heart, waiting to sprout. He had been a monster inside long before the warpstone had given him a body to match.

These last weeks had been foggy, if not in the city then in his mind. He remembered the feel of Trudi, the feel of her flesh...

And he did not want to remember any more.

He must have been weird-juicing last night. Purple squiggles still came and went in the periphery of his vision. And then he must have been brawling. One of his teeth was loose and he had bled from cuts on his face. But not all the blood on his clothes was his own.

On the floor of the cabin he found a docker's hook, like the ones carried by the waterfront gang. It was blooded.

For some reason, he took it with him when he left.

Emerging onto the deck, he found that the barge was moored near the Three Toll Bridge, at one of the public quays.

He took three crowns from his pouch, to cover the damage, and left them by the wheelhouse, under a coil of rope so they wouldn't shine and attract attention.

The barge was on a loose mooring, to rise and fall with the river, and it was played out. The rope was stretched tight and the quay was ten feet away. There was nothing for it but to get wet.

He lowered himself into the icy waters, almost relishing the shock of the cold, and got a strong grip on the rope. The current pulled at his legs. There was a surface mist trailing off the water, joining the thick fog in the air.

He could barely see the dock.

He worked his way, hand over hand, feeling the rush of water washing him clean.

He hauled himself up and stood on the planks of the jetty. He tried to shake himself dry, like a dog, but his shirt and britches hung on him like ice slabs.

He wanted to go back to Trudi, but wasn't sure that was a good idea. He could not remember what their argument had been about, but it had been a bad one. He thought he had used his hands on her. Again. And that made him burn with shame.

Dripping, he walked off the docks, fumbling his way in the fog...

THERE WERE RUFFIANS fighting on the Street of a Hundred Taverns, but it was more serious than the usual Hooks-and-Fish or Students-and-Dockers clashes. Those did not usually leave many dead, but Dien Ch'ing could tell that at least five people had been killed in the fighting so far. It would be a good night for his lord.

Disdaining the ostentatious carriage that was his right as ambassador, he had chosen to go for a walk in the fog. At the palace, there were those who thought he must be mad, but the ways of foreign diplomats were not often questioned.

The duel this morning had given him quite an appetite.

He honoured the purpose of Lord Tsien-Tsin and heard in his head the orchestra of the Fifteen Devils. He longed for the Pagoda, and to be far away from this barbarous and cold country. He remembered the sweet teas and fragrant blossoms of his homeland, and wondered humbly how soon it would be before his master chose to summon him back to Cathay to work towards the downfall of the presumptuous Monkey King. That monarch had reigned for too long over the greatness of the east, and it had always been the intention of Tsien-Tsin that he be brought low. Ch'ing had promised himself the position of executioner and imagined the scimitar describing a graceful arc towards the throat of the Monkey King and the look in his enemy's eyes as his befuddled head was expertly detached from his unworthy neck.

His pleasant thoughts were interrupted.

'You,' said a rough voice, 'Green velvet!'

There were three of them, each taller than he. They blocked his path. They were indistinct in the fog, illuminated by the fires behind them. He looked from outline to outline. Two men and a woman. They each held docker's hooks in their fists.

'Off your patch, aren't you?' said the one who had already spoken.

Ch'ing bowed. 'Might I humbly request that you let my meagre and contemptible self past. I have urgent business.'

They laughed at him and he sighed.

'We don't want your sort here,' said the woman.

'Palace scum!'

'Parasite!'

'Yellow dog.'

A hook sliced out of the fog at him. He clapped his hands over it, halting it an inch from his nose.

'Moves like a rabbit,' someone said.

He let the hook go and it was withdrawn.

He saw the dagger coming and tapped it away with his palm. It struck a wall.

The fog swirled around them as the three Hooks spread to surround him. The fire nearby was rising and Ch'ing realized that there was a carriage overturned in the street, burning steadily. He could see their stupid faces. They all had grotesquely large noses, skins the colour of a pig's belly and peculiar moon-round eyes, and the men were disgustingly bearded, with thick hair like growths of moss about their chins and necks. Typical unwashed barbarians.

He drew up his knee and spread his arms in the crane position.

'He's a loony,' said the woman.

He hopped into the air and kicked where her voice had come from. She was out of the ring instantly, consciousness knocked out of her.

Ch'ing landed a little unsteadily on the cobbles, but quickly regained his balance.

'Did you see that?'

'What did you do to Hanni?'

'Slit-eyed swine!'

The two Hooks circled him and he turned, preventing either from getting behind him.

Finally, he became tired of the game.

For the one who had spoken first, he employed the Drunken Master technique, weaving unsteadily from side to side, then head-butting the Hook to the ground and stamping on his face, as if trying to put out a burning patch of lamp-oil. It was most comical.

For the other, he switched to the Sleeping Fist. Yawning loudly, he stifled himself with the back of one hand and leaned backwards, as if falling into a hammock. His outstretched elbow smashed into the Hook's ribcage, breaking a few bones. The man coughed and fell, and Ch'ing sliced his neck between his scything legs.

He left two dead and one sleeping. Sparing the woman was his concession to the mores of the Empire where, for some extraordinary reason, it was not considered polite to kill a female. Not, of course, that that stopped anyone. This Beast fellow, for instance...

Standing over his fallen enemies, he heard someone clapping.

A creature scurried monkey-like out of the fog, its hands slapping together.

Ch'ing bowed. He recognized Respighi.

'My master sends his greetings, Celestial.'

'They are accepted with thanks.'

'He is busy elsewhere...'

There was a sound from across the river. It was a large building gently bursting into flames. There were a lot of fires in the fog. In the distance, people were shouting.

'...but has asked me to accompany you to the Matthias II. I am to represent his interests.'

Ch'ing spread his hands. 'We all have the same interest, Respighi. The greater glory of Lord Tsien-Tsin.'

'Tzeentch.'

'As you will. Names do not matter. We all eventually serve the same purpose.'

Respighi giggled.

IV

HAVING DECIDED TO accept de la Rougierre's invitation for the
evening, Johann was now faced with the problem of making
his attendance at the soirée not seem extraordinary. He had
cultivated, he now realized, an unusual unsociability, regularly avoiding the balls and receptions that proliferated
around the Imperial court. It was not that he hated these
things so much, but that he had been away from the world
of titles and etiquette for so long that he no longer had the
desire to enter it. The latest dances, current fashions in hem-
lines and the petty schemings of rival court factions simply
did not seem important, or even interesting, to him.

And yet, it was now clear that he must be at the
Bretonnian ambassador's soirée. He knew, with a certainty
that was unusual, that this was not just an innocent social
occasion. The scent of the Beast was in the air.

In the afternoon, he had encountered Leos von Liebewitz,
who was in ominously good spirits, and discovered that the
viscount and his sister were also on de la Rougierre's guest
list. Leos had offered him a place in their carriage and he
had accepted with practiced off-handedness.

Johann found it creepy that the undemonstrative, unemotional, humourless viscount was only able to be anything approaching friendly if he had spilled blood that day. Before leaving him, the youth had clapped Johann on the shoulder and shaken his hand. He fancied that Leos had kept up physical contact a moment or two longer than was necessary. There were stories told about the viscount, not to his face... Stories about why he had rejected the undeniably appealing Clothilde of Averheim as a marriage prospect, or even as a sweetheart-of-the-month...

De la Rougierre was away from the palace, making preparations, so Johann had to ask around to discover who else would be at the table. That meant paying his respects to the Countess Emmanuelle and listening to her for longer than he would have chosen to.

The countess was genuinely the most beautiful woman he had ever seen, but she was so self-absorbed as to qualify also as one of the most boring. He found her surrounded by a flurry of notably unattractive maidservants, endeavouring to make a choice between seven equally magnificent, overly decorated and borderline immodest gowns. She had been relying on the judgement of Mnoujkine, the guests' steward, to assist her and the man was notably relieved to have a superior to take over the duty from him. She asked Johann to give advice and he had to sit in her rooms while she darted behind a screen to struggle out of and into each in turn. Mnoujkine, with the tact of a born underling, withdrew to leave his betters unchaperoned.

All the while, she talked. Johann learned that the party was to be graced by the presence of future Emperor Luitpold. Mikael Hasselstein was due to make an appearance and Dien Ch'ing, the Cathayan ambassador, and Grand Prince Hergard von Tasseninck. Also, the Marquess Sidonie of Marienburg, which prompted Emmanuelle to remark that 'the Bretonnian would have to be careful with the seating arrangements since Leos killed her husband last year on a matter of honour.' Johann wished the countess would take the trouble to watch her brother butcher his opponents and then try to talk about matters of honour.

Three electors, the future Emperor and a Lector of the Cult
of Sigmar. If one was to assume that Luitpold could influence his father, and that Hasselstein was more or less
charged with the powers the Grand Theogonist was neglect-
ing to wield these days, then one would see that this small,
exclusive gathering concentrated more political power in
one room than had gathered since the last meeting of the
Electoral College. The thing that puzzled Johann most was
where the Celestial fitted in. What could be the common
interest of Bretonnia and Cathay? Also, it was well-known
that de la Rougierre had little actual power at the court of
King Charles de la Tete d'Or, the ridiculous perfumed dwarf
having been appointed to the ambassadorship as a cruel
joke against Karl-Franz that no one had yet had the nerve to
explain to the Emperor.

'Which do you prefer, baron?'

He paid attention. The countess was in her robe again,
playing artfully with her lapels to show off her well-shaped
bust.

'The green velvet,' he said, distractedly.

She seemed surprised and chewed a strand of her hair like
a teenager. It was well known that the countess had been
twenty-nine for some years now.

'Very well, the green velvet. A good choice. Traditional.
You have an admirable eye, Johann.'

He shrugged, uncomfortable. He did not know where to
put his hands and opted to leave them in his lap.

She gave her maids directions in a low, serious voice. The
dress was to be cleaned, pressed, aired, perfumed and laid
out. She listed the underwear and accessories that went with
it, and handed one girl the key to her jewel-box, with
instructions to fetch several bracelets, brooches and rings,
and a specified tiara-and-necklace combination. Obviously,
the life of the Countess-Elector of Nuln was one tough decision after another.

Johann made an excuse and left.

He thought about Wolf. And he thought about Harald
Kleindeinst, wondering if he had done the right thing by setting the watchman on the trail.

It was too late to step back.

In an hour, he would join the von Liebewitzes and venture out into the fog.

Perhaps there would be answers out there.

THEY WERE WAITING for him at the Wayfarer's Rest. He had been delayed by the business with Joost Rademakers. Dickon was being stupid and would suffer for it later. He should have known that Rademakers on his own wouldn't have a chance against Filthy Harald. The captain always had underestimated him.

The whole city was going mad in this fog. The Luitpoldstrasse Station had been snowed under with bleeding citizens, complaining of assaults, robberies and arson. Harald had seen three Knights Templars roughing up a couple of Fish and left them to it. There were Imperial Militiamen hanging around with the watch, getting in the way.

Dickon had sent a runner to the fire-fighters, to help with the burning carriages in the Street of a Hundred Taverns, but he had either got lost, got killed or found the fire service busy elsewhere.

He could tell straight away that Rosanna and Elsaesser had news for him.

'Out with it,' he said. 'Elsaesser, speak slowly, no repetitions, no gabble.'

'Trudi Ursin's missing boyfriend is Wolf Mecklenberg...'

'Von Mecklenberg,' put in Rosanna.

'The elector's brother.'

Harald bit down hard on the nugget, to see how it tasted. It wasn't good.

'But the baron was interested in the Beast *before* Trudi turned up dead,' he reasoned. 'Which suggests that he knows something we don't.'

'There's more,' said the scryer. 'It's common knowledge that the baron's brother was abducted as a child, by Chaos knights...'

'It was a bandit called Cicatrice,' said Elsaesser. 'I'd heard the story, but never made the connection...'

'Wolf was rescued,' explained Rosanna, 'and purged of the warpstone. But maybe there's still something inside.'

Harald imagined a young man in a frenzy, tearing at a girl with claws and teeth.

'Scryer, is Wolf the Beast?' he asked.

She thought hard, not wanting to say anything until she was certain.

'I'll put it this way: do you *think* he's the Beast?'

'It's… it's not impossible. I've been through some of his clothes, trying to find traces. He has an aura of violence, of confusion. Also, he suffers from terrible guilt.'

'But that doesn't make him our killer?'

'No,' she admitted. 'There are a lot of violent people in this city.'

She was looking at him. There was still a splash of Rademakers's blood on his coat.

'That's true,' he said.

'What should we do?' asked Elsaesser.

'You take Baron Johann,' he ordered. 'Get over to the palace and stick to him like a lashworm in case his brother shows up. Tell him I've sent you for his own protection. Make up some story. Convince him that there's a rumour going around that he's the killer and the vigilantes are after him. That's probably true. There are rumours going around that everyone's the killer. Dickon is trying to convince the Hooks that it's me, and hopes they'll put me out of the way.'

Elsaesser saluted.

'Rosanna,' Harald continued, 'you stick with me. We'll try and find this Wolf of yours. He may not be the killer, but he's certainly got some questions to answer.'

'He's a Leaguer,' Elsaesser said. 'You could start at their hall. It's not far.'

'Also,' said Rosanna, 'he's on weirdroot. He might be trying to buy some of the stuff.'

'That's something to start with.'

Elsaesser pulled on his peaked cap and left.

'Lad,' Harald said after him, 'be careful.'

The officer said, 'I will be,' and left.

Harald felt the aches of his fight with Rademakers disappearing. The old copper feeling was coming back. It wasn't just nausea, it was a tightness in the pit of his stomach that he recognized as excitement.

'You want him, don't you?' said the scryer.

'Yes, I do.'

'Dead or alive?'

'Either way, Rosanna. Just so long as we stop him, I don't care.'

'Dead, then.'

'That's safest, I admit.'

'Dead, yes. I agree. Dead.'

'SELECTING YOUR SWORD, viscount?'

There was a perfume in the air that he recognized. Knowing he was in for a tedious scene, Leos ran a chamois leather along the edge of his blade and turned to pay attention.

'Dany,' he said, pointing at a comely throat with the foil, 'do not overestimate your importance in the order of things.'

The favourite pouted, ringlets shaking.

'Testy this evening, aren't we?'

'I have to go out.'

'With the countess? You are much in her company.'

The sword point did not shake. It was fixed in the air. He was still in perfect condition, the muscles of his shoulders, arms and legs gave him pleasure as he stretched, extending his steel. Von Tuchtenhagen's champion hadn't strained him at all.

'I could kill you, you know. Quite easily.'

'But would that be honourable?'

'Honour is a matter for gentlemen. Between us, it's different.'

Dany laughed, a girlish giggle, and brushed Leos's sword away.

'It certainly is, dearest.'

Leos scabbarded his blade and felt its weight on his hip. With his weapon in place, he felt whole again.

'You killed this morning?'

'Twice.'

'Did it give you an appetite?'

Dany tried to kiss him, but he pushed the favourite away.

'Not now.'

'Temper, temper. You know, Leos, when you are angry I can quite see the quality in you that made poor Clothilde of Averheim swoon so dramatically. I hear the little fool is ruined for all other men after your callous treatment of her. Such a shame. Hot little bitch too, I'd heard. The young men of her city must curse you in their prayers.'

'Dany, you can be extraordinarily tiresome at times.'

'I thought I had a certain degree of license. After all, I am an *intimate* of the family…'

Leos felt the killing chill in his heart.

'You're sailing into choppy waters, Dany. You might well encounter the odd wreck.'

'Wrecks by the name of the Graf von Tuchtenhagen, or the Bassanio Bassarde, or… what were the other names?'

'You know them as well as I do.'

'Not quite as well. No one ever forgets their kills.'

Dany was playing with silk handkerchiefs, running fingers under them, examining the shifting patterns.

'My sister has tired of you, you know,' Leos said, spitefully. 'She has a more important admirer.'

'Bitch,' spat Dany.

Leos gave one of his rare laughs. 'Hurts, doesn't it? Have you met the current paramour? Very distinguished, they say, and highly influential. Between them, the countess and he could decide the fate of the Empire.'

Dany made a fist, crumpling silk.

'Before von Tuchtenhagen and Bassarde, I had to kill others. You are right. I remember the names: Cleric-Captain Voegler of the Order of the Fiery Heart, young von Rohrbach, even a commoner or two, Peder Novak, Karoli Vares…'

Dany tried to counterfeit a lack of fear.

'It's a long list. Perhaps my sister provokes too many insults for her own good. But many of them were quite close to her at one time or another. The ways of her heart are unpredictable.'

The favourite looked away.

'And so, Dany my dear, are the ways of mine.'

Leos took the favourite's shoulders and turned a pretty face around to look into his eyes. Dany's pupils were contracting, a sign of overfondness for weirdroot.

'Aren't my hands strong, Dany dear?'

Leos forced his mouth against Dany's and kissed him. The viscount tasted the favourite's fear.

'Maybe you won't be the favourite much longer?'

Dany broke away and wiped his mouth with his silk, spitting into it. He had been shaking, but now his confidence was coming back.

'I'll never duel with you, Leos,' he said.

Leos smiled. 'And I'll never ask you.'

'After all,' Dany said bitterly, 'now the countess has done with me, it is not as if I lacked for female company?'

The favourite smiled.

'And my girlfriend's name is still von Liebewitz.'

Leos backhanded Dany across the mouth, rouging his lips with blood.

'You should be more careful, family favourite. If it ever entered your head to tell what you know, or what you think you know, you would be dead before the first story crept out of your mouth. Remember that.'

Dany slunk away and flung himself face-down upon the bed. He was not crying out loud.

Leos finished dressing. Johann would be waiting at the coach. Emmanuelle would be late, as usual.

Leos was interested in spending some time alone with the Elector of Sudenland. The man had a mysterious, attractive air.

And he was after something.

V

'Etienne,' said the dancer, Milizia, 'is this appropriate?'

The Bretonnian ambassador cast an eye on the girl's costume. It was tight in the right places and cut away to display her body. It was a gravity-defying miracle.

'Wondrous to behold, my sweet,' he said, 'now leave us alone. We men have business that must be discussed. The landlord will feed you in your dressing room and I shall send for you later.'

Milizia curtseyed, setting herself wobbling like a jelly on a plate and withdrew. De la Rougierre felt his amorous spirits rising again and fingered the waxed ends of his moustaches.

'The lady,' began Dien Ch'ing, 'is most substantial.'

De la Rougierre laughed out loud. The Celestial was a sly one.

'You have no women the like of our Milizia in Far Cathay, I'll bet.'

'No, indeed we do not.'

'More's the pity, eh? Tell me, those sailors' stories about the girls of the East…'

Ch'ing waved his serious anthropological inquiry aside and tapped the papers on the desk.

'This treaty, de la Rougierre. Tonight, I would like to see our guests put their seals to it. It is most important.'

'Of course, of course, but nothing is more important than love, my friend, nothing...'

The Celestial gave a thin smile. 'As you say.'

'But after love, there must be war, eh?'

De la Rougierre thumped his barrel chest. 'The Bretonnians are as renowned for their prowess on the battlefield as in the boudoir, my friend. The foeman trembles when the armies of Charles de la Tete d'Or III are on the march.'

'So I am given to understand. I am a poor stranger in these lands, but even I have heard of the high reputation of the Bretonnians.'

The dwarf clapped his hands like an excited child and lifted his goblet. The Celestial was a fine man, a fine diplomat.

'This treaty will be the start of a great campaign against the Dark Lands, a campaign that will strike at the goblins in their homes. It will be magnificent.'

'Of course,' the Bretonnian agreed, 'with a de la Rougierre in it, it could hardly be anything but magnificent!'

'That is indeed so.'

'I'm glad to hear you agree with me. I'll call for another bottle of this establishment's best Quenelles rosé and we'll drink a toast to our victory over the dark.'

Ch'ing laughed softly, almost under his breath.

For an instant, de la Rougierre felt as if someone were tickling his skeleton with a rocfeather. There were shadows in this room and he could swear that there was something small lurking up in one of the corners, hanging from the ceiling, spying on them with glittering eyes. When he looked again, there was nothing there.

The wine arrived.

'Our guests will be here soon,' de la Rougierre told the landlord. 'Make sure they are conducted up here with no trouble. These are important people.'

The landlord, who was taking more money for this private party than he usually did in any given three month period, was nervously obsequious and assured the Bretonnian that all that could be done would be done or he would know the reason for it and be using a stick on his staff.

The Celestial sipped his wine.

'Wonderful vintage, is it not? The best wines in the world are Bretonnian. And the best wine-drinkers.'

De la Rougierre drained his goblet, then refilled it.

He thought of Big Women.

GETTING ACROSS THE city to the palace had not been easy. Two of the main bridges had been blocked, Emperor Karl-Franz Bridge by the wreckage of a couple of carts and an armed band of Hooks, and Three Toll Bridge by the Knights Templar and the Imperial Militia, who had sealed off each end and were keeping some unfortunate travellers penned between their positions.

In the end, Elsaesser found a lone ferryman and paid him over the odds.

Out in the fog, everything seemed peaceful. But he could see the flickering of distant fires in the East End and hear shouts of anger and pain.

'Bad fog,' said the boatman, 'worse than the coronation year and that was as bad as it's ever been.'

A rowing boat floated by, keel-up.

'Nothing as bad as fog, unless it's torrential rain with thunder and lightning.'

There was a series of splashes. Some people were being thrown off one of the docks.

'Maybe an earthquake would be worse, if we ever got them. Or the Southlands hail where the stones are the size of coaches.'

Everyone was busy tonight: the watch, the Templars, the Hooks, the Fish, the militia, the fire-fighters.

That would make things easy for the Beast if he wanted to venture out.

'Of course, an invasion of hideously altered beastmen would put a bit of a dent in trade and spoil everyone's day.'

To Elsaesser, it was personal now. He felt as if it were just him and the Beast. That wasn't true, of course. There was Captain Kleindeinst and Rosanna.

'And a rain of fire from the skies, called down by a black wizard, would be just *awful*.'

And Baron Johann? He was with them, wasn't he?

'You have to look on the bright side in the ferry business.'

Elsaesser was sure the baron wasn't trying to protect the Beast. That would not make sense. Even if his brother were the killer, the baron would want him stopped, if not necessarily executed.

'Here you are, sir. Have a nice evening.'

He paid the man and ran all the way to the palace. He passed more Knights of the Fiery Heart, marching from the Temple, armour clanking.

Reinforcements. They were talking about taking on the enemy and putting them to the rout, but none of them seemed to know which enemy. After some discussion, they decided they were probably supposed to put down a rebellion in the notoriously slack and untrustworthy palace guard.

The portcullis was down, but Elsaesser had wound up with Baron Johann's imperially-sealed document and that was enough to get him into the palace. None of the men on the gate knew where the baron was, and neither did the steward he bumped into in the courtyard.

Elsaesser had never been inside the palace before and was surprised at how big it was. You could fit his entire town into its walls. Even without the fog drifting through the courtyards, it would be easy to get lost in the place.

He saw a slim young man striding across towards some outbuildings, looking as if he knew where he was going.

'Excuse me, sir,' Elsaesser asked.

The man turned. He wore one of those damned green velvet cloaks that were causing such trouble.

'I beg your pardon,' he said, 'do I know you, officer?'

'No,' he admitted and the courtier sneered, as if Elsaesser were committing a grave offence by talking to someone to whom he had not been introduced.

The officer remembered Professor Brustellin's lectures. This man was typical of the aristocratic cancers the great man had diagnosed, handsome in an unmanly sort of way, with a bred-in-the-bone contempt for anyone without a lineage.

'I'm with the watch,' Elsaesser explained. 'I need to see Baron Johann Mecklenberg.'

'Von Mecklenberg, I think you mean.'

'Yes, of course, von Mecklenberg,' said Elsaesser, impatient. 'Do you know where he is?'

The youth looked amused. 'I'm going to meet him now, at our carriage. Is it really necessary that you disturb him?'

'Oh yes, he'll thank you for conveying me to him. It's to do with the Beast.'

The aristocrat dropped his effete pose and looked serious, a single line appearing between his fine brows.

'Viscount Leos von Liebewitz,' he said, not extending his gloved hand. 'Come on, hurry up.'

They walked through the fog and soon the outlines of a coach were discernible. The baron stood beside it.

'Elsaesser,' he said, 'what are you doing here?'

The viscount stood back, faint in the fog, and Elsaesser wondered why the man was so brittle. There was more than just aristocratic distance in it. He was acting like a jealous girl.

'Captain Kleindeinst sent me. I'm your bodyguard.'

The baron laughed, not unkindly.

'You don't seem the type.'

'Sorry, sir.'

'No, fine, it's a good idea. You can fill me in on your progress…'

Elsaesser knew that would come up and wondered whether he should tell the baron what they had learned about his brother's relationship with the last victim.

'You've met Leos, I see.'

The viscount emerged from the fog, his face a mask.

'Elsaesser and I have been hunting the Beast.'

'The murderer of commoners? I'm surprised at your interest, Johann.'

Elsaesser felt something pass between the baron and the viscount. All these titles confused him and the subtle tensions that went along with them were worse. He was glad he only had to deal with Hooks and Fish, and murderers.

The baron ignored the viscount's implied criticism and turned to talk with Elsaesser. 'Leos is a champion swordsman. He'll be useful in the fog, I think.'

The viscount smiled sheepishly and tried to shake off the compliment.

'Leos, will you throw in with us? Will you join the hunt?'

The man was uncomfortable, torn between two impulses. He wanted not to have anything to do with a nasty common series of killings, but he desperately needed the baron's approval. In the end, he did not have to make a decision, for someone arrived to interrupt the impromptu conference.

'Elsaesser,' said Baron Johann, 'may I present the viscount's sister, the Countess Emmanuelle.'

A lady, wrapped up in transparent gauzes to protect her dress and face against the fog, appeared out of the gloom.

Elsaesser's knees went unaccountably weak.

He was travelling in distinguished company. He wondered what Mrs Bierbichler would say.

Undoubtedly, he would be told that he could die.

THE BEAST SMELLED *the fog and crept out of the man-shell, claws extending.*

It tasted the blood in the air and howled for joy. With each night, this city became more hospitable.

Tonight would be magnificent…

VI

THEIR CART RATTLED through the streets of the East End, drawn by two stolen horses. He stood up, no longer even needing to speak. The crowd was with him, surging behind the cart. In the back, Stieglitz was making torches with efficient skill, using his teeth to compensate for his missing arm. Dipped in pitch, they were then handed to Brustellin and Kloszowski to be lit and, flames growing, to Yefimovich and Ulrike to be thrown.

A torch spun into the air, spinning wooden end over flaming head, and disappeared into the fog. He heard it land and then the soft whump! of the flames spreading.

'Down with the green velvet!' shouted Ulrike, her long hair streaming behind her, her face aglow in the torchlight.

A hundred voices in the crowd echoed her.

This was her moment. She was like Myrmidia, Goddess of War, leading her armies against the Chaos Powers.

Of course, Ulrike, unknowing, was serving those same powers.

Yefimovich could capture a crowd with his words. As he had discovered, there was even a sexual charisma to his fire-breathing. He could pull people in and make them his, convert them to any cause. Tomorrow, he could enlist in the service of the Emperor and turn these people around, making them into ardent supporters of the aristocracy. His slogans came from dozens of mouths and seemed to have been born there.

But he would never have what Ulrike had.

She was truly the Angel of the Revolution. In her, the madness glowed like the fire of the gods. She believed with a passion in the cause and her belief was contagious.

Of course, she was beautiful. Of course, she was young. And, of course, she had suffered mightily during her rise from house-slave to angel. But there was something else, something inside. Some actors had it, too few leaders of men, and all gods.

There was not a man in the street who would not follow Ulrike to the death. Men as disparate as Kloszowski, Brustellin and Stieglitz were desperately, hopelessly in love with her. It was rumoured – incorrectly, as it happened – that she had enslaved electors, courtiers and even the Emperor with her looks.

She sang songs of the revolution and her high, clear voice could be heard above the chorus of the crowd.

She gently tossed a torch through a second-storey window and cheers went up as the flames grew.

The crowd were hailing her even as she set fire to their homes. There was nothing a woman like this could not do.

Yefimovich's inner fires burned. The face Respighi had found for him was not settling well. He would need another before morning. That was an annoying distraction. There were too many important matters to take care of tonight.

'They'll be trembling in their palaces,' said Kloszowski. 'I'll write poems about this night. They'll live when the House of the Second Wilhelm is forgotten.'

The cart stopped. There was a press of bodies in the street.

'What is it?' Yefimovich asked.

'Templars,' said one of the ringleaders, a Fish called Ged. 'Blocking the bridges, trying to keep us on this side.'

Yefimovich grinned. There could not be enough of them.

The fires had been started in the East End, the smallest of
the three triangular wedges within the city walls that made
up Altdorf. To one side was the wedge with the palace and
the Temple and to the other the one with the docks and the
University. His plan was to take the docks and swarm
through the Street of a Hundred Taverns to link up with the
radical students of the Ulli von Tasseninck School. He had
anticipated, even counted on, the blockade of the bridge.

'Stieglitz,' he said. 'You're the tactician. We have the weight
of numbers. Can we break through?'

The ex-mercenary fingered his stump. He grunted. 'Boats.
We'll need boats. And archers.'

'Done,' Yefimovich said. 'Ged, get him what he needs.'

'And you,' asked Kloszowski, 'what will you do?'

'I shall get across and make sure that we can surprise the
Templars from the rear. I'll take Ulrike. She can stir up some
support on the docks.'

'It's a good plan,' said Brustellin. 'Similar to the tactics of
Bloody Beatrice the Monumentally Cruel in her campaign
against the Thirteen Rebel Electors.'

Ulrike wasn't hearing them. She was still singing, still
exulting in her communion with the crowd. Yefimovich
pulled her down and helped her off the wagon. People got
out of her way, treating her respectfully. A young man threw
himself at her feet and kissed the hem of her dress. She
smiled and made of him a radical for life.

Yefimovich's gloves were itching. His inner fires were troublesome tonight.

'I have a boat ready,' he told Ulrike. 'It's disguised. We're
meeting friends on the other side.'

Ulrike allowed herself to be led like a child through the
cheering multitude. It was slow going, but she did not stop
too often to dispense blessings or accept embraces.

Five or six city blocks were burning now and the fires were
spreading through the close-packed tenements. There would
be plenty of burned meat for Tzeentch.

Finally, Yefimovich got Ulrike to the boat. Respighi had
killed its owners earlier and had it covered with canvas,
moored unobtrusively at a near-derelict jetty. People flowed

by, swarming towards the bridges, as he pulled away the covering and helped Ulrike step into the boat. She shouted encouragement at them, but they mainly couldn't hear. Amid the crowds, they were strangely alone.

'Get down low, we don't want you to be seen.'

She crouched, looking up at him with adoration. He took a satisfaction in that.

'Here,' he said, 'roll this up and use it as a cushion.

She took the cloak. 'It's green velvet,' she said.

'Come the revolution, we'll all wear green velvet.'

She laughed. 'Come the revolution…'

He began to row. His gloves chafed as he worked the oars. He would have preferred to have someone else do this, but Respighi was busy at the Matthias II.

The oars slapped water and the fog was all around them. Beyond Ulrike, Yefimovich could still see the glow of the fires in the East End.

'Are we there yet?' Ulrike asked.

'Past the half-way mark.'

They were well away from any of the bridges. He could not see the fog lanterns on either bank.

This was about right.

He upped oars.

'What is it?'

Yefimovich took the hook from under his seat.

'The Beast, Ulrike…'

'What? Where?'

He stood up. 'The Beast is about to kill you.'

He struck. Blood spurted and his shoulder felt wrenched.

The look of surprise stayed in her eyes, even with the hook sunk into her forehead.

He pulled the weapon free and began his Beast-work.

VII

THE LUITPOLDSTRASSE STATION was a bedlam. When Harald had been there in the afternoon, just after his fight with Joost Rademakers, there had been a loose crowd of annoyed people outside, hurling curses and pebbles at the front of the building. Now there was a tight crowd of furious people and they were hurling more than words and small stones. The front windows had been smashed out and flaming torches were being lobbed into the station, lying on the floor to be stamped out by one of the officers of the watch. Harald wished he had not taken the trouble to push through the crowd to get into the place, since the crowd seemed to have closed behind him like a trap. And, to cap his carelessness, he had brought the scryer with him and needlessly subjected her to danger. This was what the Second Siege of Praag must have been like.

'Damn it,' said Thommy Haldestaake, an old skull thumping copper, 'I'm going to break out the crossbows. That'll dispel the bastards.'

Thommy looked at Dickon, who was sitting glumly in the corner, having evidently given up on the whole thing. He had a steaming pot of tea on his table and was occasionally gulping down cups of the stuff.

The captain didn't stamp on Thommy's suggestion and so the officer picked the station keyring off Dickon's desk and walked towards the armoury, sorting out the keys to the double lock.

'No,' said Harald.

Thommy stopped and turned round to outstare him.

Harald stood up and rubbed his forehead, where he still wore one of the bruises Rademakers had given him, and let his hand fall to rest on the hilt of his Magnin knife.

When he was first appointed to the watch, he had been partnered with Thommy. The old officer had shown him all the ways that a cunning copper could augment his salary, by accepting the occasional crown or two and turning his back on the odd crime, or by insisting on a modest cut of the profits of any pimps, dicers, weirdroot vendors or pickpockets who wanted to stay in business on his beat. Harald had gone straight to Captain Gebhardt, Dickon's predecessor, and set out his evidence against the bent watchman, and been surprised when Gebhardt simply turned him out of the office.

Thommy explained that he had forgotten to mention that, in addition to making a profit, it was traditional for a watchman to tithe a portion of his personal earnings and turn them over to the captain. Then Thommy had tried to beat Harald to a bloody pulp.

That had been a long time ago and Thommy had been younger. But it had been an even match and neither had emerged the clear victor. Thommy's cheekbones were still asymmetrical and Harald still had the trace of a knife-slash across his hip.

Thommy put the first key in the lock and turned it. The works creaked.

'Thommy, I said no.'

The old copper turned, growling, and came at him like a wrestler.

This time it would be decisive. But Harald didn't have time for a head-to-head. So it would also have to be quick.

Harald pulled out his Magnin, tossed it in the air, caught it by the blade and hurled it.

He was merciful and the hilt slammed into Thommy's skull, stopping him in his charge. He blundered forwards, but was already senseless. Harald picked up his knife. Thommy was in an instant deep sleep, stretched out on the rough wooden floor.

Dickon didn't complain. His tidy world of regular bribes and comfortable corruption was falling down around his helmet. He swallowed some tea.

A torch came through the window and Harald caught it in the air, returning it to the foggy night with a powerful throw.

He and Rosanna had come back to have Dickon put the word out that Wolf von Mecklenberg was wanted for questioning. But the captain was no longer able to take care of that simple job, or even interested in Harald's case. The Beast was taking a very low priority this evening.

'Dickon,' Harald said, 'this place will catch fire eventually. Get your men out.'

Dickon looked up, but didn't seem to know where he was.

Harald stood over him and slapped his face with his open hand. The captain mumbled.

Rosanna stood by him. She picked up Dickon's half-full mug and sniffed the tea sloshing in it.

'Weirdjuice,' she said.

Harald tipped Dickon's head back and looked into his eyes. The captain wasn't seeing anything real.

'You dolt,' he said, with feeling. Dickon smiled, drooling a little.

There was a crash and a wagonwheel smashed through the window, sweeping in most of the casement. There were burning rags tied to it. The whole thing had been soaked in lamp-oil.

Thommy moaned and tried to get up.

The keyring was dangling from the armoury door. Harald got it and tossed it to Rosanna.

'Find someone half-decent and have him open up the cells. There'll only be whores, drunks and vagrants down

there. Get the prisoners out and tell any watchmen you find
to leave as well.'

The scryer went without question.

Harald looked at Thommy and Dickon. It was up to him
to make sure that neither of these deadweights got burned
to death in a fire.

He was tempted to leave them, but resisted.

The fire was spreading from the burning wheel. Dickon's
potted plants were aflame and the blaze was spreading to a
cabinet stuffed with arrest scrolls. The Luitpoldstrasse
Station was a lost ship and it was up to Harald to get everyone evacuated.

Outside, people were shouting, 'Death to the watch!'

Great.

Harald picked up Thommy in a fireman's hold. The old
officer accepted too many bribes in pies and cream, and
Harald's knees buckled. But he stayed upright.

'Death to the Emperor!'

In the narrow passage outside, there were drunks and
watchmen scrapping with each other and trying to get out of
the front doors. They were emerging into a hail of cobblestones and bits of wood.

A lieutenant of the Imperial Militia was trying to keep
order, rattling off tactical instructions which everyone was
ignoring.

'Down with green velvet!'

Two coppers were deliberately stripping their tabards and
insignia, arguing over a civilian's cloak. That was one way to
resign from the watch.

'Death to Sigmar!'

Harald butted his way through and dumped Thommy on
the steps of the station, rolling him towards the crowd. A
pebble stung against his hand and he heard the crowd call
for his blood.

'Death... Death... Death!'

The militiaman came out of the station and his shiny
breastplate made a fine target. Stones put dents in it and the
lieutenant staggered. Harald pulled him out of the way and
tossed him into the crowd.

It was like a game. Once you were part of the crowd, you weren't the enemy any more. Harald heard the lieutenant shouting, 'Death to the watch!' with the worst of them.

He fought against the thinning stream of watchmen and petty criminals, and got back into the station. Almost everyone else was out. There were fires everywhere now, steadily growing. A wall collapsed and a ground-cloud of dust swept around his shins.

'Death to everyone!'

Rosanna came up from the jail area. 'All the cells are empty now,' she said.

'Get out,' he said. 'I'll find Dickon and follow you. We're closing down this station. It was a shithole anyway…'

Dickon staggered into the passage. One sleeve was on fire, but he couldn't make his hand work to smother it. He rubbed against a wall but the flames persisted.

Harald ripped the captain's jacket off and threw it away. Dickon looked offended.

'Good coat, that,' he said. 'Briechs Brothers of Schwarzwasserstrasse.'

Like a child, Dickon allowed himself to be led out of the station.

As the three of them came out of the station, the roof fell in and a cloud of hot air, smoke, dust and cinders exploded through the doors behind them, pushing them down the stairs.

The crowd was retreating now. A few watchmen were down in the street, being thoroughly kicked. Harald saw one of the officers who had been struggling into civilian gear standing shoulder to shoulder with the mob, putting the boot in to his former sergeant.

'Death to the tyrants!'

The whole quarter was in flames.

He looked around for Rosanna and saw her struggling. Two militiamen and a Fish wearing the insignia of the Revolutionist Movement were fighting over her like dogs arguing over a scrap of meat.

They all wanted death for someone-or-other, he had gathered that much.

Harald thumped one militiaman and pulled Rosanna out of the melée. The revolutionary raised a club, but caught the look in Harald's eyes and backed off.

'Filthy Harald,' he muttered, panic growing, 'Filthy Harald is back!'

The revolutionist – whom Harald could not remember ever having met – turned and ran, spreading the news.

Harald felt a kind of exhilaration in the man's instinctive fear. The urge to shout was contagious.

The mob was breaking and retreating. 'I'm back,' he shouted at them. 'Filthy Harald is back!'

The fog was still thick, but the fires made it easier to see things. The crowd was swarming away from the burning station, flowing like a tide of molten lead, streaming into side-streets.

There were cloaks and coats underfoot. People had ventured out wrapped up for the fog and found themselves next to the bonfires. There would be chills and fevers when the blazes died.

Rosanna was saying something. 'There isn't one Beast… they're all Beasts…'

The rioting had passed on to some new battlefield. It would hit the Street of a Hundred Taverns in force next. Later, it would run and either sweep across the river to the palace or head north towards the University. Maybe it would split in two. Maybe it was not that localized. It could be happening like this all over the city.

Luitpoldstrasse was empty now and a terrible quiet fell. Harald heard the crackle of burning buildings and the low groaning of people in pain. There was blood in his mouth. He spat it out.

Thommy was lying face down and bloodied. He might have been alive. Dickon was sitting cross-legged in the street, trying on a succession of cast-off garments to replace his Briechs Brothers coat. He was a broken man, which at least saved Harald the bother of breaking him.

The fog was agitated, still swirling to fill in the spaces so recently occupied by the mob.

He turned to Rosanna.

She was standing stiff, arms by her sides, as if fighting a sudden paralysis. The vein in her forehead was pulsing and her eyes were wide.

He reached out to shake her, but stopped himself before he touched her. He didn't want to break her contact, whatever it was.

'What can you see?' he asked.

Her lips moved and she croaked a word. He couldn't understand.

'What is it?'

Despite the fires, it was a cold night. Harald felt a chill.

Rosanna croaked again, clearer this time.

'Near,' she said, 'near.'

VIII

THERE HAD BEEN some rowdiness out on the street, but nothing the Templars couldn't handle. He had charged Cleric-Captain Hoven with keeping order and knew he could depend on the man to be a true servant of Sigmar.

As his coach trundled through the checkpoints, Mikael Hasselstein was deeply troubled.

He had not heard from Yelle all day. His nerves were drawn as tight as bowstrings.

At the Matthias II, the green velvet carpet was laid down in the street. There were footmen with torches to light the way through the fog to the inn.

Hasselstein hurried across the pavement and through the doors. The Matthias II was empty of its usual patrons, being staffed only by footmen and waiters in the livery of the Bretonnian ambassador. It had been redecorated in the colours of Bretonnia for the occasion and a buffet was laid out against one wall.

'Lector,' said de la Rougierre, bowing low, 'welcome…'

Hasselstein was polite to the silly little dwarf and presented his ring of office to be kissed.

'You are the first of my guests. The company tonight will be most distinguished. Can I interest you in a Bretonnian vintage?'

'No, I think not... well, maybe, yes.'

The ambassador grinned broadly and snapped his stubby fingers. A servant girl in a tight bodice decanted a full goblet of sparkling Vin de Couronne.

The drink might relax him a little.

The girl flounced off and Hasselstein noticed just how close the cut of her uniform was. He suspected that the buffoon dwarf had had a hand in the design of the outfits worn by his female servants.

Leos von Liebewitz might be the best duellist in the Empire, but Etienne de la Rougierre could lay claim, in another sense, to being the most prominent swordsman.

He thought of his mistress and her moods. She was as unpredictable as an Altdorf fog and as dangerously deep. Tonight, he must confirm his position with Yelle, or risk madness.

Of course, de la Rougierre must have some diplomatic scheme or other to propose, and he should pay attention to that as well.

The next to arrive was the future Emperor Luitpold, attended by two huge guardsmen in full armour.

'Rough night,' he said. 'Half the city is on fire.'

The young man was still a child in many ways and prone to exaggeration.

'Really, highness?' Hasselstein said, politely. 'You surprise me.'

'It's the fog,' the young man said. 'It always makes people funny in the head.'

'The fog, yes.'

He was thinking of Yelle, of her lips, her eyes, the delicate softness of her...

'Fog.'

The serving girl gave the Prince a drink and he thanked her. She nearly swooned, obviously smitten with the young man, for his stature as future Emperor if not for his ordinary good looks. For his part, Luitpold was equally obviously staggered by her, especially when she leaned forward to fill his goblet. The palace maids certainly didn't look like that.

'You know,' the heir to the Empire said, 'I could have sworn I saw something in the corner of the room... something small, with bright eyes...'

De la Rougierre was offended. 'Highness, that is impossible. I had all the rats caught and killed this afternoon...'

...and they would be gracing the table this evening, if Hasselstein's prejudices about Bretonnian cuisine were to be confirmed.

'...I have ensured that this establishment is fit for the most high-born and courtly of guests...'

The dwarf winked, his grin taking on a lascivious tone.

'...if, however, graced with a manner of entertainment one would not find at the stuffier court sort of affair.'

De la Rougierre was practically dancing a jig. He would be more fitted to the position of jester than ambassador. It really was time the Emperor protested to King Charles about the little idiot.

'I've secured the services of a variety of entertainers the like of whom one rarely sees. They appeal, I hope, to the more *sophisticated* tastes, to the more *liberated* palate...'

Hasselstein thought he knew what the dwarf meant and was a little annoyed. He had Yelle to think of and did not want to be distracted by some cheap Bretonnian peepshow.

Another carriage arrived outside, and Hals and Hergard von Tasseninck were admitted. The Grand Prince had a handkerchief clapped to his forehead and was bleeding into it.

'Someone threw a rock at father,' said Hergard.

Hasselstein's goblet was empty and he decided he would like a refill.

This had the makings of a very tiresome evening.

'NEAR...'

Rosanna felt like a tiny fish in the presence of a whale. The creature they hunted was nearby and hungry.

The contact had come out of nowhere and latched onto her brain. She wondered if the Beast had been among the

crowd in Luitpoldstrasse. She could have looked into the
murderer's eyes and only now be feeling the effects.

The presence was overwhelming, freezing her to the spot.
Her bowels wanted to let go, but she fought to control her
body.

Kleindeinst stood back, concerned.

There was violence around him too. He had killed a man
this afternoon and she couldn't look at him without feeling
it. Over and over in her head, Joost Rademakers's throat
crunched under his fist.

Then, she was free.

Gasping, she said, 'He's near. Very near…'

'Where?'

She tried to scry a direction, turning in a circle.

'That way,' she pointed. It was the direction the crowd had
taken.

'Towards the Street of a Hundred Taverns?'

'Yes.'

She imagined the Beast loping along among the crowds,
unseen by them, inflamed by their savagery. He would have
had a taste of blood by now.

'Captain Kleindeinst,' she said.

'Yes?'

She remembered the dark heart of the thing that had
touched her mind. It had been like a concentrated cloud of
blackness, with spears of silver lightning inside it.

'The Beast is getting ready to kill again.'

IX

JOHANN WAS ABLE to arrive without too much fuss, because the Countess Emmanuelle had to make a grand entrance before any of her escorts. She had stepped out of the carriage as if expecting a cheering crowd and been disconcerted by the surly few standing by the inn, growling evilly.

Descending to the green velvet carpet, Johann could feel the hostility radiating at him. A man with a Fish insignia hawked a lump of phlegm onto the carpet and stalked away, disgusted.

Leos half-drew his sword, but thought better of it. If even the Deadly Blade was thinking twice, then something must be seriously wrong.

Elsaesser fussed nervously and tried to hurry them across the pavement. There were shouts off in the distance and they had passed the fire-fighters several times, dashing from one disaster to another.

Inside, Johann accepted de la Rougierre's greetings and took the measure of the company.

Mikael Hasselstein was as near drunk as Johann had ever seen him. He lurched towards them when they came in, but held back. Hals von Tasseninck was showing off a bandage, surrounded by serving girls, and his son was sulking about something. Dien Ch'ing, the Celestial, was sitting calmly, picking at a plateful of food. Marquess Sidonie dropped her glass when Leos walked in and looked around for a weapon, but was unable to find anything.

'Uncle Johann,' said Luitpold, 'how nice to see you.'

Johann bowed a little.

'And you too, Leos, of course.'

The viscount clicked his heels.

'I was afraid it was going to be a dull evening,' the future Emperor said, too loudly, 'but now I see we have a fine crew here tonight.'

Luitpold had had a little to drink and he wasn't used to it. Johann knew that he was honour-bound to look out for the heir. That gave him something else to worry about.

A few surprise guests showed up: Oleg Paradjanov, the Kislevite military attaché; Snorri Svedenborg, one of the legates from Norsca; Mornan Tybalt, gloomily muttering about the sense of his thumb tax bill; and Baron Stefan Todbringer, son and heir to the Graf Boris of Middenheim. That was two more major foreign powers, an important minister of the court and another electoral seat.

He exchanged conventional pleasantries with the dignitaries and tried to watch everyone.

Elsaesser was standing by the door, nibbling on a cold chicken leg, stranded somewhere between servant and guest. Kleindeinst had sent the officer to watch over Johann, but as a spy or a guard he was not sure. The sharp young copper might be useful.

Hasselstein was in a corner with the countess, talking intently, illustrating his points with firm gestures. She looked bored. That would make a change, a man boring Emmanuelle von Liebewitz. At another time, Johann might have derived some amusement from the reversal. But not just now. Where was Wolf? And the Beast?

He had begun to suspect everyone. Most of the people in the room, except obviously Luitpold, were highly likely candidates.

He remembered the scrap of green velvet he had found in the alley adjacent to this place. He was almost tempted to go through all the cloaks in the hall and look for a torn patch. But nothing was ever that easy. Except in bad melodramas.

'Baron Johann,' said the Marquess Sidonie, 'might I speak with you? I'm getting up a petition to present to the Emperor and I was wondering whether you would consider lending your seal to it. As an elector, you have a lot of influence.'

Johann asked the thin-nosed woman what her petition was against.

She sniffed and said, 'Duelling, elector. It should be banned.'

There was a clapping sound and Johann turned to face the small stage at one end of the room. De la Rougierre was standing up, laughing.

'Honoured guests,' he said, raising a goblet, 'welcome to this magnificent affair. I trust that you've all been properly fed and watered...'

Snorri, who had drunk a quite considerable amount, roared his approval.

'That is what I like to hear. Bretonnian hospitality is, as you know, legendary.'

'That's true,' muttered Hasselstein, who had turned away from the countess, 'in the sense that you can't prove it ever existed.'

The dwarf gave the Lector a nasty look and continued: 'I have selected only the best entertainment for your pleasure tonight. Permit me to introduce you to a lady whose talents are substantial...'

The lights dimmed and the curtains parted. A flautist began to play a familiar old tune.

A dancer stepped out onto the stage, but Johann was more interested in the faces of the guests.

Looking at them, as they gazed with expressions ranging from the rapt to the disgusted, he wondered.

Which, if any...?

* * *

THERE WAS FIGHTING throughout the docklands.

Wolf couldn't understand what the fuss was about and couldn't find anyone sane enough to tell him.

He tried to keep out of the way, although he could feel his blood rising. His wet clothes had dried on him like a second skin.

He smelled blood and fire, and gripped his hook as if it were a part of him.

The Hooks and the Fish had formed a temporary, unprecedented alliance and were throwing people off one of the docks. A large crowd cheered with each splash.

Wolf saw that the victims were all in uniform or armour. Templars, militiamen, palace guards, officers of the watch.

'Death to Karl-Franz!' shouted a rabble-rouser.

The men in armour were struggling in the water, trying to cut the leather ties and let it fall off their bodies before it dragged them down. They were thrashing up a white foam.

He couldn't understand it at all. Before the fog blew up, the city had been normal. Now everyone was blood crazy.

A bully laid hands on him and he instinctively lashed out, not with a fist like a man but curved fingers like an animal.

'We've got one that scratches here, lads,' said the bully.

Wolf concentrated hard and made a fist. He broke the man's nose and stuck an elbow in his chest. The man dropped to his knees, hands clasped over his bleeding face.

Wolf ran, hoping to be well away before any of the bully's friends rallied round and decided he could do with another cold bath.

He had his hook in his hand now and would be ready for any further trouble.

He did not know the way to the Wayfarer's Rest and kept looking for an inn or a building he recognized so he could get his bearings.

He collided with a group of young men and knew he was bound for the river. He held up his hook and tensed for a struggle.

But it never came.

'It's von Mecklenberg,' a familiar voice said. 'Wolf.'

Otho Waernicke loomed out of the fog and embraced him. The party were all Leaguers.

'We thought you were done for, for sure. With what happened to Trudi, we were certain the Beast had got you.'

Trudi's name was like an arrow sinking in up to the feathers.

'Trudi? The Beast?'

Otho didn't have time, or the desire, to explain.

'The wine-drinking contest is off,' the student leader said. 'Three hundred years of tradition scuppered. It's terrible.'

'We're fighting for the Emperor,' a student declared. 'The call has gone out to all the Leagues. The forces of revolution are inside the walls and we must all stand up or fall into perdition.'

It was a fine speech and would have been finer if the deliverer hadn't slurred almost all his words, been supported by two of his fellows and breathed out Estalian sherry in its gaseous form.

'Where's Trudi?' Wolf asked Otho.

The student leader couldn't conceal anything. 'Dead, Wolf. It was the Beast. Last night...'

Wolf dropped to all fours and howled. The yell of his grief rose in his throat and escaped into the night, reverberating throughout the quarter.

Otho and the Leaguers stood back, amazed. The patriot was dumbstruck.

Wolf stood on his hind legs and tore at himself. His hook ripped his shirt and ploughed through his chest hair. He didn't feel the new pain, for his heart had already been pierced.

He turned from his friends and ran, more animal than man. He ran through fog and fire, his mind racing ahead of itself, trying not to believe what he knew must be true.

He was the monster. He had always been the monster. Even before Cicatrice.

In his mouth, his shifting teeth hurt.

X

As MILIZIA DANCED, de la Rougierre's mouth filled with spittle. The big woman was monumental, magnificent, magisterial. For her, he would usurp a kingdom, slaughter a brother, betray his honour.

And tonight he would have her all to himself, to do with as he saw fit.

ROSANNA LED HIM. His knife out, he followed her.

'This way, this way, this way,' she muttered, over and over.

She was dowsing for the Beast.

They were in the ladder of streets running parallel to the Street of a Hundred Taverns, zig-zagging closer to the main thoroughfare.

Occasionally, they passed people running one way or another, but a look at Harald's knife convinced them to keep going and leave the odd pair alone. An animal had screamed a few moments ago, but it was silent – dead? – now.

He could feel it too, now. He had never thought of himself as having a gift, but the turmoil in his stomach must mean something. The Beast was near.

Harald gripped the hilt of his Magnin and saw the fires gleam in the polished surfaces of the blade.

His guts gnawed at themselves.

When they caught the Beast, the murderer would live only long enough to confess before witnesses. Then, it would be ended. Harald's justice was neater and more final than that of the courts. No cells, no lawyers, no ropes. Just a quick, clean thrust.

Maybe then he would be able to eat again.

At the end of the street, someone stood, looking up into the sky, panting as he tried to peer through the fog.

Harald's stomach went quiet.

'Be careful,' he told the scryer.

She was still muttering, still leading him.

The man in the fog let out a cry that could not have come from a human throat.

Rosanna stopped and Harald stepped in front of her.

He had taken no chances with his weapon. When commissioning his knife, he had instructed Magnin to stir a little silver into the steel. Nothing, living or dead, would survive its sharp kiss.

The thing that had howled hunched over, its arms touching the cobbles like forelegs. A claw-thing was scraped on the stone.

It advanced, more like an animal than a human being.

Harald held up his knife for a throw...

They could see its yellow and red eyes, glowing in its dark face.

Rosanna touched his arm, holding him back.

'No,' she said, 'don't kill it yet. We have to be sure.'

Dead would have been sure enough for Harald, but the scryer had been right so far.

A fire flared up to the left of them, windows exploding from a house, and light spilled into the street.

The thing's face was human, and recognizable from Rosanna's sketch.

'Wolf,' she said, 'give yourself up.'

The Elector of Sudenland's brother crouched, tensed to leap. Harald's knife went up and his eye fixed on the madman's exposed, bloody chest. One flick and the blade would be through his heart.

'Wolf,' Rosanna said, soothing...

Von Mecklenberg stood up. His claw was nothing but a docker's hook.

He was confused.

Harald knew Rosanna was doing something.

'Usually, I pick up,' she whispered, 'but sometimes I can send...'

Wolf looked panicked. He was shivering. He might have been a monster, but now he was just a frightened young man.

'What...'

'I'm sending him Trudi's death.'

Wolf howled again.

EMMANUELLE VON LIEBEWITZ, Countess-Elector of Nuln, was bored, and boredom made her angry.

She had not ventured out on this hell of a night to watch some cowlike creature shake her udders all over a stage.

It was most disappointing after the magnificence of the von Tasseninck ball. Most disappointing.

And Mikael was being tedious beyond words. Lector of Sigmar or not, he would have to join Dany and the others in the doghouse.

Of course, she could always pass him on to Leos. She would like that, even if Mikael would be disgusted.

No, with this one, that would be too big a risk.

'Yelle,' he whispered to her, loudly. 'Yelle, answer me...'

She pretended to be interested in the show.

Yes, Mikael was on the Out List.

WOLF CLAPPED HIS hands over his ears – his hook scraping his scalp – but could not shut out the pictures in his head.

It was the red-headed girl. She was doing it.

The tall, wide-shouldered man's knife shone.

He sensed, *saw*, Trudi dying. In his mind, he was murderer *and* victim. It was too much to bear.

Trudi!

He choked back a howl. He was a man, not an animal.

The blood gushed and the flesh tore. It was extended, painful and played over and over again. It was slow and fast at the same time, like a weirdroot rush.

With an effort, he broke away from the girl and fled.

He could hear them coming after him, but he ran on strong, swift legs. He thought he could outdistance the pursuers.

He was quarry and huntsman in one.

LUITPOLD HAD NEVER seen anything like Milizia. He did not believe, even in his most secret dreams, that there were actually women like her.

In the palace libraries, there were various locked volumes devoted to the arts of amorousness, and he had been a skilled lockpick since his childhood. He had always assumed that the illustrations were exaggerated. Certainly, none of the women he had had contact with could have hoped to fill out their fantastic frames. Not even the Countess Emmanuelle, who had briefly taken a slightly creepy interest in him – because of what he would be rather than who he was. But Milizia was a woodcut come to life. And, with each scarf, more of her was disclosed.

Luitpold's mouth had gone dry.

He crossed his legs to prevent embarrassment.

When he was Emperor, he thought, he could have anything he wanted. He tried to keep a straight face.

A servant girl, almost as generously proportioned as Milizia, brought him some more wine and he smiled at her like an idiot.

A duel to the death in the morning and now Milizia. In his secret diary, he would mark this down as a Five Star Day.

ULRIKE WAS HEAVIER dead than she had been alive. Luckily, he had had the cloak to wrap her in.

He walked slowly through the crowds, as if shattered by the shock, the corpse in his hands. He let her hair trail on the ground and had exposed her pale face, with the red hole in the forehead, to the air.

As the people realized who it was he held, they fell silent. One or two devout atheists made the sign of Sigmar or some other god. Hats came off heads and were held to breasts. More than one revolutionist fell into a fit of sobbing.

At the entrance to the Street of Many Taverns, just across the way from the Old Emperor Bridge, he ran into Prince Kloszowski's brigade of student insurrectionists. They had just successfully broken through the positions of the Imperial Militia and were enthusiastically tossing soldiers into the river.

Kloszowski saw Ulrike's face and was stopped dead.

'I shall commit suicide,' he said, with feeling.

Yefimovich held the corpse up, so everyone could see who it was.

'No,' Kloszowski shouted, changing his mind, 'that would be too easy. I shall become a celibate and dedicate myself forever to the memory of the Angel of the Revolution!'

Yefimovich laid her down and opened the cloak to disclose the extent of the mutilation. There were gasps of horror.

'No,' said the Prince, 'that too is mere cowardice. I shall write an epic poem about her life. Through me, Ulrike shall live forever.'

'What happened,' asked Brustellin, 'for Sigmar's sake, Yefimovich, what happened?'

'It was the Beast,' he replied. 'He struck her down.'

The crowd hissed. 'The Beast, the Beast, the Beast!' Yefimovich could feel the emotions running through the mass of people, grief, horror, anger, hatred.

'Death to the Beast!' someone shouted.

'Yes,' cried Yefimovich, 'death to the Beast!'

He snatched at the bloody green velvet and held it up.

'I didn't see his face,' he said, 'but he wore this!'

Everyone knew what that meant.

The mob would comb the city for aristocrats, courtiers, palace servants, diplomats. Even anyone who wore green. Then, there would be a glorious bloodbath. A revolution.

'Death to the green velvet,' he shouted.

...and tomorrow, when the Emperor's people woke up, there would be reprisals. The city would be ruined by the upheaval, the great made low and the meagre raised on high.

'Death to the green velvet, death to the Beast!'

They lifted him up, taking up and amplifying his shouts. He heard the word 'death' over and over, coming as one voice from the mob's thousand mouths.

The crowd walked over Ulrike and marched up the Street of a Hundred Taverns.

Yefimovich offered up this, his concrete prayer to Tzeentch, the Changer of Ways, and knew that the Chaos Power was pleased with him.

XI

MILIZIA THREW IN every move she knew and let the music ripple through her. She might be big, but she had a lot of muscle control. She knew exactly what she was doing with her body.

Etienne was a conquest already, so she let him alone, targeting others.

As usual, stepping out into the light, she immediately picked the prospects. Young men were best, especially if they were quiet, withdrawn, a little embarrassed. Those were the ones who turned to fire most rapidly, who reached most easily into their pouches and came up with the coin.

This afternoon, the dwarf had given her quite a workout. She wondered if she was up to another session, with a more normally-sized lover. In the end, it was worthwhile. Each pfennig got her nearer to escaping from Gropius and the Flamingo Club.

There were two good prospects.

First, there was the young man sitting near the stage, barely restraining himself. She found that the music often took her near him and she took care to lean over and make

226

her shoulders work hard. She let a scarf drip away from her big ridiculous tits and stroked herself. That always gave the customers a charge, the fools.

The Number Two possibility was a little older and a lot quieter. Sitting back a way, his face was in darkness, but she got the impression of a softly handsome man. He was feigning total lack of interest, but she could see through that. He was so elaborately not looking at her, that she knew his interest was keen.

The Front Seat Boy would be easier, but perhaps Number Two would be more rewarding. Once he was started, he might be a real swordsman.

This was a strange commission, she thought. The Bretonnian dwarf and his Celestial friend were up to something. Everybody in this room wanted something and was working hard to get it. She was no different.

She climbed the strong curtains and scissored her legs in the air. The big Norseman yelled his approval and the beautiful woman sitting in front of him looking angrier and angrier glanced death at her.

She went back to the Front Seat Boy and gave him some more interesting views. She unpeeled a scarf from around her middle, allowing the paste gem in her belly-button to catch the light, and gently flicked out with it, brushing the boy's nose. He was startled, but laughed.

Kneeling down, she looped the scarf around the boy's neck and worked away. His eyes were firmly fixed on her chest, and she noticed that he wore more jewelry than most ladies of the court. His face was familiar, but she did not know who he was.

Two men in armour were marching towards them, seriously intent on protecting their charge from strangulation.

She took back her scarf and stood up, working her hips from side to side.

Suddenly, she knew where she had seen a face like that before. In profile, it was somewhere very close to her heart. On one face of the Karl-Franz crown.

That put the Front Seat Boy out of her dicing league. She was ambitious, but she knew her limitations.

The future Emperor was disappointed, but his metal covered bodyguards obviously felt better.

Maybe in a few years, she thought, he would give the household halberdiers the slip and search her out. Even Emperors are men, in the end.

The flautist was in a frenzy now. Milizia had heard he was half-elf, or something. She moved faster, loosening the remaining scarves.

Her chest was tired of jiggling and she had an ache in one ankle. But she danced on.

Etienne was clapping in time to the music and the Norseman was singing along. At least half the audience was appreciative.

She wondered about the Celestial. Miele at the Flamingo had been with a Cathayan once and claimed it was a fantastic experience. He had supposedly been the master of some mystic art or other and it turned out to have applications beyond the obvious.

No, the Celestial was too wrapped up in his own schemes even to pay attention.

That left Number Two.

She vaulted off the stage, almost cartwheeling, and strode towards the Shy Swordsman.

He would be hard to draw out, but she had never failed yet.

'Milizia,' Miele had said, 'you could seduce the statue of Sigmar outside the Temple.'

She poked out her tongue and licked her lips.

Number Two shrank back into the darkness.

Gently, gently...

She had worked up a sweat and it was rolling like oil down her body.

It would be a struggle, but she would dance on...

WOLF RAN, TRYING to escape, trying to escape the witch and the knifeman, but also to escape from the thing inside him.

Trudi was dead. And the witch had shown him killing her.

He was on the Street of a Hundred Taverns. A mob was surging down it, calling for blood.

He was overwhelmed by the smell of fear, of anger.

He was pushed against the wall of Bruno's Brewhouse by the press of people. His chest hurt where he had cut himself.

He tried to struggle free and heard a scream, sharp and pained, close by his head.

He realized he had dragged his hook up through a man's back.

He tried to apologise, but could only gabble. He was practically sobbing.

His hook came free and the man staggered off, blood flowing, apparently without noticing his wound.

There was a green velvet carpet down by the Matthias II. The mob snatched it up and it was torn instantly to shreds.

'Death to the green velvet.'

Wolf didn't understand.

He saw Yefimovich, the agitator, among the crowds, his arms waving.

He staggered into the alley between the two inns, making his way towards the sound of flowing water.

He was free of the crush.

His hand went through an open window and, on an impulse, he pulled himself through into the darkness.

There was darkness outside, but it was the dark in himself that made him terrified.

DE LA ROUGIERRE watched Milizia trying hard with young von Liebewitz and felt sorry for the silly girl. There was no way she could know she was wasting her time on him.

Still, this was proving to be a most interesting and rewarding evening.

'OUT OF OUR way,' Harald said, 'let us through.'

Rosanna supposed there were very few men in the Empire who could make themselves be listened to in a situation like this.

The Street of a Hundred Taverns was a battleground again, but on a larger scale than before. The Hooks and the Fish were fighting side by side, following Yefimovich's revolutionaries. And the League of Karl-Franz was pitching in to

back up the Knights Templar, the palace guard and what little was left of the watch.

She realized that more people were being killed within
her sight at this very moment than the Beast had managed
throughout his rampage.

Captain Kleindeinst shouldered his way through.

Wolf still left a trail and she could still fix on it.

The poor creature was mad with fear. This was not the
predator she had imagined.

They were very near where this had all started for her, the
alley where they had found Margarethe Ruttmann.

HELMUT ELSAESSER COULDN'T be less interested in Milizia. Even
the Countess Emmanuelle didn't hold much attraction for
him this evening.

It was in the air, like ozone. A kind of excitement that was
terrible and wonderful at the same time.

The music gave him a headache.

Inside, he felt feverish, but his face and hands were cold,
almost shivering.

Near the door, he could hear something of what was
going on outside.

A lot of people were shouting and there was great destruc-
tion.

He should do something. But he was under orders to stay
with the Baron Johann.

Very well. He would follow the example of brave Sigmar
and hold his position to the last.

XII

PROFESSOR BRUSTELLIN'S HEART was broken and so he had thrown himself into the conflict, determined to end his life and lie next to his beloved Ulrike. Without an Angel, the Revolution was doomed, but at least it could die heroically, setting an example. The flame he had lit would burn steadily for a long time. And the fuse would get steadily shorter. The Empire would explode in the end. It was a historical inevitability. Nothing ever stays the same.

He had a hook in his hand and was fighting with the watch. He saw the face of Professor Scheydt, who had had him flogged and expelled, in every watchman he dragged down and ripped.

He recognized some of his former students, fighting on both sides. The old faithful inkies were with the revolution, and the decadent League of Karl-Franz fought for the standard of the oppressors.

He never felt the swordthrust that killed him.

It was accidental, the Hook who struck the fatal blow being unused to the weapon he had taken from a fallen Templar. The man knew what he had done, but never told his comrades, simply taking to drink whenever the names of the martyr heroes of the revolution were recited.

Scythed through the neck and trampled underfoot, Brustellin left behind a book that would inspire revolutions, in the Empire and in distant lands, for centuries after his death.

Of course, that was little comfort to him.

WHAT IS THIS fool woman doing?

Leos von Liebewitz was outraged. If he was being insulted, then the dwarf would pay for it.

The ridiculous woman continued to flaunt herself.

Leos was disgusted.

HARALD FOUND THE open window.

'He went through here?'

The scryer told him he was right.

He stabbed into the darkness, then pulled himself through. His shoulders scraped.

He flicked his tinderbox and found himself in a store-room.

'He's not here. Come in.'

Rosanna squeezed and he helped her.

The room was neglected and there were footprints in the dust.

'An easy trail?'

'Careful,' she said.

'I know. A cornered Beast is dangerous.'

They pushed through a door. There was music coming from somewhere.

THE BEAST WAS *straining inside the man-shell, aching for blood, for flesh. The music excited it.*

Its claws popped out.

THE FRONT DOORS of the Matthias II gave way like boxwood.

Yefimovich led the mob into the inn. It could not have been better. In the hallway, three very frightened footmen were clustered by an overburdened coat rack.

There was a line of green velvet cloaks.
The crowd screamed.

WHAT WAS THIS accursed interruption?
De la Rougierre vowed that the landlord would suffer for allowing this to happen.
Even Milizia was distracted enough to miss a few steps.

JOHANN STOOD UP and signed to Elsaesser. His first duty was to protect the future Emperor.
There must be a back way out of this place.
He looked around. There were four visible doors, not counting any that might be behind the stage curtains.
That might be the safest route, through the dressing rooms. There was bound to be a performers' entrance.
The young officer stepped forwards, but tripped. There was a flood of people into the room. Countess Emmanuelle screamed. She hated being in a room with commoners.
Elsaesser was struggling.
'Highness,' Johann said, 'come with me.'
Luitpold had been in a daze, but Johann pulled him out of it. Taking his hand, he dragged him up onto the stage. The heir's bodyguards saw what he was doing and tried to block the surge of the crowd with a few prods of their halberds.
There was a backstage door.
'Highness,' he said, 'through here...'
'But–'
'No arguments. Do it. Now.'
The future Emperor went before him.
Johann had a sword in his hand. He would be turning into Leos von Liebewitz next.
There was a great deal of shouting out in the banquet room. The word 'death' was being used a lot.
Johann wrenched open the backstage door, not caring whether it was locked or not.
Someone was behind the door.
He pushed forwards, squeezing between Johann and Luitpold, as if running from his own mob of would-be executioners.

Johann felt the old phantom knife in his heart.

'Wolf!'

His brother was startled by his own name and half-turned...

There were more people coming through the door.

Harald Kleindeinst. Rosanna Ophuls.

Johann had a bad feeling about this.

'Wolf,' he said. 'Wolf...'

Then he didn't have anything more to say.

Wolf was frozen, not sure whether to turn to or away from him.

Then, the curtain fell down and everything went dark.

YEFIMOVICH WAS CARRIED away by revolutionist zeal.

He didn't care if he killed for Tzeentch or for Social Justice, just so long as he killed.

Fires were set around him and he strode through them.

'Green velvet,' he cried, looking around the room.

A woman caught his eye, trying to get through a door side-ways to avoid getting her dress trapped.

Jewels sparkled on her bosom.

Daggers drawn, he went for her...

DIEN CH'ING SAT quietly and let whatever would come come.

Someone tried to put a knife into his eye, but he swept it away with a simple movement.

After that, he was left alone.

This was much more amusing than the clumsy, grotesque-bodied dancer had been.

ROSANNA FOUND JOHANN and helped him struggle to throw off the thick red curtain.

They didn't have to talk about Wolf. A touch was enough for the exchange of views.

If Wolf was the killer, Johann wanted him caught. Not killed, but caught.

Fine. He could argue with Captain Kleindeinst later.

When they were free, the inn was a hell of tangled bodies. Everyone was shouting at the top of their voice.

She sensed a very powerful, very evil presence. Another one.

EMMANUELLE LIFTED HER skirts and ran. The horrible man was chasing her, daggers slicing through the air.

She was in a dead end. Backing down a dark passage, she had come up against a wall.

She prayed to all the gods. She asked for forgiveness. Mama, Papa, forgive me! Leos, forgive me!

The horrible man – Yefimovich the fire-breather – was coming slowly now that she was trapped, enjoying himself, making passes in the air.

'Snick-snack,' he said.

As he came into the darkness, she saw that his features weren't quite natural. Something was shining under the skin, making his face look like a luminous mask.

There was something with him, something small and horrid that scuttled along the ceiling.

She screamed.

Yefimovich laughed.

LEOS HAD HIS sword out and was holding off the mob.

'Look out,' someone said, 'he's dangerous.'

The fool woman was clinging to his shoulder, using him to shield her naked body. She might get in the way if it were to come to a slash-up fight.

He prodded the air in front of several revolutionists.

Their enthusiasm for the overthrow of the aristocracy was pricked and they backed away.

Cowards! He should have expected no more from peasant rabble.

HARALD SLICED THROUGH the curtain with his blade and stood up, shaking the heavy folds off his shoulders.

There were a lot of dangerous people in the room. But Wolf wasn't one of them.

'YELLE,' HASSELSTEIN SHOUTED, charging down the corridor.

The fire-breather was standing over his mistress, cackling.

The Lector was not a man of action. He was a strategist, a tactician, a politician. Within the Cult of Sigmar, he had chosen the Order of the Anvil over the Knights of the Fiery Heart, studying the Law rather than the Arts of Combat.

But he picked up a chair and ran down the corridor, shouting.

The chair smashed into Yefimovich and came to pieces. He found himself holding a leg and bludgeoned the agitator's head with it.

Yelle was screaming at the top of her lungs.

Her hands reached out and grabbed at Yefimovich's face…

…and it came off.

It was like a burst of light in the passage.

Emmanuelle shut her eyes, but the fiery face still burned in her mind.

XIII

ELSAESSER HAD BEEN forced into a backroom. He looked
around for something useful as a weapon and found a
kegspike.

'Look,' said a hard voice, 'it's an inky!'

Two Leaguers were in the room, armed with heavy clubs.

'Let's spill his swotty brains!'

He recognized them.

They had applauded at Brustellin's expulsion, and stolen
the library's copies of the professor's books to use as privy
paper.

'Stay back,' he said, waving his spike.

'What have you got which could make us, quill-head?'

Elsaesser reached into his jacket.

'This,' he said, producing his copper badge.

'Now,' he said, 'up against the wall and spread your legs,
ape-men!'

YEFIMOVICH'S FACE WAS gone.

The cleric of Sigmar was a trembling wreck. And the
countess-elector a screaming harpy.

Respighi opened the hidden door, releasing the catch at the top.

The High Priest of Tzeentch stepped into another room.

NUMBER TWO WAS a wash-out, Milizia decided, and gave him the shove. She could tell he wasn't interested in girls much.

Her first mission now was to get out of this mess.

No, make that second. First, she needed some clothes.

Gallantly, the Norseman threw his fur waistcoat at her. Belted around her waist, it was like a dress.

Now, escape.

She made a run for the door.

THEY HAD HALS von Tasseninck down on the floor and were kicking the teeth out of his head.

The Grand Prince's idiot son was trying to force a window and shrieking whenever anyone tried to touch him.

Harald waded into the brawl and pulled two people away from the elector's boot party. He knocked their heads together and dropped them on the floor. The rest of the kickers backed away.

Harald picked the Grand Prince up and looked into his battered and bloody face.

'Good evening, elector,' he said. 'Remember me?'

MILIZIA WAS IN the dark. She was outside the inn, in an alley. The cobbles were like ice chunks under her bare feet.

At least she was safe now.

THE BEAST WAS *savage, but it could be calm when it had to be.*

Its chosen prey scented, it stalked her, ignoring the other blood scents whirling around in the air like fog.

Its claw was out.

THE FIGHTING WAS dying down now, dwindling to mere confusion. Johann had been shielding the Prince with his body, but the young man had slipped away somewhere. He prayed to Sigmar that Luitpold was sensible enough to stay away from knives and fires.

'Yefimovich's an altered,' someone had said.

'It's true, I saw him. His head is a living flame.'

'What?'

The revolutionists were getting rapidly disillusioned with their leader. No one was sure what was going on.

Suddenly, Johann was surrounded by strangers. Harald was there, with the von Tassenincks. And so was Rosanna, over with the Norseman, the Kislevite and the blue-faced, parrot-nosed Marquess Sidonie. Mornan Tybalt was sobbing and rubbing injured hands; someone had clipped one of his thumbs for him, reducing his taxable digits by one half.

But everyone else in the de la Rougierre party had spilled out into the dark.

MILIZIA WAS ALMOST out of the alley when she bumped into him.

'You,' she said, 'out of my way.'

The shape stood firm and then stepped forwards. She backed away.

Its eyes were shining.

She felt a scream beginning...

THE CLAW STUCK into Rosanna's mind.

'Johann,' she shouted, '*it's happening now!*'

THE BEAST'S CLAW *stuck into the girl's stomach and her eyes clouded.*

There was no time for a proper job.

HARALD AND THE baron collided in the door Rosanna was pointing at.

He swore and helped the elector up.

Rosanna was with them.

'Which way?' he asked her.

'The alley. The way we came.'

The passage was full of bodies. They had to struggle.

Harald realized that Rosanna was screaming.

'*It's killing me!*'

* * *

IT WAS KILLING her!

JOHANN THUMPED SOMEONE out of the way, but it was useless. The failed revolutionists were streaming against them, pushing them backwards.

Tears were pouring from Rosanna's eyes. Her screams scratched at his mind.

It was if he could feel it too.

ELSAESSER HAD KNOCKED the Leaguers out with a tap apiece from his spike and was feeling quite chipper. That was a blow for the inkies, if not for the revolution.

There was an empty barrel in the room, standing up like a tub, its round lid resting against the wall.

There was a small, square door, bolted, at the rear of the room by some casks. He guessed it was for rolling in barrels.

Outside, a sharp scream rose and was then cut off.

He cursed himself for standing about feeling pleased.

The bolts were rusted, but he knocked them free with his spike and put his shoulder to the door.

It fell out of the wall and he stumbled into the alley, knocking his head on the opposite wall.

There was blood in the water again. He remembered this place. Number seven, Margarethe Ruttmann.

He saw the two figures at the mouth of the alley.

And now, number nine.

The corpse slapped the cobbles, falling like a loose-jointed dummy.

Elsaesser got a good grip on the spike and stepped forwards.

Impossibly quick, the Beast was coming for him.

He raised the spike, but the killer had his wrist in a shackle-like grip.

The Beast pushed him and they both fell back through the barrel door.

Elsaesser felt something sharp slice across his stomach and then his neck. He heard rather than felt his throat opening.

He had failed. He had failed everyone.

The Beast picked him up and swung him around. He felt
his shins strike wood and then he was dropped.

The Beast had shoved him into the barrel.

He was pushed down. His front was soaked with blood
and he couldn't cry out. He just made a *'gack gack'* noise as
he gasped for breath.

The lid came down on the barrel and he heard the blows
of the cooper's hammer.

He was forced down into a squatting position, his knees
up against his chest. Blood was pooling around him.

He was seeing colours in the dark.

Mrs Bierbichler had been right. He could die.

But he would die having seen the face of the Beast.

PART FIVE
BESTIALITY

I

THE COMMISSION OF Inquiry decided officially that the Great Fog Riots petered out sometime soon after sunrise. Actually, the incidents continued for several days, as stragglers from various factions set about each other with leftover weapons, and the Hooks carried out a series of opportunist robberies. The fires in the East End were finally brought under control in the late afternoon, and a lot of people returned home to find their homes weren't there any more. The Commission more or less decided that this was their own fault for getting mixed up with a riot and, upon the advice of the one-thumbed minister Mornan Tybalt, opted not to crack open the treasury to provide the newly-homeless with funds for food, shelter and refuge. Whereupon there were a few more riots and the Imperial Militia, by now a great deal better experienced, moved in and restored order with a modicum of unnecessary brutality. By the end of the week, the city's population of beggars had increased by one-third and there were nightly scuffles outside the Temples of Shallya as indigents fought over the limited number of cots made available by the Clerics of Mercy.

The riots ended mainly through confusion of purpose. Rumour and counter-rumour spread through Altdorf with a supernatural rapidity. However, it was almost immediately general knowledge that Yevgeny Yefimovich was an altered and a devotee of the Ruinous Powers, and that he was also the murderer of Ulrike Blumenschein, the Angel of the Revolution. This was a heavy blow to the radical movement and Prince Kloszowski dashed off several poems excoriating the fiend in human shape who had perverted a just cause and a good woman to his own diabolical purposes. There were a few die-hard Yefimovites, but they tended to get more involved in violent feuds with the Kloszowskists than with the authorities. Professor Brustellin's body was found in the street and buried outside the city walls, a permanent shrine erected above his remains as a reminder of his great works. The watch mainly left the radicals to their own quarrels and concentrated on sorting out the debris.

It was clear that Yefimovich had killed Ulrike in an attempt to stir up the people against the Imperial court, and the Commission ruled that it was therefore proven beyond all manner of doubt that the revolutionist monster was also the murderer known as the Beast. Popular resentment against the aristocracy dwindled to its usual level of mild seething and it was safe again to walk the streets of the docklands in a green velvet cloak.

The fog began to thin, but only slightly.

Cleric-Captain Adrian Hoven finally managed to get into a room with the relevant commanders of the city watch and the Imperial Militia, and various disputes of jurisdiction were settled to everyone's satisfaction. A joint action was mounted and any remaining disorder was speedily quelled. The last disorder was ended when a discreet bribe was passed into the hands of Willy Pick, and the Hooks ceased their campaign of outright looting and vandalism.

The Commission would abandon its attempt to list all the casualties of the Great Fog Riots and no two estimates of the damage would ever tally. The Emperor Karl-Franz was reported to be 'most upset' by the whole affair and called for all the citizens of Altdorf 'to display that old Imperial spirit

and rally through just as Sigmar would have wanted us to.'
Grand Prince Hergard von Tassenick lobbied for the flogging
of all people suspected to have been involved in the rioting,
but this suggestion was rejected on the grounds that it was
'too impractical.' In the end, Rickard Stieglitz was caught,
then tried for and convicted of insurrection, and given a
public ear-clipping before being imprisoned in Mundsen
Keep. Nineteen other individuals were jailed for various
crimes, ranging from arson to seditious libel, committed
during the riots. Prince Kloszowski left the city before the
watch could take him and continued to write. His epic, *The
Blood of Innocents*, would become an underground classic,
especially after it was banned in every city and state of the
Empire.

A list was posted in the Konigsplatz of all the watchmen,
Templars and militiamen killed or injured. Buried in the roll
of honour was the name of Helmut Elsaesser.

The Beast, of course, was still at large.

II

THE BEAST HAD come for her. It seemed to be made of solidified fog, draped in an enveloping cloak of green velvet, complete with a hood. Evil eyes stared out of the blackness where the face should have been. She could feel its rage, its hate, its violence. It moved not like a human being, not like an animal. It had a queer grace, a delicacy of gesture, and yet it radiated strength, menace, hostility. In its clouded mind, the lust for killing burned as fiercely as the weirdroot addict's need for his dream-drug. Fixed to the spot, she could not run. The fog was as thick as cotton and she could not fight through it. She was a little girl again, far from Altdorf, somewhere in the forested mountains. Behind the Beast, she sensed her parents, making no move to save their daughter. They were thinking that it would be best if the witch cuckoo were dead. Then, they could stop blaming each other for the freak. They could be part of the village again. Father could return to the tavern and hoist tankards with his friends, mother could supervise her other daughters – her real daughters – and turn them into good little dressmakers. They urged the Beast on. Rosanna was sweating, already feeling the pain the Beast would visit upon her. Her sisters were there too, with their pinching fingers and slapping hands, like the Beast's attendants. The fog stung her eyes like woodsmoke. They were in the alleyway now, between the two inns, and the murderer's hand was around her throat, its knife slicing upwards.

Rosanna woke up, her heart kicking like a baby in her chest.

There was no Beast, except in the memories she had sampled. The memories of the killer's victims.

She had been dreaming it over again, scrambled up with her own dreams.

She was crouched against a wall in the Matthias II, with a cloak – green velvet, of course – flung over her. She could not remember going to sleep.

Baron Johann von Mecklenberg was pouring out cups of tea. Harald Kleindeinst was sitting down, carving bread with a knife less impressive than the one slung on his hip.

It would have been a cosy breakfast scene were it not for all the men-at-arms milling about and the annoyed dignitaries huddled together.

The baron had thought it wisest that everyone stay in the inn for the night, under guard. Obviously, he was as much interested in penning up potential suspects as in keeping de la Rougierre's guests safe from the rioters.

Of course, Wolf was gone. And so was Yefimovich.

The Countess Emmanuelle, still in last night's ball gown, was posed like a statue, attended by her brother and the Lector. She was looking irritated, as much because the Beast was drawing attention away from her as for the inconvenience and indignity of spending a night away from her luxurious accommodation at the palace.

Some time last night, Mikael Hasselstein had given Rosanna a gold crown and told her to stay close by. The gesture annoyed her and she was reconsidering her future at the Temple. It was becoming obvious that there might be conflicts of interest between the causes of Justice and the cult of Sigmar. And the cause of the cult was especially vague just now, overlapping unnervingly with that of the Lector. The

whores whose minds Rosanna had shared all charged a lot
less than a gold crown for their services, but their clients had
not pretended to be buying anything other than the temporary use of their bodies. Hasselstein seemed to think he
could own her outright.

The Bretonnian dwarf was up and shouting, abusing various servants and militiamen for their clumsiness. The
Celestial simply sipped tea and smiled.

The function room was a mess. The guest rooms upstairs
had been turned over to Luitpold and his instantly-assem-
bled guard and so everyone else had had to spend the night
downstairs. Some of them must have relished the chance
not to be alone, but the countess, at least, was steeped in a
cold fury.

The baron smiled and brought Rosanna some tea in a
goblet. The inn was running low on cups and there was broken crockery underfoot.

'Well?' she asked.

'Wolf is gone.'

'Baron, was he the Beast?'

The baron looked pained and she read genuine confusion.

'Call me Johann,' he said.

'You don't know?'

'No. I fear, but I don't know.'

'Last night, someone was saying it was Yefimovich.'

Harald said, 'He's not human.'

Hasselstein, overhearing, stepped in. 'The fire-breather
tried to kill the countess. Then he escaped, killing the dancer
in the alley. He is the Beast.'

Rosanna tried to think, tried to scry. She had only seen
Yefimovich briefly and had not had time to probe him.
There had been the aura of an inferno about him.

'Miss Ophuls will confirm his guilt,' Hasselstein said.

Johann looked at Rosanna.

She thought carefully. Yefimovich had been an altered
and, she scryed, an initiate of one of the Proscribed Cults.
She fixed on the memory of his bright presence. Even trying
to recall him made her eyes hurt, as fires appeared to dance

in her vision. He had left a very strong impression behind him. She felt his devotion to the Dark Powers, to Tzeentch. There were countless crimes to his credit, each a flame in his body. But she could not fix him as the shadowed Beast she had scried from the dead women. Yefimovich was fire, while the Beast was darkness.

'No,' she said, 'I'm not sure… I do not think Yefimovich is the Beast.'

The Lector looked at her as if she were the Beast herself, and his lips went tight, all colour squeezed out. She felt his anger boiling. He had thought he could count on her, and now he was feeling betrayed. He was prepared to be quite self-righteous about it. He could enforce all manner of penances upon her.

'Yefimovich was the Beast,' he said.

The Lector stared at her, trying to force his will into her mind. All he wanted was for her to agree with him, to wrap up the mystery, to end the investigation. It would have been so easy, and it would have satisfied everyone. She could not be sure of her intuitions. Maybe Yefimovich was the killer. He was certainly a killer.

'Yefimovich was the Beast,' Hasselstein repeated.

Rosanna gave him back his crown and answered, 'No.'

Anger flared in the Lector's mind and he gripped his coin in a tight fist. Had Harald and Johann not been there, he would have struck out at the impudent scryer. He was not used to being defied and he did not like the taste of it. He turned and walked back to the countess – his secret mistress, Rosanna realized – trailing his wrath behind him like a kite.

'What was that about?' Johann asked.

'I think I've just been excommunicated from the Cult of Sigmar.'

For the first time since she left her village, she felt free. It was a dizzying, slightly scary feeling, like walking a rope in a carnival with no safety net. She was, she realized, home-less, masterless, unemployed…

'Don't worry,' said the elector, 'you have my protection.'

Rosanna wasn't sure about Baron Johann's sudden offer, sincerely meant though it was. Practically, it might serve

some use if Hasselstein were to prove vindictive. But she had
relished her taste of liberty and the prospect of serving
again, under the colours of a noble house rather than a reli-
gion, was disappointing. Besides, she bristled at his casual
assumption of her helplessness.

But the men were thinking of other things now. She could
see the same name in each of their minds. Wolf. Johann was
seeing a lost youth, confused and afraid. Harald was remembering the twisted young man, barely containing his animal
heart, they had encountered last night.

'Yefimovich is not the Beast,' Rosanna said. 'The mystery is
not solved.'

'You're sure?' Johann asked.

Rosanna nodded.

'A pity,' said the baron. 'It would have been simple.'

Rosanna shrugged.

'The Blumenschein woman,' said Harald, 'the so-called
Angel of the Revolution?'

Rosanna concentrated. There had been blood in
Yefimovich's mind. New blood. He was a strong presence.
She had been able to read a lot – too much – from him dur-
ing their brief contact.

'I think he killed her. But not the others.'

Harald swore and the baron looked troubled. They all
knew that Rosanna's intuitions would not prevent the
authorities from misidentifying the Revolutionist Monster
as the Beast. That left them on their own against the real
murderer.

'Baron,' said Harald, 'if the Beast is your brother, then
what?'

'Then he must be stopped. That is all.'

'Is it?'

Johann was trying to do the right thing, Rosanna saw. It
was something bred deep into him.

'No,' he answered the captain, 'of course it isn't. Wolf is
my brother and I shall do all I can for him.'

Harald was grim. 'If it comes down to it, would you stand
between us?'

'Probably. Would you go through me to catch him?'

'Probably.'

'Then we understand each other, captain.'

De la Rougierre, who had quickly forgotten his dalliance with the dead dancer, was insisting that his guests be allowed free. He called Harald 'a stupid policeman,' and then backed off.

The streets had been quiet for a few hours now. Johann had sent a Templar to the palace for carriages. The coaches the guests had come in were burned-out wrecks and the horses fled.

Finally, the coaches came and de la Rougierre's guests were ferried back to their secure walls and well-armed retainers.

The last to leave was Leos von Liebewitz. The youth seemed torn. 'Johann,' he asked, 'can I help here?'

It was difficult for him, but he felt some obligation, if not to the commoner who had died then to the aristocrats who had not.

'No, Leos,' the baron answered, 'perhaps later.'

With the guests shepherded out, they were left alone at the inn.

Rosanna, Johann, Harald.

It took them a while to work out who was missing.

III

THEY FOLLOWED THE girl as she led them out of the function room, through a short passage, and towards a store-room. The place was mainly above ground, but it had the atmosphere of a cellar. Rosanna was in a half-trance, feeling her way along a cooling trail. The baron was by her side, like a courteous gentleman helping a blind person not to bump into walls, gently steering her round obstacles. Harald's stomach was beginning to ache and he felt the recent violence as surely as the scryer did.

'He's here,' she said.

'Where?' asked the baron.

'In this room.'

They looked around. This was the way they had come into the Matthias II last night. The window was still open, as was a barrel-door. The place smelled of old beer.

'We looked here last night,' the baron said. 'Those two Leaguers were unconscious in the corner.'

Harald's stomach complained.

Rosanna went around the room, touching things, frowning.

'He's here. Very close.'

She touched a barrel that was standing on its end and leaped back as if it were a heated stove.

'What is it?' the baron asked.

Rosanna pointed at the barrel. 'Inside,' she said.

Harald held up the lantern. The barrel was split near the base and blood had poured out through the taphole. It was sticky on the flagstones.

'Merciful Shallya,' the baron swore.

Harald found a cooper's hammer and tapped the barrel-lid. It gave, and he pulled the wooden circle out whole.

Helmut Elsaesser looked up, his face white, his eyes empty.

JOHANN COULD NOT help but feel responsible. He had, after all, intervened to keep the young officer on the Beast case. Rosanna had flinched away at the sight of the corpse and he had instinctively embraced her. He felt her body pressed warm against him, and a charge crackled from her hair, so close to his face. She relaxed for a moment and then stepped away from him, leaving only the memory of a touch. He wondered if she had seen anything in him that made her want to break contact. She was making herself look at poor, dead Elsaesser.

'Number ten,' Kleindeinst said, respectfully.

'Get him out,' said Johann.

'No, don't,' insisted the captain. 'Not yet.'

'What is it?'

'He didn't die straight away. He bled. There may be something.'

'I don't understand.'

'A message from the grave,' suggested Rosanna. 'Here.'

She was holding the barrel lid up to the light. It was stained with blood. Something was written on it.

'He may have seen his murderer, recognized him…'

Johann looked at the scrawl. There were letters. No, numbers.

As he was dying, Elsaesser had dipped a finger in his own blood and drawn numbers on the lid of his makeshift coffin.

317 5037.

'Is it a code?' he asked. 'Why would Elsaesser use a code?'

'He was there when Dickon burned the cloak, wasn't he? He may have expected the message to be found by someone who would want to hush it up. Or even by the Beast himself.'

Rosanna suggested the simplest code. 'Perhaps the numbers are letters of the alphabet. 1 for A, 2 for B and so on. That would read CA... er, G... E...'

'Yes? What's the nothingth letter of the alphabet, scryer?' asked Harald.

'Obviously, it's not so simple. Elsaesser was just out of the University, wasn't he?'

Johann tried to solve the riddle. 'Perhaps it's a map reference. At the University, they use the grid system. Elsaesser could have been pointing us to the murderer's house...'

Harald looked doubtful. 'What's the grid reference for the palace, baron?'

'I don't know.'

'And you live there. How could a simple copper know exactly a map reference in seven digits?'

'You have a point.'

'Maybe the numbers should be in bunches. There's a gap in the middle, and a smaller one here. 317. 50. 37. It could still be an address. 317 could be a house number, and the other two a street and a district.'

'I don't swallow it,' said Kleindeinst. 'Poor Elsaesser was dying, his stomach opened, his throat cut. He must have been in terrible pain. He wouldn't have had time for numerology games. It has to be something obvious.'

'There's something about the number 317 that's familiar.'

Kleindeinst snapped, 'Of course there is, that's the code number for this district.'

'Code?' Rosanna and Johann asked, at once.

'Watch code. Every watch in the Empire has a number, like a regiment of the militia. 317 is the Luitpoldstrasse Station.'

'And do individual officers have numbers?'

'Yes but you would be hard-pressed to find any watch in the Empire, much less in a slum like this, which had over five thousand men.'

'317. 5037.'

'3. 17. 50. 37.'

'3,175,037.'

'This is silly' said Rosanna. 'Maybe he was just delirious and doing mathematical problems in his head. People die with strange things in their minds. I should know.'

They looked at her and she knew what they were thinking.

'Yes,' she said, resigned, 'of course I'll try to scry him.'

HELMUT ELSAESSER HAD died gasping for breath and thinking of his landlady. There were a lot of other things, but no coherent thought.

Rosanna was still not used to violent death. She supposed she would have to go through Milizia's death, too, and still not be able to identify the Beast.

'It's almost as if the murderer can blot himself out of his victims' consciousness.'

'Is that possible?'

'Anything is possible, Johann. It's not like opening a book. It's like trying to count heads at a ball, with all the dancers on the move. I could tell you a lot about this poor boy, but I think it's best to leave him some privacy.'

'Girl,' said Harald, 'if you ever do this professionally, you'll learn that one of the things murder victims don't have is privacy.'

The thought made her unutterably melancholic.

'It's not like the melodramas,' Johann said, 'where murderers leave clues and the clever watchman sleuths them out.'

'This number is a clue,' Rosanna said. 'I'm sure of that.'

'And that green velvet Dickon burned,' said Captain Kleindeinst.

'It's a shame you didn't get to scry that,' said Johann. 'It must have come from the Beast. I held it in my hands, but I've no gift. You know, I can see it now, in every detail...'

Rosanna felt the curtains open in her mind. It happened sometimes.

'And so can I.'

'What?' exclaimed Kleindeinst.

'The velvet, I can see it. Worn along the bottom edge.'

'Yes, that's right.'

'The bottom edge?' asked Kleindeinst.

Rosanna and Johann agreed.

'But, those cloaks are thigh-length. How could it be worn along the bottom?'

Johann made a gloved fist. 'It would be worn like that, if the Beast weren't a normal-sized man...'

In her mind, Rosanna saw a dwarf...

THE COUNTESS EMMANUELLE was determined. They would be leaving for Nuln as soon as possible and remaining there until this frightful business was forgotten.

She told Leos as much in the carriage and charged her brother with making the arrangements. 'Have Dany supervise the packing of my gowns,' she said. 'He'll like that.'

She had been in this city too long, staying away from her social and political responsibilities to be close to the heart of the Empire.

Mikael had kept her here longer than she had intended. In the beginning, the intense cleric, whose desire for power was as urgent as his desire for her, had been an interesting conquest. Now, he was becoming a bore. Perhaps worse than a bore.

Mikael would be a problem. He was being too ardent. He might prove unpredictably troublesome if he were not cast loose with some tact.

In her dressing room, free from her maids, she scrubbed at her face, removing last night's fading paint. Her dress was ruined. She would never wear it again. And her tiara had been stolen while she slept.

Upright in a chair, no less! She was lucky to come away from the Bretonnian ambassador's soirée with her life.

Behind her, the door opened and a small figure slipped in.

Outraged, she turned.

'De la Rougierre!' she exclaimed. 'I hope you have some explanation for this uncountenanceable intrusion.'

The ambassador grinned and, for the first time, it seemed to Emmanuelle that he really was more dwarf than Bretonnian.

He bowed, his hat swept mockingly low, and sauntered across the room...

IV

JOHANN FELT AS IF his mind had been scooped out. Rosanna was apologetic, but more taken with Kleindeinst's suggestion.

'Yes, it could be? The cloak must have trailed on the ground a lot. Don't you think so?'

Johann stammered an agreement. He felt a fool for not noticing himself.

Kleindeinst spoke deliberately. 'There was a rumour that the Beast was a dwarf. And most of the knifestrokes were upwards...'

He made an underarm stabbing motion.

'Elsaesser said that the Bretonnian ambassador was intimate with several of the victims,' said Rosanna.

Johann's mind came back to him. 'And he certainly knew the dancer last night. The murders started just after he was posted to Altdorf...'

'De la Rougierre,' said Kleindeinst, his knife out. The copper rolled the name around in his mouth.

'It's just,' Johann began, trying to pin down a doubt, 'it's just that he seems to be such a clown, you know. The absurd little creature pretending to be a man. He's like a stage

Bretonnian, all perfume and silly gestures, with that exaggerated accent, those ridiculous moustaches, the endless chatter...'

'He's still a dwarf,' said Kleindeinst. 'They can be vicious bastards. I should know, I've had to kill enough of them.'

'There is more than one dwarf in Altdorf.'

'That's true enough. But only one has been cropping up throughout this investigation.'

'He's an ambassador. This will be a big scandal. Relations between the Empire and Bretonnia are always questionable. King Charles won't like us executing his envoy.'

'Then we'll let him do it. A Bretonnian headsman's axe is just as sharp as an Empire blade. Just so long as the toad is squashed.'

Rosanna cried out, a wordless gulp of noise. Johann and the captain looked at her. She had her hands knit as if in prayer. 'I'm an idiot,' she said, slowly, 'and you are too...'

HASSELSTEIN PUSHED HIS way in without knocking and his heart shrank into stone. Yelle was not alone and the prospect of her companion replacing him in her bed made the Lector want to vomit bile.

'What are you doing here?' he said.

The dwarf turned away from Yelle, his hand going to the hilt of his ridiculously short sword.

'Both of you,' the countess said, 'get out. You are here uninvited.'

'I merely wished to apologise for last night, countess elector,' said de la Rougierre, dripping Bretonnian smarm.

Hasselstein laughed bitterly.

'I'm sure that was the extent of your motive, ambassador.'

Yelle had her face off and was snarling like a cat.

'I said "get out", if anyone's interested...'

'Lector,' said the dwarf, 'you are a cleric, but your deity is a warlike one. I am not honour-bound not to fight you. Remember that.'

Leos appeared at the door, his ready hand on his sword-hilt. He looked at Hasselstein and de la Rougierre, unsure which to kill first.

Yelle screeched and flung an enamelled brush at them.

'Mikael, ambassador... *out!*'

'IT'S NOT FROM a cloak...'

She should have known straight away. Before the Temple came for her, she had been apprenticed to her mother, the seamstress. She had hated every minute of it, preparing ridiculously decorated outfits for the local lord and lady. Her fingers were still grooved and scarred from the rough needles.

'...it's from a dress.'

'What?'

'The stitching is completely different. The hem is higher. Even the thickness of the velvet is wrong.'

'A dress?'

'Yes, a formal dress. Maybe a ball gown.'

'Merciful...' began Kleindeinst.

'...Shallya,' completed Johann.

'Are you trying to tell us that the Beast is a woman?' asked Kleindeinst.

Rosanna reached into herself, combining the images of the murderer she had picked out of the victims' minds. It was dark, slim and a sharp edge sparkled like a jewel.

'No...' she said. 'Yes.'

'Which?'

The Beast came out into the light and Rosanna saw her face.

'Yes.'

The Beast was beautiful...

'The palace,' Rosanna said, 'now!'

...beautiful and terrible.

THE MAN-SHELL SHRANK, the boy-shell shrivelled...

All the former selves were dead. There was only the Beast.

It takes its claw and prepares for the last of them. The last of the disgusting women. The worst of them.

It is not sure whether it is hunting, or waiting. Anyway, it will be over soon.

This is the last of the grudge kills.

The Beast pads through the palace. It is proud to walk in the light. It – no, *she* – does not need to hide any longer.

There is someone else in her mind, troubling her. A woman, a filthy woman! The Beast sees red hair, a pretty face.

There's a number, too. 317-5037. The woman presence doesn't understand. 317-5037?

The Beast is puzzled, for a moment. Then, it becomes clear. And she laughs...

THERE WAS A watch carriage outside the inn. Harald commandeered it and took the reins, while the baron helped Rosanna up onto the seat.

The scryer was almost in a trance, her open eyes twitching. She was like a human dowsing rod. She didn't speak, just sat rigid.

Harald whipped the horses and the carriage tore through the fog. He hoped that the vehicle made enough noise to warn people to keep out of the way.

He imagined the map of the city and took the shortest route to the Emperor Karl-Franz Bridge and then on to the palace.

'It's Emmanuelle,' said the baron. 'The Marquess Sidonie was with us all the time last night.'

Harald didn't say anything. Nothing was proved yet.

'There were no other women in the company.'

A horse reared up in the fog, looming. It was one of the runaways, as yet not rounded up.

Harald pulled back hard and kept his own animals on course.

The stray was panicked, but galloped out of the way, fading into the grey murk.

'But the countess? Why?'

They were over the bridge and the streets were wider. There was mercifully little traffic, what with the fog and the leftover from the riots.

'Kleindeinst,' the baron said, 'earlier, you claimed that a womanslayer was the worst kind of criminal there was.'

Harald grunted a yes.

'Well, could you become one?'

Harald thought of the Countess Emmanuelle, tried to imagine her with knives in her frail hands, tearing away at the dead women, cutting young Elsaesser's throat.

He still couldn't answer the baron's question.

Ahead of them, its massive outline clearly visible, a stone hammer raised high above the structure, was the palace.

And inside was the Beast.

'I THINK MY sister wants you to leave,' Leos said, calmly.

De la Rougierre and Mikael Hasselstein looked at the viscount and were chilled into silence. Leos took his hand away from the hilt of his sword and everyone breathed again.

'Yes,' said Emmanuelle, 'that's right.'

His sister was frayed around the edges. Without her paint on, the delicate lines around her mouth and eyes were visible.

The dwarf and the cleric both wanted to protest, but Leos counted on their taking his swordsmanship seriously.

De la Rougierre broke first. He clapped his hat on his head and left the room, attempting to draw himself up to a dignified height.

'Yelle,' Hasselstein pleaded, 'can't we-?'

'No,' Emmanuelle said, 'we can not. Please go.'

The cleric made useless fists in the air and backed out of the room, grinding his teeth. He looked as if he would scream as soon as he got out of earshot, or take out his anger on a servant. His robes of office brushed the floor as he walked.

The door closed behind them.

Emmanuelle's face was twisted. Her hands were up in the air, sharp nails pointed like talons.

'Yelle,' Leos said, 'it is over…'

Emmanuelle screeched.

Within seconds, Viscount Leos von Liebewitz was dead. And the Beast had killed him.

V

A PAIR OF guardsmen stood in the middle of the gateway, with their pikes crossed, barring the road.

Kleindeinst shouted a warning, but made no attempt to stop.

Johann wondered if the two men would stay and be trampled. He held his breath.

Rosanna was mumbling and painfully gripping his arm.

The guards decided on survival over honour and Kleindeinst lashed the horses. The carriage rushed through the gateway.

Someone had unlocked the portcullis chain and it rumbled down behind them, spikes spearing the stone.

A guardsman drew his sword, but Kleindeinst pushed his badge in the soldier's face.

Johann showed his face and the guardsman saluted.

'Elector,' he said.

'I'm sorry for this,' Johann said, 'but it's urgent. I'm on the Emperor's business.'

Rosanna snapped out of her trance and vaulted out of the carriage, landing well.

'Follow us,' Johann ordered the gate guards.

Rosanna led the way, as if she knew every stone of the palace, and Kleindeinst and Johann had to stride to keep up with her.

She was taking them to the guest apartments.

At the main door of the block, they ran into Mikael Hasselstein. His face was stony and his knuckles white. Rosanna pushed her former patron out of the way without seeming to recognize him and pulled open the door.

'In there,' she said. 'The Beast.'

Hasselstein took notice. 'What?'

There was no time for explanations.

The party marched through the passageway. Along the way, they picked up Mnoujkine, the guests' steward. Johann told him to have all the other servants and guests evacuated.

'We think we have a killer trapped in here.'

'Countess Emmanuelle?' Hasselstein said. 'Yelle?'

Rosanna stopped outside the door of the von Liebewitz apartments as if she had walked into an invisible wall. She pointed at the door, her hand shaking.

'What is this about Yelle?'

The door was locked.

'Break it down,' Johann ordered.

Kleindeinst put his shoulder to the door, but rebounded with an oath.

'That's solid oak, with iron crossbars.'

A guard stuck his halberd into the crack, between the hinges, and tried to prise the door open. The shaft of the weapon snapped.

Beyond the door, there was feminine laughter. The sound squirted icewater into Johann's blood.

Johann kicked the door and uselessly jarred his bones.

'Get axes,' Kleindeinst ordered.

'Yelle? Yelle!'

'Shut up, Lector,' said Johann. 'Rosanna? What's happening in there?'

Rosanna was flagging. She had made it this far, but the strain was showing.

'Dying,' she said, 'she's killing... dying... him...'

The axes came.

'This door dates back to the time of Wilhelm II,' said Mnoujkine, 'it's a valuable antique. The Emperor will be most distressed.'

'We'll buy him a new one,' said Kleindeinst, hefting the first axe.

A chunk of wood flew out of the door and the passage shook.

'Stand back,' said Johann, pulling Rosanna out of the way. She clung to him, like a child.

He was glad he was not seeing in his mind what she was in hers.

Kleindeinst smashed the wood around the lock and the door began to split.

There was still laughter.

The door came apart, falling in three pieces. Kleindeinst threw the axe away and pulled out his knife.

'After me,' he said…

INSIDE THE VON Liebewitz apartments, everything seemed ominously in order. Cloaks and coats were hung neatly in the hallway. There was an open fire in the reception room and a book was open on the dining table. *The Treachery of Oswald*, by Detlef Sierck.

'Careful,' Harald said, cautioning the others.

The laughter was coming from somewhere.

'Lector,' Harald said to Hasselstein, 'where is she?'

The cleric had to be shoved by the baron to make a reply. 'Her dressing room. It's just down the corridor.'

A woman who killed women. That was something new in his experience. There were always surprises, although few were ever pleasant.

'Countess,' he said, loudly, 'this is the watch. We would like to talk to you.'

The laughter stopped.

'Emmanuelle,' said Baron Johann, 'it's important.'

Quiet.

Harald looked at the baron and guessed that he received the elector's approval.

He stepped sideways into the corridor, pressing his back against the wall opposite the row of doors.

'Which one?' he asked, softly.

'The third,' said Hasselstein.

Harald edged down until he stood opposite the door.

Johann and the three guards cautiously came into the narrow corridor. Harald hoped that none of the company would have to die.

He touched the point of his Magnin to the door and pushed hard. The door was not latched, it swung open.

First, he saw someone lying, dead or in a faint, by a dressing table, a green velvet cloak thrown over them.

Then, he saw the Beast. The murderer came at him, her train flying behind her. She was veiled and wore a richly decorated ballgown. There were some contraptions fitted over her hands, gloves with sharp hooks. The Beast had claws.

He raised his knife to slash, but his hand was slammed out of the way.

Mikael Hasselstein had crammed himself through the door and thrown himself at Harald's arm, dragging him down. He sank his teeth into the watchman's hand.

Harald slammed the Lector with his elbow, but Hasselstein kept his grip.

The Beast stood still, poised, claws ready.

The baron tried to haul Hasselstein off Harald, but couldn't get a grip.

The wiry cleric was fighting as if possessed. Hate could do that, or love.

Incredibly, Hasselstein off-balanced Harald and pushed him back into the corridor, tumbling in a bruised bundle with Johann.

'Yelle,' Hasselstein said, dropping to his knees before the Beast, 'Yelle, I love…'

The Beast slashed him across the face, her claws sinking into his cheek and hooking onto his skull. He was lifted off his knees and hurled aside, a cloud of blood blossoming around his head.

The Beast laughed like a little girl, then howled like a wolf.

* * *

317 5037.

The number rolled in Rosanna's mind.

Johann crawled across the floor, trying to disentangle himself from Harald Kleindeinst.

She saw the number written in blood on the underside of a barrel-lid.

317 5037.

Rosanna had her hands under Johann's arms and was pulling him up.

The Beast was still laughing. Hasselstein was yelping, his hand to his bloody face.

She got her arms around Johann and got him upright. She felt his body close to hers,

317 5037.

The lid circled.

Urgently, Rosanna kissed him. He was astonished, but responded.

As their mouths met, so did their minds.

Suddenly, without any communication in words, they knew a lot more about each other. She saw Johann in the woods, firing his fatal shot, and at the top of the world, facing the monster that had been, and would be again, his brother.

He saw her as a little girl, resented by her sisters, kept at a distance by her parents, impressions flooding into her mind from everywhere.

Rosanna hoped they would both survive.

Together, they saw the numbers.

317 5037.

The lid was rolling across a floor, revolving like a wheel.

317 5037.

They had read it wrong.

The lid rolled and fell, so that they could see what Elsaesser had written rightside-up.

It was obvious now. There was no clever code. The officer had just tried to write, but been unable to finish, the name of his murderer.

Not 317 5037.

LEOS LIE...

Their minds parted. Johann and Harald were standing up again, facing the Beast. Hasselstein was not in the way.

The Beast's veil slipped.

VI

THE VISCOUNT'S FACE was painted, his lips rouged. He looked like a younger version of his sister. He had been a handsome young man, now he seemed to be a startlingly beautiful woman.

Johann, his mind still reeling from the touch of Rosanna, tried to understand. Leos was mad, and dressed as his sister. He was the Beast, a murderous she-creature with razor claws. But he was still Deadly Leos, the calculating duellist. Two murderers, the brutal and the elegant, in one body.

Leos slashed at the air, snarling.

Harald parried with his knife. The Magnin clashed with Leos's claws and there were sparks.

Not hampered by the ball gown, Leos moved fast, striking out and just missing Harald's throat.

The watchman stumbled over a carpet and sat down, his knife spinning away across the polished floorboards.

Johann had his sword drawn. He thrust in front of Leos, preventing him from bending over Harald and tearing out the man's throat.

Leos hissed and turned on Johann.

The Beast held up its claws and rattled them together, like a woman showing off her painted nails.

Johann was reminded of the man-woman altered he had duelled with at the top of the world.

For a moment, Leos was back. He stood up straight, the dress hanging absurdly on him, and beckoned with his right hand, his left reaching behind him.

Too late, Johann saw he was picking up a sword from the top of a chest. The weapon had been neatly placed on top of a pile of folded garments. Leos's clothes.

The claws didn't affect Leos's grip. His blade came up.

Finally, it had come to this.

Johann made the first strike and Leos effortlessly brushed it away. They both had the measure of the fight and joined in serious swordwork.

The dress didn't slow Leos's feet, but there was a certain awkwardness about his carriage. Johann tried to work on the weakness, but Leos defended perfectly, turning every attack with contemptuous ease.

Johann recognized the echoes of Valancourt of Nuln. He had seen the great teacher give a demonstration for the Emperor once. But Leos had improved upon his mentor's moves. There was a cruelty that undercut his elegance. He was less artful, but more dangerous.

As they fought, Johann looked into Leos's empty face, searching for an answer. Rosanna would scry one, he hoped. For now, there was only the fight.

A double thrust slipped through his guard and he felt his cheek sting. He knew the cut was deep.

He had forgotten Leos's claws. With a snarl, the Beast latched its left hand to Johann's shoulder, biting deep. Leos pulled back, trying to get the distance between them for a decisive thrust.

Johann drove his knee into Leos's stomach and swiped at his opponent's rapier, ignoring the pain in his shoulder.

The hooks came free and the duellists were apart again.

Kleindeinst was up, with his knife ready, but Leos was moving too fast to give him an opening. He was standing in front of Rosanna, protecting her.

With a flurry of moves, Leos advanced, inflicting a dozen tiny rips upon Johann's clothes, scratching the skin beneath. That was for show, but also to wear him down.

Johann had not fought seriously since the Top of the World. He had never considered it a fit amusement. But now, the instincts came back to him. What Leos had studied in gymnasia and duelling courts, he had learned in forests and battles. With each hurt, he felt stronger, faster. Technically, Leos was the greater duellist and the savagery of the Beast powered his attacks. But Johann was the skilled survivor.

Johann picked up a candelabrum with his left hand, his shoulder protesting, and jabbed at Leos with it. The flames were snuffed, but the feint distracted the murderer.

Johann saw his opportunity and took it, raising his swordarm in a muscle-stretching salute, then slicing down, chopping through the air with a whipping whistle. Leos tried to step back, but – for the first time in his career as a duellist – was caught by the end of the blade.

The point of Johann's sword slipped into Leos's flesh just below his collarbone and drew a line down across his torso, tearing cloth and skin. The cut would be too shallow to do anything more than itch, but Johann hoped the flapping dress and the blood would slow him down, make him defeatable.

Surprise flared in Leos's pale eyes. The dress tore and Johann stepped back, bringing his sword up for another thrust.

The dress gaped open, just as Johann's blade was aligned for the heart-piercing move.

Johann saw Leos's white skin and couldn't move. He willed himself to make the fatal strike, but couldn't.

He had won, but he had lost also…

THERE WAS NOTHING else for it.

Harald tossed the knife around, grabbing the blade firmly, and then threw it.

The Beast was caught, the knife sunk into the naked skin just below the heart.

'Sister...' Leos said and collapsed.

For the first time, Harald was unsure about killing a murderer. He felt like a womanslayer.

Rosanna slipped past him and went to the viscount.

He was still alive...

The dress was torn, from neck to waist.

Baron Johann stood still, his sword trembling, his mouth open.

'Sigmar's holy hammer,' swore Mnoujkine.

Viscount Leos von Liebewitz had been a woman.

Rosanna was holding his head, like a cleric trying to shrive a distracted sinner.

'This isn't enough,' she said. 'We have to know why.'

'No,' said the baron, 'Rosanna, don't...'

She ignored him and kissed the dying Beast. As their mouths joined, a shock ran through the scryer's body...

'Help her,' Johann said.

Harald didn't know who he meant.

VII

As THEY DIED, Rosanna lived the Beast's life...

'But I don't want a little sister,' a pretty child said, *'I want there to be only me.'*

Her father protested, but mother – already a convert to the cause of her eldest daughter's position as the Empire's greatest beauty – was insistent.

'What my little Yelle wants, my little Yelle shall have.'

Their father, the old Elector of Nuln, knew what his wife and daughter wanted was wrong, but he had always been a slave to women.

In the end, he was glad to have one less in his household. And he had always wanted a son. If he had lived, he would have found an ally in the 'boy,' Leos, who grew up to hate women so much...

'Don't touch yourself there. That's disgusting!'

Then blows. Leos was taught with whippings to cover her body at all times. She came to think of herself as a boy. He suppressed the memory of his brief life as a girl. He played with wooden swords, not dressed-up dolls. He wanted to be a swordsman when he grew up and face hordes of goblins

or trolls single-handed, leaving mountains of green-skinned
dead wherever he adventured.

Father, Chancellor of the University, would lock himself
up with his books of history, while mother supervised the
children. Yelle would be rewarded, Leos would be beaten. If
she transgressed, he was punished. He came to tolerate the
punishment, then to yearn for it. The idea of punishment
appealed to him. Later, he would approach it from another
angle and become the chastiser rather than be the chastised.
It was only right.

When Yelle was seventeen and Leos eight, mother died in
a coach accident. Leos was properly a boy by then, but the
Beast was growing inside him as he had grown inside his
mother. The Beast was not the girl he would have been if
raised as one, but the girl that had been imprisoned, tortured, suppressed. And she was angry.

Shortly after the death of her pet cat, Yelle stopped beating the boy. She was his mother now and could have him
sent away or punished at will. She used her power over him
sparingly, remembering just what she had created in her
brother.

Besides, Leos was now devoted to his sister. If he ever
fought with the local boys, it would turn out that his opponent had angered him by insulting Yelle. And if he ever
fought, Leos would win. Emmanuelle became quite protective of Leos, mothering him far better than their real mother
had.

The Beast had tasted blood already. The two men, who
didn't matter, and sweet, ripe Natasha. When her claw had
slipped into Natasha's peach-soft flesh, she had known what
her purpose was. Women (Yelle excluded) were disgusting.
Creatures of Evil. The Beast was born to kill women, to be as
great a scourge to them as Sigmar had been to goblinkind.

At the University, Leos was taught swordsmanship by the
great Valancourt, and soon his blade was blooded.

The Beast felt strange about the blade. She loved to lick it
sometimes, gently scratching her tongue to get the taste of
the blood, but it was not a claw. And the boy-shell's duelling
partners were men.

The first claw was a hunting knife that had been father's. The Beast loved that claw and still cherished it. After the first kills, when the blade was still wet, the Beast would hold the knife between her thighs, feeling the hilt against her forbidden place. It made her feel complete.

Later, the Beast had fashioned more suitable claws and come out of the boy-shell more often. Yelle had so many pretty dresses, so many pretty jewels, so many pretty things… And the Beast's knife-gauntlets matched so many of her sister's dresses.

The Beast still thought women were disgusting. They were weak and foolish, not like herself. The Beast wanted to couple only with men, to feel their rough, hairy bodies. Even the boy-shell had no romantic interest in the feeble girls of the court with whom he danced at balls. He was rumoured to have broken the heart of Clothilde of Averheim through his cruelty, but actually the hurt was done by a simple lack of interest. Sometimes, the Beast would try on her sister's gowns and feel the killing lust flare in her heart.

Usually, she could hide inside Leos, coming out when she had to strike. But on her hunting expeditions, she would frequently dress up as if for a ball, selecting a green velvet gown with a matching cape.

But Leos hated himself for having the Beast's desires. Later than the Beast, he became a killer too. He killed elegantly with his sword, while the Beast ripped with her claws. They never really became one, and would fight continually.

The Altdorf victims were only the latest in an unbroken chain of corpses. Lately, the Beast had raged more, been less cautious, given Leos less time to clear up and cover the tracks.

The fight for control of the body became a constant thing.

In the end, as was inevitable, the Beast won.

VIII

THE COUNTESS EMMANUELLE'S dressing room was filled with
people. From somewhere, more guards and servants had
appeared. As an Elector, Johann was in charge of the situation.

Mnoujkine had called the palace physician and Mikael
Hasselstein was lying on the countess's daybed, having his
ripped face seen to. He might lose an eye, and his upper lip
was so badly torn that he would have trouble talking, but he
would live. Emmanuelle herself was unharmed, but she had
fainted and been covered with Leos's cloak while her
brother – it was still hard to think of him as a her and as the
countess's sister – dressed in one of her gowns.

Johann and Harald were most concerned with Rosanna.
She was in another trance state, dreaming furiously. Leos
lived for a few minutes with Harald's knife through her
heart and died without saying anything.

'We'll never know why,' Harald said.

Johann knew the captain was wrong. 'Rosanna will know,'
she said.

'Maybe it would be best if she didn't...'

Kleindeinst gently eased his knife out of the Beast's breast, wiped it on the cast-aside velvet cloak, and slipped it into its sheath.

'Green velvet,' he said, rubbing the rich material between his fingers. 'This has been a lot of trouble for such rotten stuff.'

Johann picked up Rosanna and carried her away from Leos's body. She was mumbling and fighting the dream.

He took her out of the dressing room and into the first bedroom he could find, where he laid her out gently. The room was sparsely decorated, as untenanted and character-less as a guest chamber in an inn. It had been Leos's room.

The only objects which suggested an occupant were a row of cameos on a dresser, small and cheap portraits of hand-some young men – heroes of the Empire, popular actors, the sons of distinguished families. Johann recognized an indif-ferent picture of himself among the collection. In a rack on the wall, there were several fine swords.

Rosanna would wake up on her own, soon. He could leave her to that.

In the reception room, the countess was surrounded by solicitous servants, her face a beautiful mask. Johann had never noticed before how closely she resembled Leos. Normally, the younger sister would have been the greater beauty. But there was very little 'normally' about this busi-ness. He wondered how much his fellow elector had known, had guessed, had suspected...

Then, he thought of Wolf. His brother was still out there, confused and hurt.

Emmanuelle was talking in a low, serious voice, giving orders to Daniel Dorrie, one of her retainers and, it was rumoured, one of her lovers. The smooth-faced young man was paying close attention.

Kleindeinst stood by the door, examining his axe-work. Emmanuelle knew he had brought Leos down and seemed to be talking with Dorrie about the officer. Killing the rela-tives of electors was getting to be a habit with him. Johann swore to himself that the captain wouldn't get into any more trouble for his action. Any of them would have done the same thing. In the end, Johann thought it was probably best for poor Leos. Earlier today, he had thought of the Beast as a monster. Already, the murderer had become 'poor Leos.'

There was a movement from behind him and Rosanna came out of the bedroom, a hand pressed to her head as if she were hung over. She was unsteady on her feet. He supported her, but she pushed away from him and stood on her own.

Johann and Kleindeinst both looked at the scryer, both asking the same question in their head.

Why?

Rosanna put out her hands to steady herself and knocked a small ornament from a stand. It smashed on the floor. Emmanuelle looked over and tut-tutted, then went back to Dorrie's orders.

The scryer took a deep breath and became fully awake.

'It's over,' Johann said.

Rosanna shook her head and, without saying anything, walked towards the Countess Emmanuelle.

Dorrie put his hand under his cloak, reaching for a knife, instinctively protecting his mistress. Kleindeinst's hand got to Dorrie's wrist before the favourite's hand got to the knife.

Rosanna took hold of the Countess-Elector of Nuln by the chin and tilted her head upwards. She looked at the other woman, hawked loudly and spat in her face...

EPILOGUE
JOHANN & ROSANNA

SHE STILL COULDN'T bring herself to explain it all to them. The Countess Emmanuelle von Liebewitz was back in Nuln with her courtiers and her conscience, her sister buried in the family vaults with an inscription referring to her as 'beloved son and brother.' Rosanna could never forget the ten deaths she had experienced during this investigation – the nine women and Elsaesser – but the lifelong death of the girl who had never been allowed to live was the worst thing she had ever known. Leos had never even had a girl's name.

The three met in a coffee house well away from the Street of a Hundred Taverns and mainly sat without talking. Johann was not pressing her to talk, but thought she would tell him eventually. Maybe she would. Harald really didn't want to know, although there was a sore point inside him, a voice that whispered 'womanslayer.'

'Don't blame yourself,' she said.

'I don't. You misread me. I killed something that had to be killed. That's all.'

It wasn't, but she didn't contradict him.

Officially, Leos had fought one duel too many, on a matter of honour, and been bested by Harald Kleindeinst. Followers of the viscount's career were surprised that he should choose to match blades with an untitled watchman, but few were interested enough to question the story. Sam Warble, a halfling investigator hired by the Marquess Sidonie to delve into Leos's character and habits in the hope of uncovering something that would help her avenge the death of her husband, eventually returned to Marienburg, having just missed turning up some real surprises. The investigator had a few questions left, but Harald had convinced Warble not to ask them too loudly and he had proved very persuasive in the matter. The marquess, pleased enough at the end of the business, had paid the halfling his full fee in any case, and was planning on erecting a statue to her husband in the Marienburg market square.

Harald drank his coffee and, impatient with them, got up to leave.

He said his goodbyes and pulled on his coat. His copper badge was on one lapel. He unpinned it and dropped it on the table.

'I suppose I shall not be needing this any more.'

Johann picked up the badge.

'I understand,' Kleindeinst said, 'that the countess-elector has petitioned for my prosecution. Doubtless, Hals von Tasseninck has forgotten the service I did him during the riots and seconded her motion. If I'm lucky, I'll be able to get my old job back at the Reik and Talabec.'

Johann handed the officer the badge.

'I have talked with the Emperor. This time, I really have. Karl-Franz isn't so bad, you know. The countess will not be welcome at the palace for a long time. He has personally blocked her paper and I doubt that she'll press it further. I have told her that if she does, I shall tell Detlef Sierck the true story of the Beast and he will cancel that Zhiekhill and Chaida play and stage instead a spine-chiller called *The Secret Life of Leos von Liebewitz*.'

Harald nearly laughed. He pinned the badge on again.

'Back to the docks, I suppose,' he said.

'Dickon has been removed, I understand.'

'Yes.'

'You'll be the new commander in Luitpoldstrasse then?'

Harald shrugged. 'I'm not a commander, I'm a street copper. Besides, there's no station in Luitpoldstrasse, remember...'

'I'll have extra funds diverted to the watch, I promise. I'll make it my business to get the station rebuilt. But it will be different this time.'

'It will have to be.'

Harald Kleindeinst walked out of the coffee house and left them together.

Johann looked tired for a moment.

Outside, the fog had completely dispersed, but it was winter. There was already a light fall of snow and the windows were frosted over. There were still plenty of burned-out buildings in the city and whole areas of the East End were ruins. There was a tent settlement amid the cinders and ashes, and the cold was already a problem. Grand Theogonist Yorri's Riots Commission wasn't doing anything about that. Yefimovich was still at large, with a thousand crowns offered for anyone who turned him in, sought for the Beast's crimes as well as his own. The insurrections had died down, but Prince Kloszowski's latest pamphlet harped on the familiar neglects and the freezing inner-city dispossessed were repeating his verses under their steaming breaths as they stamped their feet, as much with irritation as the cold.

After Leos's death, there was a rash of singular occurrences, which Rosanna thought of as omens in reverse: Dien Ch'ing, the Cathayan ambassador, disappeared from the palace; Detlef Sierck announced a horror play which would give the rest of the city the nightmares Rosanna had already been having to cope with; Etienne de la Rougierre was recalled to Bretonnia and rebuked by King Charles Tete d'Or for his licentiousness; Ch'ing's proposed expedition to the Dark Lands, suspected as a scheme to distract the Empire from subtler evils closer to home, was abandoned; Mikael Hasselstein resigned his position as Lector and entered a secluded branch of the Cult of Sigmar, taking a vow of silence as part of a self-induced penance; by night, the network of streets between the docks and the Street of a Hundred Taverns again became thick with women soliciting; people still lived, suffered and died...

'I never found my brother,' Johann said. 'He's not returned to the University.'

'He's hurt and confused, but he'll mend. I scry him occasionally. He's still in the city. He knows he's not the Beast now. I promise you.'

Johann let his coffee cool. 'I must find him,' he said. 'He was the reason I got into this thing. I must see it through. I think he still has a trace of the warpstone in him. You must have felt that when you touched his mind.'

Rosanna agreed. 'But the warpstone isn't the only thing that can twist a person out of true, Johann...'

'You are right. There are worse ways of altering than to have a face of fire or daemon's horns or a little wolfishness.'

Rosanna thought of Leos and was angry again. The girl inside the boy-shell had been a walking knot of agony. Then, she looked at Johann and calmed herself. The baron needed a scryer and she was without a position.

She centred herself and tried to reach out with her mind...

The city teemed with hurts and resentments, with plenty and poverty, with nobility and savagery, with devotion and injustice, with Law and Chaos. She brushed hundreds of minds as they were tossed around like peas in a soup, each sealed in its own little shell of skull. She was wary of letting any of them in. The taste of Leos was still too strong with her. Over the last weeks, she had often found herself dreaming Leos's dreams, choking on her memories. No matter how much she tried to dispel, her gift still gave her a curse. Also, she had flashes of Johann's past, of Elsaesser's, even of Wolf.

She knew the feel of Wolf's mind and searched for it. Her senses swelled to encompass the whole of the city. It would be like picking out one particular pea in a lake of soup, but it could be done.

Johann noticed her distraction. 'Rosanna, what is it?'

'I can help you, Johann,' she said, laying her hand over his.

ABOUT THE AUTHOR

Besides his contributions to the Games Workshop
Warhammer and Dark Future series, the seldom-
seen Jack Yeovil is the author of a single novel, *Orgy
of the Blood Parasites,* and used to fill in occasionally
as a film reviewer for Empire and the NME. Kim
Newman seems to have Jack under control at the
moment, but the stubborn beast flesh occasionally
comes creeping back.

INFERNO! is the indispensable guide to the worlds of Warhammer and Warhammer 40,000 and the cornerstone of the Black Library. Every issue is crammed full of action packed stories, comic strips and artwork from a growing network of awesome writers and artists including:

- William King
- Brian Craig
- Gav Thorpe
- Dan Abnett
- Barrington J. Bayley
- Gordon Rennie

and many more

Presented every two months, Inferno! magazine brings the Warhammer worlds to life in ways you never thought possible.